CONFIRMATION BIAS

BRUCE DRAVIS

THE PAPER HOUSE
PUBLISHING

Published by The Paper House
www.thepaperhousebooks.com

Printed in the USA

DEDICATION

This book is dedicated to the passengers and crew of United Airlines Flight 93.

At 8:42 a.m. EDT on September 11, 2001, Flight 93 left from Newark, New Jersey, bound for California. Four minutes later, the first passenger jet hijacked by Al Qaeda struck the North Tower of the World Trade Center in New York City, followed by a second plane that struck the South Tower at 9:03 a.m. Hijackers took control of Flight 93 at 9:28 a.m., just before a third plane struck the Pentagon outside Washington, D.C.

The passengers and crew of Flight 93 were from no single background or race, or single political or sexual orientation. Armed with knowledge of the hijackers' intentions, they banded together, formed a plan to fight back, called their loved ones to make farewells, and—within thirty minutes of their plane being seized—counter-attacked the cockpit.

United 93 crashed in a field near Shanksville, Pennsylvania, by 10:02 a.m. A bare 76 minutes after the first Al Qaeda attack, America achieved its first victory over the terrorists, administered by their intended victims.

There was one more action taken by the United 93 heroes before they made their charge against the cockpit. They took a vote on the plan. There could be no stronger affirmation of their faith in America than their instinctively practicing democracy before their final actions. A vote is a prayer, and not everyone votes for the same candidate or the same outcome, just as not everyone prays to the same god, and yet—with no certainty of success or survival, vote they did. Pray they did.

May America always be worthy of their example, their courage, and their sacrifice.

CONTENTS

PROLOGUE TO PART I

July 2004
Fallujah, Iraq

HERE IS *what Anthony Rogers remembers: Knowing at the start of the attack how it will end.*

Adrenaline spikes. Time slows. There is no analysis, only pure reaction. The stranger is 50 yards ahead of the American patrol, entering the street under the midday desert sun.

The man's movements falter. He reaches the center of the road, then stops. His leathered face bears an expression of uncertainty and sorrow.

Rogers calls over his shoulder to Mac, perched in the turret of the armored vehicle trailing Rogers' open-top Humvee. "Situation!"

"On it!"

The man wears a cap with the Manchester United logo. Western-style pants and shoes. A thin cloak of material that looks like burlap. Rogers can't tell if there is a bomb vest underneath.

"I am not a rich man, or a mighty one," shouts the man in Arabic. It is as though he is beginning a speech. Along the street, the crowd immediately begins to clear.

Mac is a sniper-level marksman. The rules of engagement don't permit firing on the man simply for looking like trouble. Another step toward the patrol will make it a different matter. Rogers knows Mac will go for a headshot.

"I welcome the stranger as a guest," the man declaims, gesturing to the sky. He addresses no one in particular. Not the Americans, certainly. "I tend to my family. To be good for the sake of good alone—that, I have done."

"Don't move!" Rogers shouts in Arabic. "If you are in danger, we can help." Next to him, the Iowa kid, Leinheimer, starts to rise. Rogers puts out a restraining hand to keep him sitting.

"Then the war came to me," says the man. "All I have done, and sought to do? Gone. Washed away by the war, like a storm."

He looks downward. As he lifts his head, Rogers' eyes meet his, and he takes a step forward.

"Don't be angry..." he begins, before he dies.

PART I
YOU PRETEND TO TELL THE TRUTH AND I PRETEND TO BELIEVE YOU

2016

July 1
Washington, D.C.

Maureen Dallas knows Talbot Mundy will lie to her.

On a sultry evening like this, the hotel north of DuPont Circle runs the air conditioning high. She wears a thin black cotton sweater while she waits near the bar. It is her favorite spot for interviews: She loves the nearby neighborhoods, quirky and possessed of elegance and the weight of history. One afternoon, decades back, a madman seeking to impress a movie star shot the President, right outside on the sidewalk.

She knows Mundy will lie because that's the game. Whatever a source may tell her, the true story is more often found in the source's motive for talking, or in the facts that are twisted or left out. Her column on how Washington really works—*You Pretend to Tell the Truth and I Pretend to Believe You*—cuts through carefully-worded misdirection to show readers the truths omitted or hidden inside, like a magician explaining a card trick.

The crowd will thin out soon, just past the dinner hour. Mundy knows the likelihood of being seen talking to her here. Perhaps the CIA deputy director doesn't care about being seen talking to the press about the hijacked airliner over Mecca that the Saudis had shot down in May, or figures he is invisible. Their discussion will be on background, not on the record. She doubts the session will be productive. She called him, which means he's likely coming to extract information from her based on her questions, and she might get nothing in return.

The hotel features eight TV screens around the bar, in sight of the restaurant area. Cable news with sound turned low or off. White décor—Maureen finds the sterility comforting. A small woman, she has picked a booth that doesn't force her to stretch to keep an eye on the entry. She sees Mundy arrive.

He is mid-fifties, rumpled, and a trifle doughy. In certain lighting, he resembles former President Gerald Ford. He is the behind-the-scenes guy, the workhorse, the CIA lifer. The CIA director, Robert Nadeau, had been in Congress. Nadeau is the show horse, the public face of the Agency. Nadeau is the Agency's Number One, but she knows the book on Mundy. Nadeau only makes decisions on matters Mundy feeds him, and Mundy handles all the rest.

Maureen met Mundy a year ago at a social event with top-end catering, sponsored by a defense-oriented think tank. Looking back, either the invite had been flattering, because she was respected enough to be cultivated by the CIA as a media contact, or insulting, with Mundy hoping for a conduit to the Post he could manipulate. She didn't know. That was all before she got her column.

Exchanging greetings, Maureen and Mundy order drinks and make small talk on the day's events. They ignore the menu's dubiously sensual descriptions of the chef's works and order burgers. Maureen sees food as fuel, not entertainment.

Mundy looks around the bar. "This place has more screens than we do at the shop."

"In this town, the definition of tragedy is when you're on TV and you miss it."

Mundy points to the open paper. Maureen had been re-reading her morning column, Treasury assistant deputy something, Harriman Brown, talking about money laundering. A snoozefest. "Good story," Mundy says.

"I've had better."

"The first time you and I talked, you told me about your official rule for Washington interview etiquette, and now it's the title for your column." He offers a smile. He's been having his teeth professionally whitened. "Have you always been a cynical woman?"

Flirting? Dear God, she thinks. He's at least 15 years her senior and looks 30 years older. She pushes her tortoise-shell glasses back to the bridge of her nose.

"I'm pragmatic."

Mundy sips his drink. "No direct or indirect quotes. Call me 'a member of the Intelligence Community.' Absolute background that doesn't even suggest you talked to someone in Washington."

"Sure. We have information that the Saudis were able to prevent the attack because they got a heads-up."

"Old news. Either the Saudi Air Force was much better than anyone knew, or they had inside information. No other explanations fit. What do you have that's new?"

For all that Maureen protests Washington artifice and pretense, she enjoys the verbal fencing. She knows she's good at it and that Mundy is a pro as well.

"We got a lead that the tip-off rumor is true."

"Real-time, ahead of the attack?" Mundy looks dubious.

"Unclear. The tip came with sufficient time for Saudis to scramble jets."

"Source?"

"Of the tip to the Saudis?"

"Of the story to you. But yeah, the whole thing needs vetting."

"Our story came from foreign service sources. Maybe just recycled embassy cocktail party chat. Don't know."

"Embassy? Any specific embassy?" Mundy asks. "Or is your source the

State Department?" As Maureen expected, he came to ask her questions but to answer little.

"Another reporter. Foreign desk. Is it true?"

"There's no way I'm going to confirm any of that story to you. Not on the record, off the record, informally, formally, or anything. There's no reason to think that the CIA knows anything about how the Saudis wound up shooting down an airliner."

"Other agencies?"

Mundy offers a grim smile. "There's no way that I am confirming, or hinting, or anything, that the United States has any knowledge at any level whatsoever about the Saudis shooting down a civilian aircraft. Period. Just to be clear, my understanding of U.S. policy is that the United States thinks shooting down passenger planes is bad."

"Are you denying the Saudis got a tip?"

"From somebody? No. But the idea that the CIA–and by extension, any other element in the U.S. government—can tell you who helped the Saudis shoot down a civilian aircraft is fucking nuts. Or if they did know, that would be a secret. Atomic bomb level secret. But on top of that, I personally never heard anything like this."

Maureen gives him a mischievous look. "Do you object if I put 'fucking nuts' on the record?"

"Yes. But it is. No agency, no government, wants to have its name anywhere near an action like that, even to speculate about it. If the Saudis believed they had to do that, it's on them. Not our problem."

Mecca is home to the holiest site in Islam, the Grand Mosque, and from around the world, Muslims travel to Saudi Arabia each year for the Hajj, the pilgrimage each member of the faith is pledged to make at least once in a lifetime. This year, a KLM Boeing 737 filled with 171 Iranian pilgrims and six crew on a tour package went radio silent and veered off course toward the Grand Mosque. The Saudi Air Force shot it down 40 miles away from the city, fearing a hijacking and attack.

The Middle East, never calm, had been on even higher alert since, with new tension and open belligerence among adversaries. Militaries throughout the region mobilized, borders were patrolled, and yet, no enemy emerged. The Saudis held firm that their duty to protect the Grand Mosque included shooting down the airliner. The official line was that their ability to get to the airliner so quickly demonstrated how seriously they took that obligation. Countries outside the region, and even some Muslim nations, had accused the Saudis of being overzealous.

Still, two months later, the mystery remained: No terror groups claimed responsibility. The day of the incident, Al Jazeera received a package with a cryptic message: "All false prophets must die, as Allah wills," but no one knew for sure if the message was connected to the plane.

"Our tip mentioned a group called the Lions of Jihad," Maureen says.

Mundy holds his poker face. No way to know if he's heard the name before. In desperation, she offered the only truly new information she had. She's resigned to it; the game works that way sometimes.

"And they were the hijackers?"

"Most likely. Involved somehow."

"Nationality?"

"Iranian, maybe. But I'm supposed to be asking you questions," Maureen says.

"A little give and take here. I've got no information connected to that name. We think the message to Al Jazeera points to Islamists. If I hear something about your group, I might be able to let you know."

"So right now, what I have is 'member of intelligence community casts doubt on confirmation of heads-up to Saudis'."

Mundy smiles. "'Casts doubt?' That's your takeaway from the words 'fucking nuts'?"

"You didn't give me an official denial."

"Yeah. Well, I'm not telling you how to do your job. But you have room to tweak that, make it a little stronger."

A vibrating phone interrupts Mundy. He listens to voicemail. His eyes narrow; his voice takes an edge. "Looks like I'm going back to Langley after all."

"Kind of late. What is it?"

He drains his drink. "You'll know. You'll guess."

He steps briskly through the tables to the exit.

Maureen watches him go. She'd traded away the "Lions" name to see if she could provoke a reaction. All she'd gotten in return was a vague promise to maybe hear back. But Mundy wasn't faking the emergency call. He'd gone pale and cut things off in less than 60 seconds. With a follow-up, she might get a story after all.

As Maureen takes a last sip of her wine, a gasp and murmur echo through the hotel bar. She turns to the TV screens. Masses of flames and smoke. The barman turns up the sound on the TV nearest her.

"....flight bound for Tehran struck the Burj Khalifa, the tallest building in the world. It is early morning here in Dubai, just before 7 a.m. local time. No one thinks it is an accident. It must be an act of terror...."

Maureen is unable to draw breath. She is in post-9/11 New York again. The grey ash everywhere. Taping photos of her boyfriend David to light poles, a prayer that went unanswered. Vaguely, she knows there are other patrons nearby. She tries attending to the sound and images from the television and fails. The long second holds and won't end. Then, finally, it ends, and her breath and focus return.

The plane struck the 120th story. Left Dubai Airport minutes before. Hijack. Lost radio and transponder contact. Boeing 737. The building still stood, but could that last?

She hears sobbing at the bar. A man places his arm around his companion, who is weeping over her Tiki drink. He glances around helplessly, unable to console her. He looks embarrassed.

Around the room, hushed whispers. Faces all turned to the screens. No one looks away.

Her phone buzzes. A text from Geary, the managing editor. Come back to office.

In the cab, she remembers the blue of the New York sky from that Tuesday long ago and her old black flip-phone with the weak battery. By the time she'd charged it, all she had was David's hurried last voicemail: "Leaving now. We're going to try to get out. I love you."

As she enters the newspaper office, she catches sight of her reflection too late. She'd been teary in the cab and smeared her eye makeup. "You okay?" Geary asks.

"Yeah. Got triggered a little. What do you need?"

"Work the phones on the intelligence and military side, find someone to talk about the folks who did this, and we'll add it to our lead story. Early guesses are Iranian involvement, after what happened in Mecca, but that's talking heads guessing, not hard facts. Don't worry about waking people up. They're awake."

"Okay."

Geary says, "We're going with wire services for the first edition. We'll try to add local comments for later editions. I need first copy by 11 p.m., we'll assess everything we have at that point, then new marching orders."

"Got it."

"What happened with your CIA guy? Anything to tie into this?"

"No. He wanted to ask questions, not answer them. He got called back for an emergency—this, obviously. No confirmation that the Saudis got a warning on Mecca."

"Anything else?"

Maureen sighs. "He said the idea the U.S. knew about a warning to the Saudis on Mecca was fucking nuts. Quote-end quote. Nothing on Lions of Jihad."

"Well, early innings. Let's keep going, work the phones."

Maureen spends a fruitless hour. She uses private numbers, or home numbers she had gathered over the years. She tries office numbers in case military or intelligence personnel she knows have returned to their desks. Either they haven't, or they aren't picking up, or they aren't picking up for the press. Then she mills around the newsroom with the other reporters to speculate and gossip. No one wants to leave.

On the other side of the world, the Burj burns through the early day. She watches the TV screen in the center of the bullpen. The networks had gotten footage of the moment of impact and play it again and again. Another video shows a stream of flaming jet fuel spurting from the ruptured plane to the floors below. It looks like a waterfall catching the last rays of sunset.

The dense black plume of smoke snakes east, dissipating miles away. Anxious broadcasters wear down the audience with redundant variations of the single comment and fear: The Burj was built after 9/11. Would it hold up better than the Towers did?

No one leaps from the building to escape the flames; there is no explanation to the viewers at home. Construction experts offer insights. The base of the Burj was engineered not to collapse, but where the plane struck, the cement core is thinner. It could crack, shifting the weight of the highest floors to steel beams whose vertical strength is being sapped by the fire. In that case, as any beam falters, the burden will shift to the beams that remain and a cascade of failures could bring the summit to its breaking point.

The top floors of the Burj lean, then lean further. They keel over just before 12:30 a.m. Washington time. The falling spire plunges down, intact, like an icicle in winter, hitting the plaza and not the lower part of the structure. The collapse plays live on TV. Where the plane hit, the remaining shard of the building sticks up like a broken fang.

Maureen is jittery and drained. It's another wound freshened.

She'll call Tony Rogers in the morning. He teaches at West Point now, Mideast stuff. He won't be close to the story, but he might provide background. It won't hurt to touch base.

-o-

July 2
Hudson River Valley, New York

Maureen's call comes during the late-morning rush at the Rogers home, Rogers preparing for a campus meeting and his wife Dub on her way to a Little League game. The Rogers family lives near the military academy at West Point, in a single-story 2,200 square foot home in Nelsonville, New York, decorated in glass, chrome, and leather—heretical in the Hudson River Valley, where antiques are so beloved, but their taste is modern.

"My meeting with Klamber should run until noon. I don't see myself lingering." Rogers moves sideways past Dub as they maneuver in opposite directions in the home's narrow hallway, careful not to knock his grandfather's framed medal from its hanging. Rogers is in a suit. His only concession to summer is omitting his tie.

"Not going for drinks afterward?" Dub asks. Rogers makes a face.

Rogers is clean-shaven, with sandy brown hair and brown eyes. His typical expression is friendly enough. When he smiles, he flashes the broad smile he learned as a boy, and only close friends notice that his eyes don't always join in. He'd been injured in Iraq and was healed in many ways but not all.

Dub telecommutes most days as an audit director with Ernst and Young. Except to meet clients in person, she declines to wear makeup, and on humid summer days like this one she wears her black hair pulled back to keep it from turning frizzy. When Dub and Rogers first met, she explained her nickname—"Short for 'W,' which is short for Wilhelmina, which is short for don't ask me about it because I hate the name." She is off the partnership track, trading career advancement for flexible hours while keeping good pay and interesting work.

"You should eat something," she says.

"I'll heat up that taco from Diablo's last night on the way out. Breakfast of champions."

Rogers sets the brown paper leftover bag into the microwave and then walks down the hall to gather papers. Dub begins shouting, "Fire! Fire!"

He rushes back to the kitchen. The sack is aflame in the microwave. Rogers pulls it out and hoses it down in the sink. "Stupid." He soaks the sack and contents. "Stupid, stupid, stupid."

"What happened?"

"Foil in the bag. I didn't look. I just tossed it in." The kitchen smells of burnt paper. Charred scraps of the bag cling to the microwave and the top is marked with soot. "The world is full of morons, and I hate when I'm one of 'em."

"You know, you've figured out how to act patient with everybody else on the planet except yourself."

Rogers shrugs. "I have a bias against being an idiot." As he throws the ex-taco into the garbage, his cell buzzes. "Maureen! How can a small-town academic help a reporter from the big city?"

"How can a West Point expert on the Middle East help me on the day after a terrorist attack?" Maureen says. "Tell me who did it."

"No idea. I'm heading off to a meeting—let me call you later?"

"Before four o'clock? I'm helping someone who's on deadline."

Stepping outside, Rogers watches his son Stevie balance like a wire-walker on the six-inch raised cement curb. Rogers recalls doing the same at Stevie's age, under his own father's benign gaze. As a boy he too had imagined that adulthood would hold constant adventure but got faculty meetings instead.

"Crossing a giant river?"

"Volcano," Stevie yells back.

"Oh, sure. Obviously. Well. Be careful."

Dub emerges from the house. "Maureen Dallas wants comments on the Burj," he tells her.

"You got any?"

"I'll fake it."

He kisses her goodbye.

"Who do you guys play today?" he asks Stevie. Their child is a weak hitter but a nimble infield defender.

"The Cubs."

"Are they any good?"

"I don't know, we haven't played them yet," Stevie says as Rogers enters his car.

Rogers believes that his department chair, Rockwell Klamber, is dishonest, intellectually and in other ways. They have a history: Rogers' distaste for bullies and phonies brings him into open conflict with Klamber more often than is practical or prudent, and Rogers can't—or won't—use diplomatic language to disguise his irritation.

Klamber received a master's degree from Wharton, specializing in organization structure, after a decade of stateside military service in logistics and PR. The wall behind his desk is a mosaic of precisely arranged expensive frames holding certificates from various special programs and seminars offered by the Pentagon and by Ivy League-level schools, surrounding and showcasing his Wharton diploma. His Arizona State undergraduate degree is tucked discreetly in a corner of the design.

Beneath the desk is a small footstool: Klamber is a short, stocky man, and has jacked up his chair to look visitors in the eye.

"I've decided on a new topic for my paper," Rogers begins, taking a seat on the other side of the desk.

"No," Klamber says.

"You don't even want to hear it?"

"If the topic's good, use it to get another grant. You got the grant for this one, so finish it. Something on terrorist organizations, right?"

"I thought it would be an interesting topic until I did enough work to find out it wasn't," Rogers says. "Leadership succession in modern Islamist terrorism, from Osama bin Laden to the Islamic State, compared to the historic rise of the Assassins during the Crusades. Hassan-i Sallah to the Old Man of the Mountain."

"I'm sorry you're not entertained." Klamber drums silently and impatiently with his pen on the papers before him. "But here's the rule: You never give back money, and you never surprise or double-cross sponsors. Suck it up and finish. Besides, terrorism was old news when you got the grant and Mecca and the Burj make the paper more relevant. You might learn something."

Ahead of the meeting Rogers had rehearsed arguments for his proposal, but in the face of Klamber's obstinance he discards them all. Klamber's ambition is to promote department research and prestige, either to rise within the Academy, or to be promoted at another school. Classroom performance counts for nothing, and Rogers' lack of research production is a mark against him. Rogers seethes, wary and silent, as happens in most of his meetings with Klamber.

"Since you're here," Klamber says, "I'll bring you up to date on another department development. Professor Howard is going on leave, and it might extend to spring."

"He's a good man. What's the issue?"

"Personnel matter. Can't get into it. But I can't leave the spot vacant."

Rogers knows Jerry Howard left an eye and an arm in Afghanistan and still has problems with pain management. Howard and Rogers arrived at the Academy around the same time, before Klamber, under a program to reintroduce wounded vets to the world. Klamber ended the program and was rumored to have called its participants "charity cases." Rogers, a Princeton grad, is narrowly in Klamber's good graces. Even though Rogers regards his training in Army intelligence and his field experience as equivalent to a post-graduate degree, he knows that in Klamber's world, winners have credentials and mere possession of skill is for losers.

While Rogers and Howard weren't close now, in their early years at the Academy Howard had introduced Rogers to lines from T.S. Eliot that had served Rogers as encouragement and inspiration:

There is only the fight to recover what has been lost
And found and lost again and again: and now, under conditions
That seem unpropitious. But perhaps neither gain nor loss.
For us, there is only the trying. The rest is not our business.

"What are you thinking?" Rogers asks.

"Howard has two spring courses: Ottoman Empire and Middle Eastern Geography. I don't see bringing someone in just to fill in one time for something that specialized. A new hire means I'd have to reassign him or let him go." Klamber paused. "If it comes to that. His leave might not extend to spring."

Conversations with Klamber were never innocent. Rogers knows he is being set up. But Howard is a friend and Rogers won't leave him at Klamber's mercy.

"I'll cover those courses, if needed. They're close enough to my subject area. I don't want Howard to be under pressure to come back early if he needs time."

"I was hoping you'd say that." Klamber leans back. "It would work out with another plan I have regarding your seminar. I'm bringing in a guest lecturer from Columbia, a social scientist with extensive primary research credentials in the field. Heavy hitter."

"For my cognitive bias course. The one I developed specifically to focus on military situations."

"Yes. He's an expert in cognitive science, and you're not."

Rogers stares across the desk. Klamber is stealing his work to recruit an academic celebrity. "My background is the value-add to that course. The whole point is to use real-world examples of military situations to help decision-making in the field." Rogers knows his memory of a premonition in Fallujah is faulty—merely hindsight making the future seem predictable, even inevitable. His knowledge of thinking biases is first-hand, not academic.

"Your war stories aren't that special. If you think you're able to learn the science, then surely he's capable of learning a few anecdotes. I want to see how an expert handles that seminar."

Rogers knows his body's reaction to stress. Angry hormones are poisoning his blood. "And that frees up time, if it turns out you need to teach Howard's courses," Klamber continues, seeming satisfied that pieces have fallen into place as he'd planned.

"We don't only teach subjects, we train future officers. The value of duty. The ability to balance competing priorities and make choices and live with the consequences."

Klamber looks at Rogers coolly. "In that regard, you shouldn't trust that your belief in your own honor compensates for other deficiencies."

"Who's the carpetbagger you're giving my course to, sir?" Rogers asks.

There is no benefit to provoking Klamber. Rogers does it anyway. "Someone you want to owe you a favor in the future? Or is it a payback?"

"Don't make charges without proof," Klamber glares at Rogers, standing to signal that the meeting is over. "I'm validating your work. You should be grateful."

Driving home from the Academy, Rogers fights to control himself against a rising rage. He tamps down the anger for a moment, and then a new wave crests and arrives. He slows his breathing, recalling techniques the therapists years before had taught him and that he wrongly thought he'd finally moved beyond.

Rogers likes the Academy. But not Klamber. And their relationship, never warm, is now arctic. Klamber didn't like being caught out trading favors.

Dub and Stevie have not returned by the time Rogers reaches home. Just as well, he decides. He isn't fit company. To give himself a chance to calm down, he walks to the park, half a mile through the tree-shaded neighborhood. His strides are angry and fast and he limps slightly. As Rogers reaches the small manmade lake with its row of planted willows along the banks, the surges of anger are slowing. He is getting to the other side of the cycle.

A neighbor passes by. They share greetings. Putting on a cordial face helps restore him. He keeps walking. A duck lands on the water. Rogers watches the ripples spread. When he is finally calm enough, he calls Maureen.

"What's your take on what's going on?" she asks.

"Big picture? Like who did it, or why? No idea." Rogers focuses on the still surface of the lake, willing himself to be equally placid. "You're still working for the Post, right? This is just old friends talking background. I'm not on the record. No quotes."

"Yes, still at the Post. Fine, no attribution. But how about insight?"

"None to offer, I'm afraid." Rogers shifts the phone from one hand to the other, fishing for a piece of gum in his pocket. "Everyone immediately thinks of terrorism, of course. For our generation, we hit adulthood and

9/11 changed everything. And while Mecca and Dubai aren't a U.S. problem, per se, if someone has cracked the code on how to use airliners as weapons, international attacks could be everybody's problem."

"An arms race. Terrorists versus the world."

"We don't know yet that it's terrorism."

"You don't think so?"

"You have to test any theory against the facts. I teach how thinking biases produce errors in military judgment. People overvalue information that fits an initial theory, and undervalue information that conflicts. We remember 9/11 and when we see Mecca and Dubai we assume 'ah, terrorists.' And that assumption reflects what's called availability bias—we compare the new attacks to the first thing we think of. But what do the facts really show?"

Rogers walks Maureen through gaps in the case for terrorism. Unlike the Twin Towers, the Burj was not a symbol of the West, and while it has no love for Islamists, the Emiratis are majority Sunni and officially Islamic.

Most of all, Rogers is bothered that no one claims credit for the attack at either Mecca or the Burj. "Terrorists brag. Silence doesn't advance the cause. It doesn't rally recruits or bring in money. Terrorism without PR is just mass murder."

"It could be that the attacks are by terrorists we don't know about yet." Maureen says.

"Yes. When someone flies a plane into a building, you want to know why. Terrorists don't do this stuff for no reason. Some of them are coerced. But most aren't."

Rogers says, "You sound tired."

"Late night. Staying on my feet using caffeine and frustration," she says. "I get your point about thinking biases. Everyone I talk to in D.C. just plugs Mecca and the Burj into their pet theories. Iran guys blame Iran; North Korea guys say it proves something about Korea. But guesses are cheap and facts are dear."

"Yes, cherry-picking data for facts that fit existing theory. Confirmation bias." Like the way I wound up in Fallujah because official

Washington was convinced Iraq was in on 9/11, he thinks. "I know lack of facts never keeps anyone from talking, not in Washington."

She ignores the jab. "How about the DOD? Do you have contacts at Department of Defense who would be willing to talk to me, either background or for the record?"

"Willing to talk? I doubt it. This is all too fresh. When there's hardly any information out there, the people I know stay quiet."

Maureen asks if Rogers would try. "I'm hitting a lot of dead ends right now."

"I'm seeing a friend this weekend. He could be helpful to you."

As the call ends, Rogers leaves the bench, comfortable that his anger has subsided. The storm is past.

-o-

July 3
Washington, D.C.

Arriving early for his meeting at FBI headquarters, Director of National Intelligence Rod Thorpe waits in a windowless conference room with a cup of coffee he poured for himself from the insulated pot on the credenza, scrolling on his laptop for music videos recommended by his secretary. He wears a conservative navy suit, a pale blue shirt, and a bright blue tie faintly embossed with a small paisley pattern. A decade earlier, Thorpe had taken firm and decisive action against a relentlessly receding hairline, a choice he reaffirms each morning by shaving his scalp as bare as a newborn's bottom.

When the briefing team finally enters the conference room Thorpe closes the computer. Special Agent Ted Brooks is the first to enter, filling the doorway at 6'6" and nearly 300 pounds, his playing weight during his four seasons in Florida as an NFL lineman. Following him is Special Agent Andy Mayfair, a wiry man who stands more than a head shorter than Brooks. Both are in dark suits and white shirts, standard FBI.

Phillip Knowlan, director of the SEC Enforcement Division, is the last to enter. The exchange of greetings is polite but brief as the new men seat themselves. Everyone is tense, but all Thorpe knows is that the SEC found evidence of stock market profiteering by someone with advance knowledge of the Burj attack, prompting Knowlan to bring in the FBI immediately. The apparent tie to terrorism led the FBI to summon Thorpe.

Knowlan wants to open with a tutorial for Thorpe on insider trading. "The SEC normally does its own investigations into insider trading," he begins. Thorpe waves him off, impatient to drill down into the case at hand. Knowlan starts over.

"In the weeks just before the Burj attack, routine SEC surveillance flagged suspicious trades in Boeing stock. A sudden influx of massive short and put option positions—bets that Boeing stock would go down. Then a Boeing hits the Burj, the stock drops, and the traders cash in. Profits are still being calculated, but might run to $100 million."

Knowlan pauses to look at Thorpe. "Real money," Thorpe says.

"A lot of the accounts are overseas, but we need to identify any Americans who were involved. My initial instinct was to freeze the accounts in the U.S...."

"No. No way," says Thorpe.

"...until the FBI explained that this is no longer a financial crime, it's a counter-intelligence case," Knowlan finishes.

"That's right. That's the key." Thorpe had retired as a SEAL and is accustomed to being perceived as a severe-looking man, since he has no facial hair other than his dark heavy eyebrows, and his weathered face seems to bear a scowl even at rest. "Identifying who broke the law is the start, not the end. We need to know who helped, who knew, and who else is still out there. And they can't see us coming."

Thorpe turns to the FBI men. "Do you agree?"

Brooks nods. "We do. Head of counter-intelligence is out of the country, or he would be here today. But he's been briefed, and his thinking is to let the traders take the money and track money flows to find the terrorists."

Mayfair concurs. "Even if the trader we want wasn't a terrorist, he represents a U.S. point of contact in the trade, and we need to know how he got the information that a second attack using a Boeing plane was coming. Our working assumption is that the leak wasn't American, given that the attacks and most of the trading accounts were overseas."

"Usually in insider trading we want to catch the guy who made the money, the trader," Knowlan says. "In this case, the guy who leaked the information that led to the trade is the priority, the tipper."

"Correct. The money can wait, and the criminal case can wait. We need to follow the money and find the bastards behind this." Brooks' deep, gravelly voice is as imposing as his size.

Brooks lays out the specifics of the SEC findings: In the weeks before the Burj attack, 238 separate accounts shorted Boeing in significant amounts. Some trades were undoubtedly innocent, made for reasons that had nothing to do with the Burj. Some might have been copycat activity by traders who spotted the unusual volume and decided to join in. Once the SEC looked through the corporate and partnership names on the 238 accounts, it handed off a list of 800 individuals for the FBI to investigate.

"Account names used by the people we're after will probably be false. We'll weed out legitimate trades as quickly as we can, but getting the information sorted is a problem of both quantity and quality," Brooks says. "There's a second, related line of inquiry. May be a dry run. Right after Mecca there were some hinky airline trades—smaller dollar amounts, and a different method, someone manipulating international airline stocks after the attack, rather than trading on advance information. Whoever it was created a one-day market panic, pulled their profits, and then disappeared."

Mayfair looks up from his notes and adds, "Feels connected, but it's too soon to know if the Mecca trades and the Burj trades tie in."

Thorpe is less concerned with fine distinctions between the two financial crimes than with the importance and urgency of the SEC information. "I believe in paranoia, not coincidence. We've got to run these trades to ground." Thorpe turns to Brooks. "How long will the securities investigation take?"

Brooks shakes his head. "No promises. Weeks at best."

"No certainty whether this is someone working with terrorists, or if it's a criminal gang, or even a state actor, like a sovereign wealth fund," Knowlan says. "A lot of countries, oil-rich, run investment pools with surplus cash. This could have been one country attacking another, making a side bet in the market."

"You'll alert me immediately for any obvious international security questions, correct? Sovereign wealth involvement, that sort of thing?" Thorpe is issuing a command even though it is phrased as a question.

Knowlan confirms. "If we find international money laundering issues, we may need to bring in the Treasury Department, but we'll see what develops."

Thorpe stresses the need for the FBI to check account names against everyone in the intelligence community, with no information sharing until the vetting is complete. "I don't want to believe that someone on the intelligence side learned of the attack and chose to make money from it instead of alerting the authorities, but we live on proof, not assumptions."

He looks around the table. "I need no leaks. No inter-agency communications—SEC and FBI excepted—and no talking with those magpies in Congress. If you get an inquiry from Congress on this, route it to me and I'll stall them. They can't keep their mouths shut up there unless something is classified top secret, and sometimes not even then."

Thorpe places his closed laptop into his briefcase. "There may be an innocent explanation. Sometimes people miss clues until after the fact. Processing data takes time. Maybe we really had no warning whatsoever."

As he stands, Thorpe frames the question from his perspective. "But my issue, my main concern...Somehow, terrorists planned two attacks and had a leak both times they conducted operations. The Saudis caught on in time to send jets to Mecca. Your traders knew about the Burj. Is it really true our intelligence community knew nothing about either attack in advance?"

-o-

July 5
Hudson River Valley, New York

The cell phone video surfaces by the end of the first week after the Burj attack.

A young girl with her parents, posing as the family goes to breakfast. A fellow tourist holds the phone. Up angle, top of the Burj high in the background. The plane hits. The family straightens. The tourist backs away, still filming. Debris—a fragment of the plane, still travelling forward at cruising speed but deflected downward—slices through girl and father. Mother screams.

The networks run the happy family and cut the video off at the moment the plane strikes the building. The web runs the whole thing. Terror porn, the blood of innocents in a continuous loop.

Rogers sees the abridged clip on TV. He reads about the full video and doesn't want to watch it.

The mother is Afghani. She is beautiful, skin the color of beach sand after high tide, framing luminous green eyes. Her grief haunts the camera. The networks and cable run her image again and again.

Across America, cable news producers smile: Each network needs a logo for its attack coverage. The human face of the tragedy just happens to look like a cosmetics model. Win-win.

-o-

July 6
Brooklyn, New York

Col. Johnston McCaulley—"Mac" to everyone except his sister Angie —arrives at her cramped Brooklyn apartment in time to help with party set-up. Angie is turning 40, but since she and Mac share a birth month, she declared it was a joint birthday party to draw Mac north from Washington to see the rest of the family. Then her husband was called away for business, making Mac's presence indispensable. As the party begins, Angie tries both to track her two-year-old and to keep food and drink flowing, to the detriment of both efforts, even with Mac's help.

The dining room table serves as the primary buffet, with the kitchen table handling the overflow. Every other flat surface—side tables, coffee table, mantlepiece, and windowsills—is in use by people eating, or to clear plates. The scene has the constant mild chaos Mac associates with his family. He feels at home.

Rogers and Dub are down from the Hudson Valley. Mac is glad to see Rogers looking healthy, probably his best in years. Their last meeting was two years prior, when local cops stopped Mac while he was driving his Mercedes in Nelsonville after dark. The usual Driving While Black garbage, and Mac still burns at the indignity. He loved the Academy, and expected better from the area where he had gone to school.

Dub heads off to find drinks, leaving Mac and Rogers alone. "How's life defending the front lines of freedom, Colonel?"

"Sucks. How's life in the ivory tower?"

"Bad days and good."

At a few inches taller than six feet, Mac is slim the way his father had been. Only the beginning gray at the temples suggests he is not in his thirties.

Mac tells Rogers he has been serving in the DIA, Defense Intelligence Agency, for about a year, most recently monitoring troop positions around the Arabian Peninsula. "Country by country and army by army, watching potential flashpoints since Mecca. Then the Burj cranked tensions up higher. Both planes had connections to Iran, one coming from and one going to. Good news is that Iran and Saudis don't share a border. No flash points to escalate into actual war, with Iraq in between."

One side of the room erupts into an impromptu sing-along as the music switches to a Marvin Gaye classic.

"That part of the world is the leading international supplier of oil and religious fanatics. You'd think the attacks were the latter," Mac says.

Rogers shrugs. "No terrorists taking credit. The dog that didn't bark."

Mac's eyes narrow and his voice drops. "You still TS?"

"Yeah." Rogers had maintained his Top Secret status in order to do occasional consulting for DOD.

Mac nods. "Good to know. I may need a second set of eyes. Things that might require your particular talents."

In Iraq Rogers demonstrated reliable instincts for identifying when superiors put personal priorities ahead of mission requirements—he resented abuse of position and despised bullies—and Mac had used Rogers' "particular talents" to push back on unwise or dangerous orders more than once. Mac can tell Rogers catches his meaning.

"Let me know. I'll help," Rogers says quietly. "You want to talk to Maureen Dallas?"

"Is that the columnist?" Rogers nods. "I read her story the other day. Were you the 'noted terrorism authority'?"

"No, I was the 'Middle East expert with military background'."

"Thank God. The other guy she quoted was a whack job. But as for me talking, the short answer is no. Longer answer is hell no."

"I told her not to get her hopes up."

When Dub returns, they all talk about their kids for a bit. Mac's son Brandon had skipped the party, remaining in Washington with Shayera, Mac's ex. Mac's contact with his son in the years since the divorce has been sporadic at best, but Mac doesn't admit that, even to old friends. "He's good. He's figuring things out."

Angie passes by to say hello. "I remember you," Angie says to Rogers. "Bad guys in a pickup truck with a machine gun shooting at Johnny behind a wall, and you crashed your Humvee into them doing sixty."

Rogers looks down and says softly, "Mac and Chris Leinheimer, that's right. Probably only doing forty. The roads were terrible."

"Johnny says that truck crumpled up like a beer can." Angie gives Rogers a fond smile. "You know I'm grateful every day."

As Rogers prepares to leave, he and Mac agree to stay in touch. Mac goes off to receive other well-wishers. As the party breaks up, Mac finally connects for a quiet chat with Angie. Like Mac, she is slim, athletic, and ageless. She worries his son didn't come along.

"Brandon is getting so big." She puts her hand over Mac's arm. "He's thinking ahead, talking about college already. Wants to study math. He told me he wants to go to UCLA on either a math scholarship or a football scholarship."

"Natural student, natural athlete, he could make it. If he works his ass off."

"I told him that. He's not interested in the military, though."

"No, and I don't blame him. He saw what happened with his mom. Shayera wasn't cut out to be a military wife. It was unfair of me, really. To let the price of my choices fall so heavily on her."

Angie feigns a stern look. "Johnny, every woman in the world is too good for the man she married. I don't know why we women put up with it. But if you want to stay married, you just have to recognize that."

"Is that what you tell your husband?"

"Elston knows it. And he knows better than to argue with me about it, too. It's a good thing you work so late all the time. It would be a shame if you somehow had time on your hands and met somebody and went on a date."

"I'm not thinking that's the way it works for me."

"You don't want to think that's the way it works. That way there's no chance you get yourself close to somebody again."

"Angie, don't."

"Don't what? Be concerned? Care that you end up alone, or stay a stranger to your boy? I work hard, but I still have time for my husband and my baby. It can be done. You're just making excuses."

"You have no idea..."

"You know that's not true. And Brandon needs more attention from you than a weekend visit two times a month. Make a phone call once in a while, you've got a phone in your office. They have women in the military. You want someone who knows what the life is like? Go fraternize with some nice enlisted women," This time Angie gives a stern look like she means it.

"Harassment claim. Not doin' that," says Mac. "Maybe family life isn't what I want."

"Everybody needs people in their lives. Even you. Especially you. And you deserve someone to appreciate you, other than me. You can lie to me about it not being what you want, but some part of you knows you do. What kind of life do you want Brandon to have? I see him. He's a smart boy. But he's a little dreamy too, and you could do him a world of good. Spend more time. You got time with Dad. Give Brandon time with you."

Leaving Angie's to catch his return train, Mac wonders how much more time he would have been able to spend, even if he and Shayera had stayed together. Mac was second generation West Point. Mac's own father had been around only sporadically in childhood. Mac is proud of his father, who rose to lieutenant colonel and retired relatively young, but his father was not the primary parent in his upbringing. Angie and Mac only got to know him after his retirement, when he had more time.

At full colonel, Mac ranked ahead of his father at the same age. The promotion was a mark of extraordinary success, which part of Mac still felt was undeserved. One evening as a lieutenant, Mac had seen his commanding officer, a major, come back to barracks drunk. The base commander's car—personal car, not official vehicle—was in the lot. The major clipped it with the jeep and dented the bumper. No one else saw. The paint was going to be on the jeep and there was not going to be a question of the sequence of events. But the major had taken a jeep that was checked out to one of Mac's fellow lieutenants. The major saw Mac nearby. "You're not telling anyone about this," he said.

Mac had maintained his silence. The accused lieutenant protested but acknowledged that the jeep was checked out in his name, and since he had no idea who had actually done the deed, the blame fell on him. Mac had failed his fellow officer, falling short of the requirements of the honor code. Worse, the major had made Mac complicit in his misbehavior. Mac's cowardice had given the major a kind of leverage over him. Mac was glad two years later that the man was dishonorably discharged for a different problem. Mac told no one about it other than his sister, who wanted no part of Mac's self-torture over the matter. "What is it?" she said. "You think you're the only man in history who got scared? You think you're the only man in history who made a mistake?"

When Mac reaches Penn Station for the Acela back to Washington, he spends his waiting time in a restaurant near the departure gate. He isn't hungry. He takes a booth near the bar. He orders a tumbler of whiskey, and then a second.

Angie doesn't know the whole story about his marriage. Shayera hated the work schedule, the travel, his complaints about the bureaucracy, but worst of all, she hated the stories about men who lost it, killing themselves or attacking those close to them.

Mac had never lifted a finger toward Shayera, but their arguments could become loud and terrible. She saw the core of hard anger under Mac's surface of placidity and control and finally she couldn't be around him. "It's all just one bad day away," she said. "I don't want to be here when that day comes."

Remembering those conversations leaves Mac weary. The victories in his job tended to be kept quiet, so bad guys wouldn't learn how the military and law enforcement caught them. It's asymmetric, he thought. The victories occur off camera and the failures are public, when one guy gets through one time. That guy draws the media attention, and his victims, the random targets of his actions, receive brief wide sympathy and then fade into vague and nameless memories.

As for the families of the men and women standing guard—no public ledger tallies the cost to them in lives or health or missed happiness.

Mac watches a baseball game displayed on the TV above the bar without taking in what is happening. It is like looking into a campfire. He finishes his drink and walks to the train that will take him home.

-o-

July 12
Hudson River Valley, New York

Rogers is waiting at the kitchen table when Dub, just home from Stevie's ball game, sets two boxes of take-out pizza on the kitchen table. "I've got a consulting project with Mac," Rogers says.

Without looking up, she says, "Can you get out of it?"

Rogers thinks, this won't go well. She's not hiding her foreboding. He'd done small projects for the military to generate supplemental income in the past, but he knows Dub thinks workaholic Mac is a bad influence.

"It's short."

"It's a slippery slope."

"He needs me to give him a second opinion on the Burj attack," Rogers says. "They created an ad hoc inter-agency task force, the Burj Action Group. The BAG. Mac's working with the BAG now."

"Tony, I know you want to do this." Dub hugs him and looks up at his face. "I know you want to avoid working on your terrorism article, too."

"Avoiding the paper is an entirely unrelated side benefit." Rogers smiles. "But this is important."

"How much work? Enough to pay for vacation?"

"Fly down to D.C. next week, spend a day, maybe a couple days reviewing material. So, yeah, I'll make enough to cover our trip, with a little left over."

"Righting the world's wrongs is not all on your shoulders." She's the family disciplinarian, using her no-nonsense voice. Protective, which Rogers mostly loves and sometimes resents.

"You know how it is, Dub," Rogers says. "I'm just tackling the problems I can."

"I'm not trivializing your sense of duty. That's who you are."

"Two attacks, maybe terror, in the most uptight region of the world.

It's my area of expertise, and I get a chance to weigh in on an international crisis in real time? Of course I want in. I need to be in."

"Yes," says Dub. "But this job may be messy, and bigger than you think right now. Once you're in, it may be hard to get out."

"It's a consulting gig. You sound like you're sending me off to war."

"I believe in the power of negative thinking. Prove me wrong. We got a slow start in life, and I don't want to take a step back from inattention, or bad luck."

Together, they'd conducted Rogers' rehabilitation after Iraq like a military campaign: First he had to recover his present, then his career, then his future. Dub started out thinking it was her job to save him until eventually they both learned it was his job to save himself.

Neither of them liked who they'd been, over those years. The worst had been the trip to see the small hand-painted portraits of soldiers killed in the first years in Iraq, lined in a row on tables single file like 2,000 canvas tombstones. Each artist had dedicated the time, brushstroke by brushstroke, to commemorate a soul now gone. When Rogers came to Chris Leinheimer painted in sepia and white like a faded photo from the 1800s, he sighed and said, "I don't have it in me." Leinheimer's death wasn't Rogers' fault. But the facts were one thing, how Rogers felt after the war was another. Dub replied: "You're just a ray of fuckin' sunshine, aren't you?"

Their marriage survived the resulting public shouting match, but it was a narrow escape. Now, possessed of careers, home, and family, neither of them wants to go through another rebuild.

Dub softens her tone. "I prioritize vigilance first and opportunity second. There's no shame in a quiet life."

Rogers says nothing. He knows what she says is true. And also that she knows part of him was never right after Fallujah, that the work he was meant to do in the world was interrupted and is still unfinished and that he is haunted by a need to discover what it is and to restart it.

She isn't telling him no, but she isn't offering encouragement.

"This is a big deal, in your area of expertise," she says finally. "I get it."

Rogers downplays her concession. "It's a gig to keep my resume current, give the school something to point to about faculty being on top of current events. Insurance to rebuild Klamber's goodwill in case the article isn't enough."

"Yeah, well, whose fault is that?"

"But you love me anyway."

"Depends on the day." She takes a teasing tone. "You're an acquired taste—you have a habit of advertising your flaws and forcing people to dig for your virtues."

She pulls the pizza wheel from the drawer and slices each pizza into eighths. Stevie won't eat mushrooms and he gets a whole pie to himself. "Go tell Stevie dinner's ready to serve. I'll set the table."

When Rogers returns with Stevie, she takes his arm and says, "Please."

She doesn't specify what she's asking. He'll get what he wants but she's warning he doesn't know the price.

Dub dishes out the pizza and says, "You're taking Stevie to his game tomorrow."

-o-

July 18
Arlington, Virginia

After playing the voicemail, Mac takes a second to get his bearings. Francisco Nino's voice is familiar from their years in Iraq, but the context is wrong: "We have the black box from the Burj."

Why is his old pal Cisco calling him from the National Transportation Safety Board test lab to talk about something that is none of Cisco's business? How did the NTSB get involved?

Mac returns the call and Cisco gives him a quick background: The cockpit voice recorder was thrown clear from the wreckage of the Burj, but so badly damaged as to make it unplayable. To get help fixing it, an investigator from the Emirates counterpart to the NTSB sent the box by

DHL courier to the American technician he had met at an international conference. Skipped proper channels.

"So here is maybe the smoking gun from the attack, depending on what is recoverable, sitting in U.S. possession," Mac says. He looks around his office. The call feels like he's fallen down a rabbit hole.

Cisco wants to stay out of trouble, and to keep his subordinate, the tech guy with the Emirates buddy, out of trouble too. "I don't think they broke the law, but they sure as hell didn't follow procedure. Who should I turn this over to?"

Mac tells Cisco he will come by and get the box to the right place. Mac isn't being selfless. He thinks the CIA is hiding some of what it knows about the attack, and Mac wants his own sources, perhaps even some information to barter.

Mac drives to the NTSB lab in Virginia in his personal car, out of uniform. Cisco is in the lobby to greet him. Mac observes that civilian life agrees with Cisco too well: Back home without military fitness regs to live up to, Cisco is 50 pounds over his service weight. They had been the same rank during their military days and fall easily into their former verbal jousting.

"Long time," Cisco says.

"Measured in belt size, yeah."

"I like to cook and I like to eat, man, you know that." Cisco makes an expression of feigned injury and the two men laugh.

"You need to do push-ups, man. The horizontal kind, away from the table."

"You see how desperate I am for a favor if I call a cold-blooded prick like you."

"I'm only this way talking to you. It's like riding a bike, it just all comes back."

Cisco escorts Mac down a series of pale green hallways into a conference room. The room is a junkyard. Cables run randomly to equipment stacked against walls and on the meeting table. In the middle of the table is a battered metal box wired to stand-alone speakers and a laptop computer.

Cisco fills in the details about the box's journey to the U.S. Dubai crews dealing with Burj debris were about to throw the twisted bit of metal away, but the Emirates technician on-site recognized the box before it was junked. The techie ran the tests he could in his own lab, but couldn't get the box to give up any data. He then called his friend from NTSB, Joey Kim, whom he'd met in Switzerland the prior year.

"No one else even knows the box made it through the crash," Cisco says. "The Emirates techie asks Kim for advice, and Kim says, 'We have equipment here, let us take a shot.' So the guy on the ground in Dubai couriers it to Kim."

"DHL," says Mac. "He has what could be a crucial part of evidence in the investigation into the terrorists who smashed into the tallest building in the world, and he drops it into DHL."

"Not my idea. Not Joey's idea, either. At least, that's what he says."

"This...." Mac is at a loss for words. The casual handling of this potentially valuable evidence is frustrating. How can anyone rely on it? Is it even the real thing? What was the Emirates techie thinking?

"We tracked everything on our end. Full documentation of all handling, every procedure we did. We're in the chain of evidence business. We know how things are supposed to be done."

"Yeah, but the Emirates contact was so flaky, it may do us no good in the end," Mac says.

Mac and Cisco sit in chairs against the wall, both looking at the jumble of wires and boxes. "It happens when you're dealing with nerds," Cisco says. "Kim vouches for the guy, says he's just a science guy, not a forensics guy, looking for results. He wasn't getting them with his own equipment, so he called in the big boys. Maybe, too, he didn't want to tell his boss he failed, and tried to go around the process to get help."

Mac pushes both hands against his head. "Maybe we'll get lucky and it'll be worthless. My boss likes details buttoned up, and I don't want to have to explain this to him. Right now, all we have is a flattened box that may or may not talk to us. Have I got it right?"

"Box got here yesterday. We have equipment to analyze damage to physical media, see what kind of restoration is possible. Kim has done a few things. I'll call him in and we'll see if it works."

"Any national security clearances for you guys?"

"No. Not an issue for our usual work. But we're discreet. We're pros."

"I'll get a waiver for you after the fact. I assume you want to listen?"

"There may not be anything to listen to, but sure." Cisco calls for Kim to join them. Mac thinks the situation through. For all he knows, the existence of the box itself might be top secret to someone—people in charge of classification sometimes have a heavy hand. But he wants to stay on the right side of it.

Kim arrives, a young dark-haired man with an eager look. Kim is proud of his work. "I got signals. I think we're going to get voice."

"This was the cockpit voice recorder, not the data recorder, correct?" Mac asks.

"Correct. Data recorder vanished, is what my colleague said."

"Could have been crushed and mixed in with other garbage. We just don't know," Cisco says.

"Shall I play what I've got for you?"

Mac asks if the room is secure.

"Take it to the Pentagon, if you're nervous," Kim says.

"What the hell. Let's see if we got anything."

Kim turns on the machine. A visual computer readout shows simultaneously with the audio playback. Kim explains there is no time stamp. He doesn't know how much data he has, or which part of the flight it is from. Total data size makes him think there are about 5 minutes of sound. Just a sliver. And at that, it might be just white noise.

Then a sudden sound comes from the speakers. English. Universal language for airline pilots. They would use English to talk to air traffic control, and if the crew was international, they would use it among themselves.

The first minute consists of crew members running through steps in a procedure. One person, co-pilot maybe, is reading from a manual and another is responding. They are trying to re-establish a malfunctioning system.

"Before the terrorists came into the cockpit?" Mac wonders aloud.

Then an attempted radio transmission:

"Tower, this is KLM 3383, we are experiencing handling issues. The autopilot has engaged itself and I am unable to override manually. Over."

Silence.

"Tower, repeat, this is KLM 3383, our autopilot has engaged itself and I cannot override. I have no control over the aircraft......Tower, can you hear? Tower?"

This is wrong, thinks Mac. Where are the terrorists? The control tower was out of touch with the plane just before the attack, and everyone assumed the terrorists were in control and being quiet. But this first piece of sound was strictly pilot/co-pilot talk, then the crew trying to reach air traffic control.

More discussion of steps among the crew. And then another attempt to radio out:

"Tower, we're turning, turning back, circling. Tower, we are approaching... we can see the skyline. We are about 10 minutes out from Dubai, at our current speed. No control over airspeed or direction."

"Can we just shut down all the systems and reboot?"

"I don't know how. If we lose the flaps we couldn't even glide. We'd just fall like a rock."

"We don't have any control now. I don't know if that would be worse."

"Tower, we are unable to assert any control over the plane. Skies are clear. No turbulence, no external conditions."

Cisco speaks over the recording: "Autopilot engages itself and no radio? That's two failures at once. That doesn't happen."

"Is there anything in the manual about physical disconnect for autopilot? Just tear the wires out? Clip 'em?"

"Still looking..."

"Tower, Tower? KLM 3383. Can you read?"

"...nothing, nothing..."

"Look."

"What?"

"Up ahead. The Burj."

"God..."

"Give me the fire extinguisher."

[metallic banging sound]

"What's going on?" Mac asks.

"Trying to smash the controls for the autopilot, my guess," says Kim.

"Tower, tower. We are on a direct course for Dubai, three miles out. No steering. We are at 1500 feet. Tower, no control here. Repeat, no..."

Silence. The recording is over.

Mac looks around the room. No one speaks. They'd all seen the footage of the moment of impact, as the plane flew near, and then into, the tower. They knew the aftermath. Emirates emergency personnel didn't have training at the level of the NYC first responders on 9/11, and the chaos on the ground was immense.

"So, we...." Mac begins.

"We heard all there is to hear," Kim says.

"I didn't hear any terrorists."

"No."

"I didn't hear any psycho pilots on a suicide mission doing the steering themselves, either," says Cisco.

"No. This sounds like remote control." Kim is up reviewing settings on the equipment, trying to tease more sound from the black box.

"Like someone hacked into the autopilot? Is that even possible?" Mac asks.

"It's impossible to hack an autopilot. The protections are way too dense. There is no way to hack ACARS, and then hack a specific plane navigation system," Kim says. "Years back, a hacker claimed he made entry into flight controls by cutting into on-board entertainment, live on the flight, but even that needed physical connection. There's no way to just dial up on Wi-Fi and turn a 737 into a radio-controlled model plane."

"But the plane was on autopilot and the pilots weren't the ones that started it," Cisco says.

"That's what it sounded like to me too."

Mac is somber. "And it flew into the tallest building in the world. That's not an accident."

Mac uses his field voice, the one he uses to command troops with no backtalk. "You gentlemen have just become privy to one of the biggest national security secrets that has ever existed. You have to maintain complete silence on this. No wives, no girlfriends, no emails, no texts, no drinking buddies, no phone calls. Nothing. Nothing. No calling the Emirates—not until we coordinate with State. Your friend who sent you this, Kim?"

"Yeah."

"You tell him nothing. You stall. You tell him it's harder than expected, and maybe you're not going to get anything at all. But get all the details about where this came from, if he'll share. Who else has seen it, who has touched it, everything. Tell him it's standard American forensics." Mac gives Kim a hard and uncompromising stare.

"Okay."

"Right now there are three people in the world who have this information. I am telling no one outside my chain of command, so if I see a word of this in the press, you are both up on espionage charges. Got it? This cannot under any circumstances leak."

The other two men nod their agreement. Mac asks if they had flight data from the Burj. Cisco reminds him that the flight data recorder never turned up. Mac asks about external data recordings, records of the flight path the doomed airliner took. Kim has a simulated flight path at hand, and his computer shows the plane taking off and then, instead of ascending to proper flying height, leveling off and taking a slow curve into the building. The men watch dots on the screen portray the final moments of a flight that ended with thousands dead. The plane flies directly to the Burj and evaporates from the screen.

Kim says, "They were maybe a couple minutes out from the Burj. Time of radio loss was around 6:30 a.m. local time. Transponder cut out too. We heard about nine and a half minutes. If their estimate on distance from the Burj was right, then our segment ended under one minute before impact. Radio contact was gone from about 20 minutes before impact."

Running his finger along the colored line of the flight path on the video display, Kim says, "We came in during the middle of the movie—here. They'd already lost radio. From here, to here. After the part we heard, they struck the tower."

Mac is already considering next steps. What he's learning is certainly not all there is to know. "You're telling me that what we just heard, about the radio and autopilot—the timing correlates with what you know, externally, about the flight path."

"Correct. Unless these pilots were the greatest actors in the world, this thing was on autopilot. No terrorists on board. Someone turned this plane into a giant fucking drone," Kim says.

"It's goofy. But it fits the facts," says Cisco.

Mac asks Kim, "The source of the Burj flight path, is that a database you can use to pull the information on the Mecca flight path too?"

"Maybe." Mac and Cisco walk for coffee while Kim searches. By the time they return, Kim has the information ready on his laptop. He pulls up a screen that depicts a flat map of the area surrounding the Grand Mosque, then superimposes the flight path.

"See, here is the flight from Iran, heading toward the airport. Then at this point, here, we see departure from flight path, vaguely in the direction of the Grand Mosque. But not on line. See? This shows the plane is off path for landing but not heading on a line for the Mosque."

"What about radio?" asks Cisco.

"Radio and transponder contact lost at around the time the plane left the path." There was a spot on the line, lit to show where radio contact died.

Mac says, "The attacks at Mecca and the Burj both had loss of radio contact."

"Yeah. But we don't have data or voice recorders from either one, except for this partial recording from Burj. Joey, where was the Mecca plane headed, if not to the mosque?"

"Nowhere in particular. No major buildings on the route."

"Straight line?" Cisco asks.

"Curved." Kim points to the arc on the screen. "See, you get the point of departure from the flight path, then the plane banks slightly to make a turn. But the turn goes nowhere. And it stays in that turn for about 30 minutes."

"Like circling a fixed point. Until they get shot down," Mac says.

"Until they get shot down, that's right," says Cisco.

"How close to the mosque?"

"At the nearest point? Maybe 40 miles," said Kim.

"No real danger to the Grand Mosque, then," Cisco says.

"The Saudis saw it differently. Mysterious airplane a few minutes flying time from the holiest site to a religion with a billion followers." Mac says.

"Sorry," Cisco says. "Not what I meant. From the data we have, when we show the flight path, there was no attempt to make the plane a direct danger to the mosque."

"Not from the data we show about the flight path, right."

Mac makes a command decision. "I better take custody of the box. Keep it secure."

"You got it. Get that damn thing away from me." Cisco has gone from being dubious about what course to take regarding the voice recorder, to seeing it as something cursed.

"Yeah. We say nothing to nobody, until you give us the word," Kim says.

"I can't tell you how long anything will take, maybe a few weeks even. It shouldn't be forever, but then, it's the government, so..." Mac offers them no assurances how long an information blackout would be. The box changes everything about his investigation.

"I got plenty of other work to do," Kim says.

"Yeah, maybe we'll get lucky, have a bus full of Cub Scouts drop into the Grand Canyon," Cisco says. "Give us something else to think about."

Mac shook his head. "God's gonna strike you dead, man."

Cisco shrugged. "Hasn't yet."

-o-

July 19
Washington, D.C.

Rogers meets Maureen Dallas and her husband John at a chophouse in the District. There are no bad restaurants in D.C. in Rogers' thinking, nor cheap ones. But his agreement calls for him to have meal expenses covered, since he would meet Mac in the morning. The restaurant is formal and old, with cherry wood paneling, dark cloth booths, and a sound system playing Sinatra and other lounge music in the background. Maureen and John wave to Rogers from the table.

Rogers knows John from meeting him at a party once. A reporter at the Wall Street Journal, John stands nearly a foot taller than his wife. No long night, they explain when Rogers sits down. Their son Mikey is with neighbors for an evening out, but they can't linger.

"How is Mikey?"

"Like the Bugs Bunny character, the Tasmanian Devil, after two espressos and a couple of chocolate bars," says Maureen. "He's playing soccer over the summer."

"Soccer's about to make it big in America you know. Any decade now," Rogers says.

"I want Mikey to get a tan and run himself ragged. He looks angelic when he's asleep."

"We know better," says John.

"We've got Stevie playing baseball. Not the same energy burn as soccer. Fresh air, sportsmanship—that's all I ask."

"How about this?" John says. "Boy-sized hamster wheels. Let 'em run it off. Alternative energy. Maybe hook it up to run a phone charger." John takes a sip of wine. "Million-dollar idea there, right?"

"John used to cover entrepreneurs. He gets ideas," Maureen explains.

"My most recent assignment is covering worldwide money laundering —huge business. The International Monetary Fund estimates that 2% to 5% of world GDP gets siphoned off between drug cartels, organized crime, and corrupt governments ripping off their citizens. Putin alone is maybe worth $200 billion. He and his buddies rob the Russian government and hide the money in the West."

"It's easier for me to imagine a giant hamster wheel than numbers that big," Rogers says. "If you build one before Stevie discovers girls, I'll buy it."

"Will you get him into rowing?" Maureen asks.

"Not competitively. That's just masochism disguised as a sport," Rogers says.

"No athletic DNA for our kid, either side. Strong genes for writing, I suppose," John says.

"You never know. My parents didn't pick me to go for history and languages. Or the military. My dad was an accountant, but I had to marry into the profession."

"How's your dad?" Maureen asks. "Your brother?"

"Okay. We see Dad next month for his birthday. Take Stevie to Disneyland, come back via Arizona. Dad's getting in a lot of golf. My sister looks in on him, since she's CFO with a company there. James wound up in foreign service. Part of the delegation to the Holy See."

"Oh, well, Rome!" says Maureen. "There's a hardship post."

"Somebody's gotta do it."

"Do you still row?" she asks.

"Now and again," Rogers says. "Not to compete. But sometimes, it's good to be out in the morning, feel the air just above the water. Then, when you get the right rhythm, the oar cuts at just the right angle and you keep up the rhythm... it's one of those perfect things."

Maureen turns to her husband. "I dated Tony's college roommate. Another rower. I was starting out on the school paper. Tony was All-Ivy in single scull and I interviewed him at the Head of the Charles Regatta."

"I had the best time in the Ivies coming into the race, but I lost. And I was furious. And you came up to me and asked me about the race."

"The key to good journalism is timing." Maureen smiles. "First you said you wouldn't talk. When I asked again, you said to me, 'I'll tell you what. I'll pretend to tell you the truth, and you pretend to believe me.' And then you said the usual bland forgettable athlete, 'I could have done better... blah blah blah.' And now I have a column where your quip is my brand."

"I saw. Should I get royalties?"

"Don't let's ruin an old friendship haggling over money."

"I was so mad. I wanted to be a good sport when I talked to you. But at the moment you came up to me, I was furious at the son of a bitch who won. Yalie. Ahead of the race, we were talking, and I used the old show business expression, 'Break a leg.' And he kicks me, right on the shin bone, and says, 'You too.' And then he walked away."

"Wait, he kicked you before the race?" John asks.

"Yeah. Sort of hurt, but mostly it was shock he'd done that. All ahead of the race and getting into the boat it got me angry that the guy was such a jerk. Then in the race I ran out too fast. I burned up all my energy, didn't focus. My strokes got choppy. Instead of a disciplined race, I was out of control, and I lost. Which I'm sure he wanted," Rogers says.

"No. You didn't tell me that," Maureen says. "You rat. That was a much better story than what I wound up writing."

"I was playing at being a good sport, even if I wasn't." Rogers pauses as the waiter begins to serve the table. "Vivid memory. I never got a rematch against the guy. It was a valuable lesson for me, on staying in control, staying calm, even when circumstances are against you. Actually, I never learn the lesson, just recognize it after the fact again and again."

"There was the war, too...." Maureen says. "But you look good now."

"Thanks," says Rogers. "A kick in the leg, you work out yourself. PTSD, to the extent you get over it, you don't do that alone."

"She's having trouble sleeping since the Burj," John says.

Rogers looks at Maureen, who gives a resigned shrug. "I'm getting help," she says.

"My roommate—the rower—was in One World Trade," Rogers explains to John.

He nods. "David. I know."

"All of Washington had PTSD for a decade after 9/11. The political class." Maureen looks around the room, a dining spot for the group she is berating. "No attempt to recover, and no effort to help the public recover either. Just macho posturing, stirring up tribal resentment for campaign purposes. They went on to other things, but I worry Mecca and Dubai will bring it all back."

"You don't have a high opinion of the people you cover, sounds like."

"Why should I? The worst of them are dishonest manipulators, and even the decent ones don't always stand up to the liars." As Maureen becomes animated, Rogers holds up the wine bottle. She gestures 'yes' for a refill of her glass and keeps going.

"FDR—he couldn't even walk, but he got people to fight back against the Great Depression, and then go fight Nazis. I despair over how much worse our politicians are, compared to the rest of the population. No FDRs out there now." She takes a sip.

"It's hard to create post-terrorism politics if people keep flying airplanes into buildings," Rogers observes.

"That's kind of my point. Attacks are political for the terrorists. For everybody else, it's like, 'Hey, I was out shopping today and some asshole tried to kill me with a car bomb.' Yes, military and government have to prevent it, but really, terrorism is just another stupid, random way to die, like being hit by lightning or falling out of a roller coaster."

"Being eaten by an alligator at Disneyworld," says John.

"See?" says Maureen. "Who expects to get eaten by an alligator at

Disneyworld? But, you know, it happened. It's sad for the people it happens to, and then...everyone has to move on. Vigilance doesn't mean being scared all the time."

"You think terrorism is just another celebrity who gets too much publicity?" Rogers asks.

"Absolutely! Over-hyped. Terrorism is just another member of the fucking Kardashian family."

John says, "Cyber-security and disruption from climate change are much bigger dangers, globally. And whatever is being done behind the scenes about corruption and money laundering, agencies and politicians never talk about it."

"My incoming cadets are so young that 9/11 is just more ancient history, like Pearl Harbor or Gettysburg. Or the Roman Empire," says Rogers.

The waiter brings the dessert menu. Maureen asks Rogers about his D.C. plans.

"Fly in and fly out, actually. I have an early meeting tomorrow so I thought I would come in early and get a chance to catch up."

"Visiting old friends other than us? Like, military friends?"

"Fishing much?" Rogers replies.

"You're a Middle East expert." Maureen is guessing about his presence in town.

"I've got a whole lot of 'no comment' on this line of questions. Mostly what I'm doing is playing hooky from working on a paper comparing modern terrorism to ancient terrorism. I could bore you with the details, but in all modesty, I predict this article will be breathtaking in its mediocrity."

John leans in. "I'll give you a new line on the whole terrorist question. From the business side. The latest rumor right now is that there was insider trading off the Burj attack. Uptick in short sales against Boeing just before the attack. Rumors in the market are overseas accounts."

"So, what are you saying? Terrorists have stockbrokers?"

"You can get a mobile app and trade from your phone in the desert," John says.

-o-

July 20
Pentagon

After Rogers clears security, a talkative corporal escorts him to the meeting room. The young man is energetic and courteous, although he looks like he should still be in high school. The corporal tells Rogers he plans to attend college on the GI Bill after his enlistment is done, and to become an engineer designing medical devices. Rogers doesn't begrudge the corporal his certainty about what his future holds. Maybe the boy will get lucky.

The path to their destination, an outer wall E Ring office on the Second Floor, off Corridor 6, near the exhibit on the work of the Defense Intelligence Agency, carries them past displays of uniforms and equipment honoring each service, and photographs and paintings commemorating each American conflict since the Revolution. The Pentagon is an office building but its corridors are also a museum.

Mac is already seated at the conference room table when they arrive. He shakes hands with Rogers and orders coffee for the two of them, omitting small talk. Mac promptly launches into a background summary. DNI Thorpe's premise in creating the ad hoc Burj Action Group—the BAG—is that Mecca and the Burj were the same cast of characters, not two separate terrorist groups. Thorpe wants to coordinate what is learned about the Burj to provide insight about Mecca, and vice versa.

"I'm DIA's representative at BAG meetings. I present a short military assessment on regional troop status, and that's it. We—DIA—are more or less cut out of investigating Mecca. Other agencies have the lead. CIA and NSA mainly. The guy calling the shots on what we get to see at DIA is

CIA Director Nadeau, and his choice on what we get to see outside of BAG meetings is, 'not much.' "

"Sounds like the bureaucracy we all know and love," says Rogers.

"The Agency has a long process before it commits to a finding—I get that. But I have a sense there is some gamesmanship, where the CIA lets everyone else declare what they know, and then CIA just echoes. That prompted my request for your particular talents. But that was before yesterday."

"What changed?"

"I'm getting there." Mac sets the context: After Mecca, all known terror groups fell silent. Islamists all deny being part of the attack, and the denials keep checking out as genuine. No one has other suspects, but the Islamist terror groups condemn the attackers as infidels and non-believers.

"And now I have new information. There were no terrorists at the Burj."

"Say again?" Rogers says.

"The plane hit the Burj due to sabotage or hacking. There were no terrorists or suicidal pilots on the plane. We got the voice recorder. And unless we have two groups of terrorists, or saboteurs, or whatever, running around the Middle East at the same time using identical techniques, that means there were no terrorists at Mecca either." Mac walks Rogers through the story of the black box and about the similar flight paths and radio behavior of the Mecca and Burj planes.

The news sounds impossible, yet at his core Rogers immediately feels it to be true. Rogers tells himself to tamp down his emotions to let pure calculation take over. "I had doubts about terrorist involvement."

Mac's face is solemn. "A change in the methodology means a change in the list of who might have done it. Sabotage or hacking lets out independent terrorist groups; the resources to develop that kind of tech would be too complex. Maybe turns it into a state action, or state-supported."

"An act of war, not terrorism."

"Possibly." Mac's voice is soft and the subject matter is grave. "Not slippery terrorists, but someone trying to start a hot war in the Middle East."

Rogers sits quietly with his old friend for a moment. The implications are immense. "Who else knows?"

"No one. The NTSB guys. I brief my commanding officer this afternoon." Mac wants a definitive write-up from the NTSB first, so as to anticipate and answer questions about the chain of custody and authenticity of the black box. Mac needs any presentation on the Burj black box to be complete, conclusive, and up to the precise and demanding standards of his commanding officer, Major General Ashton Smith.

Mac knows from experience not to bring material to Smith without being fully prepared. "You haven't lived until you've had Smith correct your sentence while you are speaking it during an oral briefing," Mac says. "You'd know him if you saw him, he just towers over everybody walking in the corridors here. He's 6-7 and maybe weighs 150 pounds, like a scarecrow, but he does Pilates and yoga, so he's actually pretty athletic. And he is very, very meticulous."

Mac looks at Rogers intently. "Originally I wanted to brainstorm on why I was getting hinky results from the bureaucracy. Now I need you to evaluate what I'm getting. I need someone whose judgment I trust and whose reports come to me alone, outside the chain of command. I don't worry about NSA or the FBI, but their priorities may not match with mine. I need intelligence that ties into military perspective."

"You think someone in the BAG is lying," Rogers says.

"Or hiding something. I need you to help me sort out who it is, why they might be doing it, and my options for doing something about it."

-o-

July 21 to July 25
Hudson Valley, New York

Rogers returns with a Pentagon-issued laptop that can access electronic files through the Pentagon firewall from a SCIF, a sensitive compartmented information facility, on West Point campus. The room is rarely used as a SCIF and instead is storage for stacked boxes that Rogers needs to move out of the way to create a space to work. Access to the SCIF needs Klamber's sign-off, which is a mixed blessing. Klamber will be pleased the Army is giving Rogers a top top-secret space to work on a high-importance project, less happy Rogers is neglecting his article.

For work at home, Rogers has a banker's box of non-classified printed material. Couriers bring a daily pouch with updated DIA materials and a copy of the Washington Post. The small study is cluttered with boxes containing the books and printouts for his academic research, along with a desk, a chair, bookshelves on every wall, and a recliner for Rogers to do more leisurely reading. Removing the recliner would create space but Rogers has his priorities, and being able to stretch out from time to time is one of them.

BAG material is voluminous if not always consequential. Reports prepared by CIA, NSA, State, DIA, and other agencies. A spreadsheet of reports organized by date and by agency, cross-tabbed to underlying Arab language documents, signal transcripts, and other source material. Rogers doesn't speak Farsi and must rely on CIA translations of material from Iran.

The core facts are not in dispute. The number of dead on each plane, the number dead on the ground. The total came to 2,053 dead, plus countless injured. Rogers knows the history and social structure of the region; he's been teaching it. But it takes days to pick up the intricacies of present-day internal politics country by country.

State Department assesses the regional political status quo as strained but intact. Borders militarized, but no likely flashpoints. Mac agrees.

After the first plane, Iran replaced its interior minister with the transportation minister, Ali Sanjani, who claimed his political enemies were in league with the Mecca terrorists and conducted a purge. Iran's defense minister, Ahmed Azel, focused on border issues, leaving Sanjani room to take over the police and Treasury. Sanjani quickly consolidated a role second only to the prime minister, eliminating political opponents and distributing billions of dollars of port infrastructure contracts along the Caspian Sea to make new friends.

NSA evaluations of signal traffic from known terrorists used 9/11 as a template. But, thinks Rogers: Signal behavior for sabotage wouldn't look anything like the "chatter" involved in coordinating live attacks. Rogers' first recommendation to MAC is that NSA re-evaluate what it has, to see if there were other anticipatory signs.

BAG minutes support Mac's observation that the CIA offers up nothing that hadn't already come first from other agencies. Given the Agency's resources, it should have something to bring to the party. Rogers sees nothing to explain why CIA wants to drag its feet. Rogers' best guess: The CIA is protecting an intelligence asset somewhere in the Middle East, and putting out new information might accidentally expose sources or methods.

The BAG participants all assume live terrorists in a 9/11 style hijacking. Once the black box enters the picture, considering sabotage means rethinking not just the question of 'who,' but also the question of 'what happened.' This vexes Rogers, sitting in the recliner with a yellow pad setting out his questions. Maybe Mecca was never a target. The flight path wasn't aimed at the Mosque. What if the goal at Mecca wasn't to damage the Grand Mosque, but to get the Saudis to shoot down an Iranian plane? And how had Saudis been able to muster jets so quickly, if the radio only cut off 20 minutes earlier?

Near the end of his several-day cram session, Rogers hears the small click of the door being opened. Only Stevie's head enters the room. "We're going for ice cream. You want us to bring you back something?"

Rogers joins Stevie and Dub for an outing. They walk the leafy streets sheltered from the summer sun. They laugh and chat and wave to neighbors. They sit at an outside table to enjoy each other's company and the cool and sweet treats. Rogers tells Stevie about Henry Hudson and the early explorers and pioneers in the valley. Stevie's features are starting to settle in—his mother's eyes, but the resemblance to Rogers is becoming pronounced. Stevie is gangly and enthusiastic and coltish. Rogers stops himself to make sure to take it all in. It is a moment to savor and cherish.

Rogers recalled a summer's night when Stevie was an infant and the windows were open and a fan was running but the humid air still held the heat of the day. Rogers awoke near midnight gripped by the sense a spirit of malice hovered nearby. The Hudson River Valley was famously home to tales of ghosts. Body tingling and slightly chilled, Rogers put on a robe and found Stevie lying peacefully in his crib. Rogers then sat in Dub's nursing rocker and held the boy against his bare skin, wrapped under the robe, and fell asleep. When he awoke two hours later he could feel the presence no more.

Returning from the ice cream outing, Rogers turns to his academic paper. Historic terror group leadership structures and succession are known well enough, from the early IRA to the post-WWII activities of Haganah and Irgun, then later the PLO, and then Al-Qaeda and ISIS. He adds paragraphs from non-classified materials to address how Mecca and the Burj differ from historic patterns. Even leaving out the flight recorder, he has room to argue that there are holes in the "terrorists at the Burj and Mecca" theory.

Turning in the article will save him one more battle. It turns out Klamber was right—Rogers learned something from doing the paper. Lack of evidence of an organization or leadership structure in the recent attacks reinforces his theory against terrorism. The Mecca message had been anonymous. No signal activity. No obvious ideology. And no obvious financial structure to support terrorist leadership or an organization. The State Department reported that Sanjani cracked down on political opponents he claimed were tied to the terrorists, but the purported 'Lions of Jihad' blamed by Sanjani were nothing more than a website. The CIA didn't challenge Sanjani's claim to have taken down terrorists, but the international community gave his claim no credence.

Someone had to benefit from the attacks, why not Iran? Sanjani never shared any intelligence about the alleged Mecca plotters, reinforcing the assessment their arrests were merely a power grab on his part.

Rogers opens the Post. On the op-ed page, there is a column, illustrated by a black and white photo of the famous grieving mother from the Burj. Even without color, her image halts the eye. The headline, though, is even more arresting: "Reaping What They Sowed."

The writer, Thomas Cutler, disdains sympathy expressed for the Muslim victims of the Burj attack. He wants Americans to keep their hearts hardened at all times against all Muslims, lest a new attack land on American shores due to weakness in American resolve.

Rogers remembers the book Cutler promoted at West Point months before. Rogers was offended by the man's self-importance. Still, as Rogers looks back on that presentation, he decides he needs to put Cutler on Mac's radar.

-o-

July 29
Washington, D.C.

The judge enters his chamber in gym clothes, blue spandex shorts, and a Dartmouth T-shirt, ahead of his morning squash game in the facilities beneath the courthouse. He hangs his robe on a hook on the back of the door, for later.

The FISA hearing is before regular court hours. If the hearing is informal, it is nonetheless highly confidential and legally precise. The government—in this case, attorneys appearing on behalf of the Department of Justice and the FBI—wants a court order under the Foreign Intelligence Surveillance Act to allow wiretaps and to intercept mail and emails. No defense attorney is present, as the goal is to keep the target from knowing what the government is doing.

"What have you gentlemen brought me?" the judge asks. The three lawyers from the U.S. Attorney's office are in full business attire. They present the judge with a bound printed copy of the brief in a brown leather folder, and a thumb drive with an electronic version.

"Requests for surveillance of two U.S. nationals and their affiliates, connected to existing interception of communications with a Russian national, currently resident in England," says the lead attorney.

"What's the subject matter?"

"Since the attack on the Burj Khalifa on July 1, the FBI has been investigating a series of securities trades suspected to have been made with advance knowledge of the attack. The traders attempted to conceal their identities and collectively made approximately $70 million on those trades. We have identified two of the traders: Jared Cain, a U.S. citizen, and Ivan Zaroff, a Russian national living in London. A third unidentified trader made approximately $10 million. We suspect that third individual is Hugh Abbott, a U.S. citizen, but that is not yet confirmed."

The judge leans in, standing. He looks impressed. "So, a total of $80 million in profits on a terrorist attack? Were these guys working with the terrorists?"

"A total of $70 million, with the third trader representing about $10 million of the seventy," the attorney corrects. "Sorry for the ambiguity. And as for the relationship to the attackers, we currently don't know."

"It's a staggering amount, either way. What's the rest of the story, in summary? I assume the full version is here in the brief." He taps the folder.

"Yes, including the securities investigation details. We first tracked trading profits to Cain, who manages a hedge fund in New York City named Herakles Investments. Through Herakles, we found another trail of profits that led to Zaroff, who operates businesses overseas. When we started tracking what Cain and Zaroff had in common, we found Abbott, who is employed by the CIA."

"Is this mostly a financial crime that has a link to terrorism, or do you think it's espionage by Abbott, with a money angle?" the judge asks.

"We don't know yet. We did discover that Abbott got the CIA to intervene to stop an investigation of Herakles by the New York Attorney General."

"Wait a minute." The judge ceases the light warm-up stretches he had been doing and faces them, then moves to his desk. "If you have the CIA actively involved, do you know whether you're getting in the middle of a CIA operation? Does the CIA know you're looking at this?" the judge said.

"It's a potential counter-intelligence matter, finding out if one of our spies has turned traitor. We'll be coordinating with the Director of National Intelligence, but for now we need to keep the investigation compartmented from the rest of the Intelligence Community."

"In other words, no, you don't have CIA cooperation. Nobody's communicating, and nobody trusts anybody else, and you're asking me to get in the middle with a FISA warrant." The judge prefers plain speaking, and if the attorneys won't do it, he will.

"No," says the attorney. "Not really," he amends.

"Explain 'not really' to me, counsel. Abbott got someone in the CIA to vouch for his operation in front of the New York AG. If you don't know what he's doing, or whether there's a problem with it, what's your basis for asking for a FISA warrant?"

"Making profits on a terrorist attack can't be an authorized CIA operation. At a minimum Cain and Zaroff are profiteering outside any legitimate work they were doing for the CIA."

The judge considers the point briefly, finally saying, "I'll accept that."

"We're working our way up the chain to find out who was behind the attack."

The judge rises from his chair. "I'll go through your brief to confirm you have a solid basis for what you've told me. My inclination is to give you a provisional warrant, but I want you to confirm that you aren't working at cross-purposes to a legitimate CIA operation, and I want either CIA or DNI approval on this. I'll be in touch by the end of the day with a temporary order, or if I have any questions. But if you don't get me the confirmation from the DNI, the order expires in seven days, and anything you collect will be off limits in court. Is that all right?"

The attorney looks unhappy but isn't going to argue. "Yes, your honor. We can work with that."

"If these guys were part of the attack, I want you to have every legal tool to go get them." The judge returns to his warm-up. "But let's exercise some discretion here, okay?"

-o-

July 30
Washington, D.C.

As Thorpe enters the conference room, he sees Andy Mayfair, the slim FBI agent, standing at the whiteboard, where he has written "BURJ STOCK PROFITEERS" ahead of the briefing. Mayfair's partner, Brooks, is nearly Mayfair's height even sitting down, and next to Brooks is Ken Robeson, the senior agent from the FBI's counter-intelligence section.

"Bottom-line this for me before class starts," Thorpe says. "I assume I'm here because you found something these past weeks."

The FBI men look at each other. "Pretty much," says Robeson.

Brooks ordered sack lunch for everyone from a shop down the street from FBI headquarters. The food is lined up on the conference table in an orderly row, sandwiches first, then chips, then soda.

"Turkey for Andy," Brooks announces. "Gluten-free."

"Thanks," Mayfair says.

"He shot a guy the day after the doctor told him he had to go gluten-free," Brooks tells Thorpe.

Thorpe looks at Mayfair. "Really?"

"Celiac. It was a diagnosis of celiac."

"Sublimated anger," says Brooks.

Mayfair lifts the pen for the whiteboard. "Let's start."

"I'm not the one who can't go out for Italian anymore," says Brooks.

Mayfair turns to Thorpe. "The guy was robbing a bank. He had hostages."

"One day you're told no more pasta, the next day a guy gets shot. I'm just sayin'."

Mayfair begins to write names on the board. "Here's the headline. The money from the Burj trade led to two individuals, an American named Jared Cain and a Russian national named Ivan Zaroff. Zaroff is ex-KGB, supposedly a private citizen now. They connect via Jared Cain's small hedge fund, Herakles, which in turn ties to a CIA mid-level manager, Hugh Abbott, and also to Cain's father, David Charles Cain. Those are the key names, and the details are important, so I'll get to those next."

To distinguish father and son, Mayfair writes "D.C." and "Jared" on separate lines. "Jared turned up first, an online account using a fake name and Social Security number, set up just two weeks before the Burj attack. We tracked money into the account just before the attacks, money out immediately after. The profit was $1.2 million. FBI forensics traced the IP address of the computer Jared used to set up the account, and the money flow between bank and brokerage accounts. Jared siphoned money from Herakles to buy put options, then returned the original cash to Herakles and kept the profit for himself."

Mayfair draws dollar signs and arrows to show which direction money flows from one name to the next. "Herakles was the mother lode for the investigation. Herakles also set up another group of accounts with Burj-related trading. Those accounts collect their winnings from Burj trades, about $28 million, by the first week of July. In those accounts Herakles profited from the attack, not Jared."

Brooks summarizes. "Herakles takes $28 million in accounts it tried to conceal, and Jared uses the fund's money to join in personally on a side bet."

"A little under $30 million in profits, total, then. Why the side bet?" Thorpe asks.

"All told, we're looking at maybe $70 million in hinky trades around the Burj," Mayfair says. "The $30 million were just the first trades we found. But there's more—Heracles turned around and immediately gave its $28 million profit to a company called Nocturne, controlled by Zaroff. Nocturne loan-sharked Herakles $23 million earlier in the year—Zaroff got paid back with $5 million of interest in a matter of months. The side bet was the only money Jared got to keep for himself." Mayfair adds new arrows to the board.

"Why the ping-pong, the money bouncing back and forth between Zaroff and Herakles?" Thorpe asks.

Brooks shakes his head. "We don't know that part of the story yet. We track money flows with bank routing numbers, but the 'why' has to wait until we see Herakles' books."

"You think Zaroff loaned money to Jared, then tipped him to a sure bet to pay it off?" Thorpe asks.

"It fits the facts," Robeson says. "Jared doesn't strike us as the kind of guy who's the first one to know things."

Mayfair adds yet another name on the far side of the board. "We also learned the New York Attorney General was investigating Herakles too, for customer complaints. That was how we found the CIA connection— the CIA asked the AG to hold off action because Herakles was part of a CIA operation."

Thorpe holds up a hand to pause the briefing. "We have the CIA protecting an American, who's doing business with a Russian—a former spy—and they both made money knowing in advance about the attack on the Burj. Is that how you put this together?"

"Yes."

"Okay. I was afraid it was going to be complicated," Thorpe looks at the counter-intelligence man, Robeson. "Do we know if the FBI has opened a counter-intelligence investigation into Abbott?" Robeson nods. "And at some level the Herakles-Abbott relationship is legitimate, because the CIA not only knows about it, they intervened to keep the State of New York away?"

Robeson nods again. "Yes, but we don't have information yet on the bona fide work Herakles did."

"All right," says Thorpe. "Tell me about Zaroff."

Robeson summarizes Zaroff's history. KGB agent in Germany with Vladimir Putin before the Berlin Wall fell. While Putin took power, Zaroff took ownership of a shipping and construction company, and for decades lived lavishly as a wealthy businessman. Homes in London and Prague, most time in London. Not known to be active as a spy, but almost certainly co-operating internationally with Russian intelligence and the Russian mob, using the shipping business to facilitate his connections to both.

"What's the CIA connection to the American? Cain Junior?" asks Thorpe.

"We screened Abbott, Jared Cain, and Ivan Zaroff against CIA and NSA personnel," Robeson says. "We looked for any overlaps in the database about relatives, line of work, education, or time and place connections. Huge number of hits, but when we concentrated on people with connections to both Jared and Zaroff, we surfaced Abbott, who is CIA Regional Assistant Operations Director for Iran."

"He's the overlap?" Thorpe said.

"Has to be," Robeson said. "Went to Yale the same time as Jared and early in his CIA career had European postings that brought him into contact with Zaroff. But the clincher was when we started looking at Herakles. It was Abbott who got the CIA to seal the New York Attorney General investigation into Herakles and Jared, saying Herakles was important to an operation he was running."

"He's our man, then," Thorpe says. "Do we know his story?"

"Just a name so far. We've been working the money side, then the names, and we have yet to work our way up to the Abbott-Herakles stuff," says Robeson. "We do know that Cain Senior shovels money into political donations, including to CIA Director Nadeau when he was in Congress."

Thorpe's eyes narrow at this news. "Go on."

"The FBI has begun around the clock surveillance and monitoring of Abbott, Herakles, and Cain Junior. We have preliminary FISA court authorization to track them and communications involving Zaroff."

Robeson pushes a copy of the FISA order across the table to Thorpe. "But we need you to confirm to the judge that we aren't crossing wires with a CIA operation. We can get authorization for warrants to move on searches and arrests based on what we have. What we need is clean investigative authority, to lead us to the terrorists."

Thorpe looks at the paper briefly and asks the still-standing Mayfair, "Who got the other profits in the Burj trading?"

"We found two main groups of accounts, 'Mr. X' and 'Mr. Y,' that collected an additional $40 million of the Burj profits. When you added the Herakles accounts with Mr. X and Mr. Y, you get almost $70 million of profits from betting against Boeing stock at the time of the attack. Another $10 million looks like normal give and take in the market. But the $70 million was dirty, trading on knowledge the attack would happen. We also know that both Nocturne and Herakles were involved in market manipulation after Mecca, too. Smaller dollar amounts, maybe a practice run for the Burj."

Mayfair uses the pen as a pointer as he retraces arrows between names. "Proceeds from the Mr. X accounts went to dealers in precious metals— and after the conversion from cash to metal, that money vanished from the radar altogether. That activity looked like espionage tradecraft, rather than the behavior of an opportunistic Wall Streeter."

"Zaroff? Or the CIA connection?" Thorpe asks.

"Likely Zaroff. Herakles tried to disguise its Burj accounts, routing them through Bitcoin and the like, but it was amateur hour compared to Mr. X."

His presentation ended, Mayfair finally sits and begins lunch.

"You haven't wasted the time since we last met," Thorpe says. "This is valuable data about the money. Now we need to turn it into workable information, by understanding the connection between the terrorists and Zaroff, Cain Junior, and Abbott." Heads nod agreement around the table.

Thorpe turns to Mayfair. "There's a chance that Abbott is Mr. Y, in your list of people who made money from the Burj attack."

"Agreed. No facts yet." Mayfair had been mid-bite in his sandwich

when Mr. Y came up. He wipes mayonnaise from the corner of his
mouth.

"You really shoot a bank robber?' Thorpe asks.

"Lifted his gun in the direction of a hostage, and I had to make the
call."

Thorpe nods and looks sympathetic.

"Another complication is David Charles Cain," Brooks says. "D.C.
Cain is tied in with think tanks, PACs, donor groups, politicians, and a
web of informal relations around Washington. He gives millions of his
own money and bundles campaign contributions from his business
acquaintances for millions more."

"Do we know if Cain Senior is clean?" Thorpe asks.

Brooks shakes his head. "Another mystery."

"We need to know. Particularly if he's got long-standing ties to
Nadeau. Will Nadeau have to recuse himself on Cain-related questions?"
Thorpe asks.

"The contributions were several years back, so probably not. We'll get
a review from ethics counsel," Robeson says.

"At some point soon I need to get Nadeau's sign-off to lift that CIA
hold on Abbott's files, so the FISA court will keep a warrant open."
Thorpe lifts the paper with the FISA order. "More important, I need to
understand the terrain. No accusations, you understand. About Nadeau.
Just caution. I don't have to mention the Burj, I'll just tell him it's
counter-intelligence. Other than that, for anybody not in this room, use
code names only for Zaroff, Abbott and the two Cains on this matter."

Robeson nods. "We have to find out what the New York Attorney
General knows," he says. "FBI counter-intelligence contacts will ask the
British intelligence services for help tracking Zaroff. No need to get
Nadeau involved there."

"Mecca involved a plane from Iran," Thorpe says. "Too soon to know
if it's connected to Abbott's work?" The FBI men agree.

Thorpe is silent as the meeting ends. He hopes Nadeau is clean. He
usually distrusts agency heads who started in politics, worrying they won't

do the work and will settle instead for the haphazard over-promising they used with voters, but his first impressions of Nadeau have been positive. Thorpe wants to cooperate with the CIA, rather than work around them or against them, but he knows that sometimes in counter-espionage he'll end up spying on people at the same time he works with them. Concealment is simply part of the job.

"We have names, we have targets." Thorpe stands to leave. He has partial information on two fronts—this trading information and the preliminary news from General Smith that the black box may have been found. Not enough to bring before the BAG, but too hot to keep quiet long.

-o-

July 30
Washington, D.C.

Crammed into one side of a narrow and windowless anteroom, the receptionist for the Americans for Common Sense on the Middle East looks like she has been forced into a closet, facing out. Her desk is nearly as wide as the space itself, with a tiny gap that forces her to turn sideways to get to her chair. On the opposite side of the reception room is a small sofa for the occasional visitor, and in the center is the door marked "Executive Director Thomas Cutler."

After Rogers suggested interviewing Cutler, Mac insisted Rogers join him to put Cutler's answers into context, which Mac couldn't pass off to the FBI. Rogers is in a suit and Mac wears a dress uniform. Lawyers working behind the scenes worked out security clearance issues in less than a week, which Rogers knows is lightning speed for the government. Evidence of how potentially serious Cutler's comments could be.

Cutler makes them wait, even though they were on time for the late afternoon meeting. The receptionist offers water. They both decline. When Cutler ushers them into his office, they can see the reception area

had been cut tiny to maximize Cutler's office. Americans for Common
Sense holds itself out as a think tank—a self-proclaimed "thought
leader" on Middle East issues—but is actually a storefront for a one-man
show, a large single room with an impressive floor to ceiling window on
the outer wall, offering a view of the neighboring mirrored glass
buildings. Cutler's workspace consists of a massive TV on one wall,
turned to muted cable news, across the room from Cutler's desk. Two
chairs face the desk, with a small table between, where Cutler displays a
laminated copy of his recent op-ed. Rogers picks up the clipping, then
puts it down.

After introductions, Cutler offers them water, and they again decline.
Cutler then offers them vodka, which he pours for himself after they pass.
"Last meeting of the day," he says. Cutler is in his late thirties or early
forties, with a salesman's bonhomie. His shaggy and ill-parted sand-
colored hair hangs over his forehead, giving him the look of a perpetual
high school jock.

Rogers begins. "I recall you from a recent speech you made on the
campus where I teach."

"That would have been part of a book tour for *The Coming Caliphate*.
Got to number six on the Times' non-fiction list." Cutler leaves out that
his think tank sponsors represented 95 percent of the purchases as part of
a campaign to make the book's ideas appear mainstream and appealing.

"What stuck out to me in your talk was when you said the day would
come when the United States could prevent attacks like the ones that
happened on 9/11, by taking over planes by remote control. It wasn't the
main topic of your speech, or your book, but that comment stayed with
me. Your old boss, Senator Mason, said you had handled oversight
briefings and classified information on defense systems. He suggested we
reach out to you, to see if you recall any specific meetings on that idea."

"It's been a long while. I went to hundreds of meetings in my
legislative career. So my recollections may not be strong." Cutler is an alert
Washington animal, and turns cagey. "And you aren't suggesting I was
giving out any top secret or confidential information about American

capabilities, are you? Any comment I made about protecting America from attacks...."

"Nothing like that. No issues about anything you said," Mac assures him.

"I'm a patriot."

"Your patriotism is not at issue. We're more curious about your memory," Rogers says.

"There was one set of meetings on point, but they were very technical and I don't have a technical background. I was a history and literature major in college." Cutler goes on to describe how post-9/11, post-Iraq, the U.S. sought ways to prevent a recurrence of the attacks, including having the CIA's Office of Technical Services (OTS) investigate electronic features to keep planes safe. "Sort of like self-driving cars, although the technology then was not as advanced. This particular project, named 'Deadbolt,' was aimed at installing an override into a plane, to let operators on the ground take command of a plane under terrorist control." Cutler takes a small sip of his drink.

"The basic idea was easy to say but implementation was horribly hard." OTS provided seed capital to create a prototype, and a consultant in Seattle got initial funding—millions, but not hundreds of millions. "But by the second meeting, it was clear that implementing the idea at scale would be incredibly expensive—retrofitting all the airplanes in the world, you know?" Cutler's eyes drift toward the talking heads on TV. The crawl line says they are discussing the lack of progress on the Burj and Mecca attacks. "Once you get a project going, somebody always wants to keep it alive, particularly when influential political donors support it, like this one. But Deadbolt went on life support really fast. Then administrations changed and it just withered and died."

"Mostly over cost?" Mac asks.

Cutler shakes his head. "Operating details were a mess—how do you transfer control of a plane anywhere in the world to a local ground operator, or to the automatic pilot? And how do you transfer control back to the pilot if the danger passes? And then there was the question on how to make the system secure. You wouldn't want hackers to be able to use the anti-hijack system itself to hijack a plane."

As he says it, the thought catches Cutler by surprise. "Hey, you don't think that's what happened at Dubai, do you? Some hackers got to the plane?"

"Unless you tell us otherwise, this project never got built," Mac says.

Cutler shakes his head. "At some point there were emails saying Deadbolt was over. I don't recall the year. At least a decade back. I was approached to join this organization, so I got off Capitol Hill and came here."

Mac asks, "Anything else you remember?"

"There were two CIA guys in the Deadbolt meetings. You'd have to get the names from the records." Cutler sets down his drink. "You know, technology moves along. Maybe the tech exists now to do this. After the Burj, maybe we need this."

Mac and Rogers look at each other and begin to rise from their chairs. Cutler reaches in the credenza behind him for two copies of his book *The Coming Caliphate*. He has plenty to spare and offers them as souvenirs of the meeting. Mac declines.

"Already read it," Rogers says. Cutler smiles, expecting praise, as is common in the circles he travels. "A few of the facts were off."

Cutler bristles. "I've heard those comments before. People with an agenda take shots at what I have to say and claim that the research was faulty, but mostly they just don't like my conclusions. I was given background material and it all looked very well researched to me."

"Not your own research."

"Oh no, that's not my skill set. I write. The sponsors of the institute bring the research to me and I put it together. But the publishers have an editing and manuscript process. That should weed out any real problems on the facts." Cutler looks at Rogers, ready to argue. "But there are some with opposing political views."

Rogers' voice is level. "Do these books support your views, sir?"

Cutler pulls out a cell phone. He shows the picture to Rogers. "My books support this view—Arlington across the Potomac, to the Washington Monument and Capitol. The view from my penthouse, paid for with the book advances and TV fees. I have an audience for what I write, and for the perspective I provide, and I give my readers what they want. I've done two books and made the NY Times Bestseller list twice. In the marketplace of ideas, my success speaks for itself."

Rogers picks up the copy of the newspaper column.

"Demand in the marketplace for this, sir?"

Cutler's voice switches from edgy to hostile. "The press eats up victim stories. Tear-jerker crap that distracts from the real issue—the Muslim world is out to kill us and they don't need our sympathy. For all we know, these attacks are phony attempts to generate sympathy for Muslims. We need to keep our eye on the real enemy, and not get distracted."

"By dead eight-year-old girls, sir?"

"When the enemy dies, we win. Maybe you teach in some liberal academic refuge where they don't see things that way."

"Huh," says Rogers. "My colleagues at West Point and I are going to have a good laugh over that one, sir."

"I'm sorry?"

"Have you ever encountered an actual terrorist, sir?"

"Live, you mean?"

Rogers lifts his pant leg to show the prosthesis replacing his left foot and lower leg. "Iraq. First-hand knowledge. And I've done my own research on the Middle East as well, and speak Arabic. Were you ever in combat, Mr. Cutler?"

Cutler doesn't like being accused of being a dilettante, but the conversation has turned. Cutler can argue, or take it, but it's clear he wants the conversation to be over. He shakes his head no.

"Ever watch someone die?"

Another headshake.

"Not like the movies, sir."

Cutler capitulates. "Thank you for your service," he mutters.

When they hit the empty hallway, Mac bursts out laughing. "Things were going okay until you started calling him 'sir.'"

Rogers faces his friend and his tone is grim. "Where's this going, Mac?"

"What do you mean?"

"Nobody looking at the attacks is talking about this CIA drone project. CIA was looking at taking over an autopilot years ago, just like you heard on the black box." Voice low but urgent, Rogers walks Mac down the corridor away from the elevator. "I thought I was going to read over some files and give you a second opinion on intelligence. And then this drops. Chasing terrorists is above my pay grade."

"Hold on, Tony. Let's not get ahead...."

"There are no terrorists in the plane, right? Maybe it's a drone, like Cutler suggested. So that needs to be ruled out. Because if it can't be ruled out, things get worse." Rogers pauses. "There's a chance American tech flew that plane into the Burj."

"I want you to help me run this to ground."

Rogers shakes his head. "It might not be just CIA tech. It might be the CIA. We could be in the middle of somebody else's trouble."

"More reason for you to stay in," Mac says.

"Or get out. If it turns out CIA was involved, I'm not going to whitewash some goddam rogue spook, just because he's on the U.S. team."

"I wouldn't ask you to." Mac is beginning to get heated himself.

"I may need to go back to writing marginally relevant papers on terrorism."

"This investigation's been a dead end for three months since Mecca. You've been on the scene ten days and we've got motion. Maybe not the right answers. Not the answers we wanted to see, for sure. But I want your help if you'll give it. It's only a couple of weeks over the summer."

-o-

August 3
Pentagon

Thorpe wants to discuss the Burj voice recorder privately with
General Smith. The DIA leader's office is drab and utilitarian, like most
Pentagon offices, decorated by a small set of family pictures and
distinguishable from other military offices by little else. Smith shows the
strain of the tense months since the Mecca attack, but Thorpe says
nothing.

Smith tells Thorpe he had required full documentation of the box's
travel from the Burj wreckage into the hands of the NTSB prior to
notifying Thorpe of its existence. Smith didn't like that the NTSB
findings were not vetted to his standards. The best the DIA team could
do, working along with the NTSB, FAA, and Boeing, was to verify that
the serial number on the recorder matched the records for the plane that
hit the Burj.

"How strong is your conviction that there were no terrorists on the
Burj plane?"

"Less than 100 percent, obviously," Smith says. "The report on chain
of custody is shakier than I want, but sufficient that the intelligence
community needs to investigate."

Smith passes Thorpe a sheet with bullet points addressing the
sabotage scenario. "We need the FAA's help, and we need Boeing to look
for vulnerabilities in their equipment and figure out how to address them.
In the end, we could be looking at plane screenings, audit of autopilot
functions, redesign of autopilots to detect and deter tampering—lots of
money, lots of time involved, but better to get started now." Smith settles
back into his chair.

"The core concern is stopping whoever did this from doing it again.
Sabotage implies a developed country. Known terror groups have savvy
engineering guys to smuggle bombs into laptops, but no avionics industry.
We're dealing with either a state actor, or someone resident in a developed
country," Smith says.

Thorpe puts the paper into his leather folio. "Anyone who flies a plane into a building is a terrorist. I don't care who it is."

"I loathe equivocation," Smith says, "but we need bets placed everywhere on the table, based on our current information. Sabotage rather than hijacking doesn't mean there isn't still a terror group implementing the action or underwriting the cost of it. If we were looking exclusively for Islamists before, our search should expand, but not stop."

As Thorpe rises to leave, Smith says, "One last thing. Colonel McCaulley has a separate lead on potential sabotage, not yet ripe to be shared. But he also thinks that the CIA is being cagey about what it shares with the BAG, and I agree with him. I was a junior officer on 9/11 and I remember the inter-agency bullshit back then." Smith makes a sniffing noise. "Getting a whiff of it now, too."

-o-

August 8
New York City

When FBI agents Mayfair and Brooks show up at her Manhattan office, Debbie Shulman barely contains her glee.

Mayfair knows Thorpe confronted CIA Director Nadeau the week before to keep a FISA warrant in place and to get the CIA to lift its hold on the New York Attorney General's investigation into Jared Cain. There had been urgent behind-the-scenes lawyering to transfer case management away from the NYAG to the FBI.

As a staff attorney, Shulman had been primed to bring the hammer down on a financial crook when the CIA intervened months before, and now shows her delight that the barrier is gone.

"So much for how helpful Jared Cain was to the feds," she says as she escorts the agents to the files. Mayfair walks next to her with Brooks behind.

"We can't comment, obviously."

"Don't have to. Cain's a scumbag and needs bringing down. Good luck and Godspeed."

Mayfair slides a photo of Hugh Abbott across the table to Shulman, without mentioning that Abbott is the subject of intense FBI counterintelligence scrutiny. She confirms Abbott held out Herakles as being essential to a CIA operation.

Mayfair and Brooks are stoic, not even exchanging glances. Witness confirmation of Abbott's involvement is important, and they both know it.

Heracles first drew the attention of the NYAG's securities law enforcement offices in the spring, Shulman tells them. Cain lost money at the end of the year and refused to honor his investors' request to withdraw funds, as they were entitled to do. The investors complained to the SEC and to the NYAG, but the SEC didn't act—"not a surprise, because Herakles was too small to get SEC Enforcement involved"—and the NYAG raided Herakles, scooped up the records, and was preparing charges when CIA counsel intervened.

"I was primary drafter of a deferred prosecution agreement between Herakles, the CIA, and the NYAG's office. We said we can't let him screw his investors. CIA said, 'if we can get the investors paid off, will you drop the charges?' We agreed to defer the charges; give him a year to get his financial house in order."

The agreement required Herakles to pay off departing investors with a $23 million bridge loan from an outside party, and not from investor funds. The other investors had to approve the deal, which they did.

This time Mayfair and Brooks look at one another. They recognize the $23 million figure as the money deposited by Zaroff's company, Nocturne.

"Cain either could make money or bring in new equity to pay off the bridge, but we needed confirmation Herakles was on sound financial footing before we would hand the files back or let him off the hook on prosecution. He had one year, so he hasn't missed the deadline yet." Shulman pulls out another set of letters and notes. "Recently his lawyer has started asking if we'll give back our copies of the files if he pays off the bridge money, so maybe he hit a jackpot somewhere."

The FBI men don't tell Shulman the bridge loan has already been repaid with proceeds from the Burj trading.

"You do nothing, just wait to see if he shows up with the money?" Mayfair asks.

"Nothing to do. We struck a deal, and there's time on the clock." She points to the boxes of files stacked in the conference room. "But he's your problem now. The records are a mess, violations everywhere. Even if Jared finds the $23 million, we still want to bring charges. Herakles was commingling funds from investors with other Herakles cash, money moving in and out of accounts. Maybe money laundering—which we guess is what the CIA was using them for."

She waits for the FBI men to comment, but Mayfair says only, "Is that your read on the files?"

"Herakles is a front for making payments whose origin the CIA wants disguised. Jared takes fees for the pool of money under management, but he also takes a cut when he moves money around—different streams of cash in different years. For about four years, there was a stream of money that came in monthly and went to an account in the name of RossTech, with a small payment out to an account called Abacus. The RossTech money stayed in the Herakles investment pool, a couple million bucks. Then a second stream began five years ago, where money came in and went back out, without any being retained in the investment pool. Abacus collected a piece of that too, maybe $2 million total over the years."

As she talks, Shulman opens the binders at pages she has marked. "There were notes about a stream of cash expected to come in and go out this year too, but that hadn't happened when we took the files."

"The other stream of payments, that weren't investment money— CIA?" Brooks asks.

Shulman shrugs. "Money in, money out, we assume CIA. We're guessing that Jared's basically a payroll processor, and his skim is a nice supplement to the main investment business. So, if he's smart—which he isn't—he doesn't kill the goose with the golden eggs. Except that late last year, he decides the being-a-delivery-boy-for-the-CIA business isn't enough and makes a big bet in the currency markets. Big leverage, big payday if he does it right. But he bets the wrong way and loses a bunch of money, gets investors pissed off, and here we are."

"The FBI forensic accounting team will make its own assessment, but your overview is helpful," Brooks tells Shulman.

Mayfair says, "Cain's dad is rich."

"People say." Shulman's tone is skeptical. Mayfair understands. Prosecutors expect the worst of people, and generally get it. "It looks like the original investment group was people who wanted to do Cain Senior a favor by putting money with his son. Until Jared made his big, stupid money-losing bet last year, they made a little bit each year, so no harm done, even though Jared has a history of drug diversions, rehabs, and various other screw-ups where other people come in to clean up his messes. A lot of court records here in Manhattan are sealed, but the cops gave us a peek at the original reports."

"There should have been family money, though," Brooks says, "so he didn't get cross-wise with the investors to begin with."

"Didn't happen. And the CIA didn't score points with us by being just another enabler for his bad behavior." Shuman closes the binders and puts them in boxes for the men to carry away. "In investment fraud prosecution, we have a technical term for guys like him. Jared's what we like to call 'a fucking idiot.'"

-o-

August 8-10
Washington D.C.

General Ashton Smith dies in his sleep of a massive heart attack. The first Mac learns of it comes as a phone call from the Secretary for the Joint Chiefs of Staff notifying Mac that he needs to take over DIA on an interim basis. Mac is shocked that the meticulous and well-organized Smith had not prepared a succession plan.

Mac accepts the position despite his misgivings. With events finally breaking in the Burj investigation, continuity of personnel is critical. While he is currently on the DIA's activities involving the BAG, he needs to learn everything else DIA is doing.

Someone else might ultimately get an acting or permanent appointment, but that is not Mac's business—for the moment, someone needs to sit in the chair.

Mac knew that, decades back, his father felt strongly that he was not only a military officer, but also a representative at every moment of all black Americans. In his father's bearing Mac saw that the man conducted himself in line with what he believed were his dual responsibilities. Older now, Mac can't escape how much of his father's manner he'd absorbed; Mac's concern for how he is perceived is a shadow that travels before him. He'll give his all, even if the appointment proves to be brief.

One of Mac's first actions is finishing Smith's effort to get records from Senator Mason on the anti-hijack device Cutler described. Sometimes people in Congress would say "no" just because they could. Mason's office is refreshingly forthcoming. They had locked down details in a matter of days and are ready to let the records loose.

Mac asks Rogers to return to Washington for the review, which is allowed only in a SCIF. No cellphone, no laptop, no pictures, notes classified. Mac escorts Rogers to the SCIF, a windowless interior office with only a metal table and two boxes containing the files.

"This is stark," Rogers says. "Are you going to lock the door from the outside?"

"If you tap the code properly on the door, the guard will let you out for the bathroom," Mac says. Mac holds up a plastic rectangle. "Key card. Food court's on this floor if you need a break."

The project meeting minutes are in paper form, all original documents or printouts. Rogers places the first folder on the table and turns the crisp pages in his fingers.

"It looks like these documents were printed, immediately filed, and have gone unseen ever since," Rogers says as Mac is leaving.

Many pages in the boxes are duplicates collected from multiple parties. The information to be gathered is surprisingly thin. At the end of the day, Rogers returns to Mac's office with handwritten pages, a report and bullet points, which Mac sends off to be typed.

"What do you think?" Mac asks, not waiting for the written version to return.

"Cutler remembered the high points pretty well, including the code name 'Deadbolt,'" Rogers says. "As shorthand, I call the anti-hijack device the 'Drone' in what I wrote up."

"Did they actually build one?"

"Nothing in the file one way or another. No formal vote to end the program. It just looks like something they did for a while, and then they stopped doing it." Rogers stands to leave.

"I'll circle back with you after I read it, thanks," Mac says.

The secretary brings a hard copy of Rogers' report within an hour. When Mac finally turns to it, he glances at the bullet points under the heading "Key Takeaways re: Project Deadbolt."

Cutler was one of four Congressional overseers and CIA provided a staffer named Hugh Abbott. CIA had a longtime contractor, RossTech, prepare specifications for the Drone and review feasibility. Communications between CIA and Daniel Ross, owner of the contractor, were not part of the Senator's file. By the second meeting, the oversight group spotted huge implementation problems, and thereafter activity consisted only of sporadic email chains, and the effort fizzled out. No formal termination, just apparent loss of interest.

Mac considers whether to interview the Deadbolt oversight participants for additional information. At a minimum, he needs to confirm Deadbolt was truly cancelled. Mac doesn't expect that the other Congressional aides are more likely than Cutler to have definitive information, but the CIA liaison might.

Interviewing any CIA personnel is a delicate question. Rogers guesses

CIA is holding back in the BAG to protect an intelligence source, which might be true, but if the Agency had a role in creating a Drone, that might explain the foot-dragging as well. Mac elects to work around the CIA for as long as possible.

The Drone is still a long shot. Having Rogers interview Ross might close out the question whether it exists and avoid altogether any need to involve the Agency.

-o-

August 10
Seattle

Rogers navigates the grid of flat-roofed warehouses and manufacturing sites, windowless square barns made of tilt-up concrete, ornamented by street numbers and an occasional business logo, parking his rental car before the utilitarian RossTech space.

From the outside, he sees a small machining area, a business office, and not much else, befitting a shoestring operation. RossTech's small scale implies low-level performance. If Rogers can rule out even tangential CIA involvement in the Burj attack, he can close down that line of inquiry, but he is determined to follow the facts as he finds them, not bend the facts to suit his preference.

RossTech has no one at the front desk. Rogers hits a cheap metal bell on the counter near the door, the kind a dry cleaner might have. From an adjoining room emerges a petite Vietnamese woman, Mrs. Ross, who is polite but subdued. He can't tell her age. She is, Rogers learns later, pushing 70; she'd been a teenager when she met Ross during the Vietnam War.

After they are seated in a small conference room, Rogers asks when Mr. Ross would join them.

Mrs. Ross says, "I am sorry that I did not speak of this before, but Danny is dead. He died two weeks ago. I was told that this was a meeting about RossTech. I am now the sole employee of RossTech, which I will have to close once I have handled all its affairs."

Rogers is simultaneously moved by her situation and irritated that she'd concealed it. He may have made the trip for nothing. "Mrs. Ross, this is very sad news. I'm sorry to hear of your husband's death. Should we even have this meeting?"

"We should," she says gently. "My understanding is that you are here for the Defense Department, and Danny did a lot of work for Defense. I believe that most of Danny's work had been completed and delivered. But if that is not the case, I will have to deal with it."

"I'm here to discuss a very old matter, actually."

"I may not know about it personally," she says, "but the files are here, and Danny was very good at keeping clear records." She speaks lightly accented English, but perfect. Her sentences are straightforward, but in her face, Rogers sees that she is not fully engaged in their meeting, as though a part of her is away still grieving.

Rogers learns the basics about RossTech: It was a consulting firm that did hardware and software specialty applications, primarily for government. Ross mostly built hardware systems but was sufficiently adept to supervise software development. Ross did not handle major systems installations or projects, but he consulted on isolated projects, or special electronics components, or customized additions to major systems—fill-in items that a major supplier would not want to do itself. Ross had no staff, but drew on independent contractors, mostly throughout the Seattle area, to develop prototypes and proof of concept projects.

"Danny had many friends, for a long time, back in D.C. He was also very active locally, particularly in recent years. Much of his life was here over the past decade, in our community, away from Washington. You know how it is: you have children, and you make friends through them. So I've been dealing with his death, with help. But I was surprised no one from Washington got in touch. And you weren't his friend." She looks at Rogers. Part curious, part accusation.

"I didn't know him, I'm afraid. I'm here in a very different capacity, as part of an investigation."

"Into what? His death?" The question takes Rogers off guard. It suggests that Ross did not die of natural causes, and Mrs. Ross seems even more curious about the visit.

"No, no. A different matter entirely, involving a program that RossTech worked on. It would have been a contract with the government, or someone contracting on behalf of the government. We are trying to find out if the products that he worked on are still around. How much of the business do you know?"

"Less than you would hope, in most cases. I know Danny had around 200 patents over the years." Rogers pricks to attention at this information —Ross wasn't some low-skill dabbler if he generated 200 patents. "Most of them he assigned to the agencies he worked for. But I don't know the details. I didn't work in Danny's field. That was all his own, although our children have both gone into high tech. They're on the business side. Finance. Like Willy Sutton, because it's where the money is. That was what Danny would say. It was a New York reference. He was very proud of being from New York."

"This program could have been classified, almost certainly would have been confidential." Rogers considers rebooking an earlier flight to go back East. He resents the hassle and the wasted trip.

"Much of Danny's work had a classified component to it. Not all, but a lot. I got confirmation from our attorney that you are allowed to see the classified material, and so if you need me to get anything out of the safe or the files that are locked, I'll do it. Danny was very careful about confidential material. He liked to tell me he worked on things so secret that he didn't even know what he knew. But I am quite certain that whatever he worked on would be in his records."

Rogers asks Mrs. Ross about the late husband's background, and the broad areas of his work. He worked mostly with cybersecurity for government records and for government buildings, and on security codes, and equipment. Ross had capability to work with radio controls. He'd started his military career in the Army Signal Corps. His background didn't include work on airplanes. Rogers asked if the files would include the names of co-workers and people who worked on different projects.

"Most likely, but he used a lot of independent contractors, so he didn't always have the same people working on projects all the time," Mrs. Ross says. "And for specific project files, I don't know how much he kept, once a project was done. Enough to document the work and to troubleshoot problems. He had to make sure that the customer was using the equipment properly and not reprogramming it and then blaming him when it didn't work. That happened in the '90s and he had a fight over it, and after that he vowed he would always have the proof with him on every project every time."

"So he was a careful man, and documented everything," Rogers says.

"Yes. A wonderful man. The world is worse without him. But, he had begun to suffer so much, for so many years."

"I'm sorry, was he ill before he died?"

"His heart was ill. He was like his father, depressed. And it took away his joy and then it took him away, completely." Again, Mrs. Ross' face shows her drifting inward.

"This last terrorist attack. He would watch the TV, and he would become angry, and then....It just affected him very much, like 9/11 had affected his father. Danny had watched his father waste away over years, and said he was another 9/11 victim.

"You see, Danny's father was a butcher, in New York, on Staten Island. And Danny's brother Joshua was killed in the Twin Towers. Joshua had tried to call Danny's father from the building, while it was burning, to say goodbye, and to tell them how he loved them, but no one was home and so the answering machine was the last they heard from him. Danny's father kept that tape and the machine for his whole life, to listen to it. But after 9/11, he fell into depression. He died a few years later," she says.

"And what about Danny?"

"He was depressed for a number of years," she says, her tone matter of fact. "Manageable. He had a heart scare 10 years ago. Health problems make everything seem worse. But, we were handling it. Then the Dubai attack made him very angry, and very sad. We tried prescriptions to get him to sleep, but he couldn't sleep. He couldn't eat. The children came for visits, tried to get him to come back to the world. And I tried. But it took him away."

"His health declined, like his father's did?"

"Oh, no. He drove his car into a bridge abutment. My husband died of suicide. There were no skid marks, no attempt to brake. He guided the car straight in. On a suicide mission. Like the planes." She speaks with great emphasis and certainty about Ross's end.

"I'm very sorry to hear that. I didn't realize...."

"He had such a hard time," she says.

"Personality change? Sudden fits of anger?"

"Yes. In many ways he was not the same man. And the anger was so sudden," she says. "But you already know something about this." She looks at Rogers.

"I was in combat. It took time for me to deal with PTSD."

"There were problems in the business that he did not discuss with me. Business was good for a long time. We are quite well off. But then near the end some of the money was gone," she says.

"He may have had a problem with a defective product that he never talked to me about. He wrote a check marked "refund." I saw the cancelled check. There was a problem. He was so proud of the quality of his work and he was very meticulous. First his mood became depressed, from how he had been his whole life, and then a month or so ago it got so much worse. This work problem was on his mind constantly. Two million dollars."

"That was the refund? Really?"

"Yes."

"That's a substantial amount."

"I know. Danny made good money and he was a very good manager. Our children are like Danny that way. Do you know they are both millionaires already, in Silicon Valley? From IPOs? And they're still in their 30s? Isn't that amazing?" she says. "They went to Stanford," she says, which to her serves as sufficient explanation. "But you know that Danny was so honest that he wouldn't want to keep money that he hadn't fairly earned, so he gave it back."

"Was there a suicide note? Are you sure it was suicide?"

"There was an envelope with all of the business accounts, and all of our personal accounts, that Danny left on top of his computer the day he died. He was an organized man. I would have found everything eventually, but him leaving it all in one place that day....I recognized that he wanted me to have everything close at hand when he was gone."

"Did he have any business partners?"

"No. A one-man show, he used to say. He would assign work to people, vendors. He worked with a few people on a regular basis, I am sure those names are in the business files. Is this tied into what you are looking for?" Mrs. Ross asks.

The light goes on for Rogers. Mrs. Ross keeps wandering off topic in conversation—but she is also keen and alert, and she has an agenda: to find out why the Defense Department called shortly after her husband had sent a sizable check back to a customer and then committed suicide. She wants to know if he is here to take the rest. She is trying to size him up, to see if the problems are bigger than she knew.

She wants to protect her husband's memory and her financial future. Rogers doesn't want to give her false hope, but is moved to want to reassure her.

"Mrs. Ross, I didn't know that your husband had died. And I had no information about the money he sent back. These may be completely separate questions from what brought me here. I came here looking simply for records on an old project."

Rogers asks if Mrs. Ross had a list of passwords on Ross' computer files. She has such a list—she reiterates that Ross had been very meticulous. This list would include financial records and websites, and personal passwords, for protected files. Most of the passwords include some variation of 'linalways,' which seemed out of character for a security conscious man.

"Oh it's a very strong password," says Mrs. Ross. "No one has ever heard of Lin. Everyone thinks my name is Betsy."

"Betsy? Your name is Betsy Ross?"

She makes an irritated face. "Yes. When I married Danny and came to America with him, he said he wanted to make sure no one ever doubted whether I was an American. Not even my children know that I was born Lin. My papers for the U.S. say Betsy." She throws her hands up. "It has always been more trouble than a help. No one believed it was my name."

She leads Rogers to Ross' office. She tells him to spend the day and call her if he has questions. There is a single computer, and a bank of file cabinets. Like many men of his generation, Danny Ross was more comfortable with paper than electronic records. Rogers asks if he could look through the files. Mrs. Ross gives permission.

He flips through file tabs alphabetically looking for Deadbolt, finding correspondence and invoices in the 2006-2009 timeframe. Ross printed out emails, most of them to Abbott, the CIA analysis liaison mentioned in the meeting minutes. Some emails went to the full oversight group. At the back of the file is a typewritten memo, prepared by Ross. They are notes from a phone conversation with Abbott.

Formal support for Deadbolt being dropped, may be able to re-direct money from elsewhere to keep going.

Private backer may support continued development. Details within the month.

Hold on to all files, specifications, computer files, etc. and physical materials.

A handwritten note at the bottom says "Rename—Python."

Looking through the files for Python, Rogers finds a development program for the continued Deadbolt activity starting in 2009. There are invoices from RossTech to various sub-contractors, which was where most of the money went; various meeting notes on development and design.

The party hiring RossTech is listed as "Snake River Corp." Emails copied to Abbott, but not at his CIA email account. Someone named Tamerlane shows up on email sometimes. In some cases, the emails to Snake River are copied to an individual named "David Cain." There are notes about meeting Cain in his New York home. Cain is the deep pocket here. Deadbolt is defunct, but Cain's money took the place of the money from the CIA to keep the project going. Snake River and Cain stay in the picture after 2012, but instead of invoices from RossTech, there were payments made via something called the Herakles Fund.

In a file for Herakles was a draft copy of a letter.

Dear Mr. Cain:

Enclosed please find a check for $2 million. It represents the current value of the account you created at Herakles for money that you paid over the years for the Python project. My conscience does not allow me to keep it.

Daniel Ross

The mystery refund. Dated two days before Ross' suicide.

Rogers asks Mrs. Ross for help accessing RossTech financial account statements. The $2 million check to "D.C. Cain" covers the entire value of Ross' Herakles account. The check was endorsed over to someone named Jared Cain.

Mrs. Ross asks if there was a refund for a non-working product. Danny was a perfectionist, she says, and he did not want to charge anyone if the product failed to perform in the way it was supposed to perform.

"It's hard to tell. It's possible the product did something different from what Danny expected, and he didn't want to hold on to the money."

The technical notes are beyond Rogers' ability to interpret. But it looks like the Drone worked, at least in the lab.

Rogers finds a shipping label from Fed Ex to Cain, years old. Not to the Snake River address, so possibly a home address. Cover letter reads "Enclosing three Deadbolt/Python prototypes and physical media containing operating software."

The words chill Rogers. He re-reads the letter.

Three prototypes. And two attacks.

-o-

August 11-12
Washington, D.C.

Rogers copies the printouts of the email traffic on Deadbolt, along with the letters covering the prototypes and the $2 million refund, to bring back to Washington. He seals the originals and the rest of the Deadbolt files in boxes for the FBI to collect. He phones Mac, but on an unsecure line says only, "What I hoped to rule out I couldn't, and it might be worse."

On the return flight Rogers writes page after page on a yellow pad to capture details of his conversation with Mrs. Ross while his memory is fresh. Then he writes bullet points for his morning one-on-one with Mac, his anger rising as the weight of the RossTech discoveries sinks in.

Landing after midnight, Rogers cabs from Dulles to his hotel, one Metro stop away from the Pentagon. The little sleep he gets is fitful. He wakes ahead of his alarm and takes a long shower. He skips the hotel's breakfast buffet, too keyed up to eat, and walks to the Metro carrying his briefcase with the yellow pad and the documents. He leaves plenty of time to clear Pentagon security, but is still just barely on schedule when he is finally escorted to Mac's office.

"A functional Drone was created—at least in a lab setting—and three prototypes were delivered to this guy Cain. Nothing in the files to show the prototypes were deployed. Nothing to show what became of the prototypes later. Nothing to show mass production of the Drone." Rogers starts with the facts, leaving his speculations and concerns for later. Mac listens somberly.

"I warned Mrs. Ross that the FBI would come to check that I didn't miss any files. I didn't want to add to her hardship, but I'm guessing the FBI will turn the business upside down. I hope for her sake she told me everything." Rogers refers to his notes as he walks Mac through his conversation with Mrs. Ross.

He concludes with what, for him, is the key point. "Even if formal CIA involvement stopped, Drone development continued, with at least one member of CIA involved."

Mac picks up the printed emails and glances at them. "So we have a new project on top of the original: Ruling out involvement of the Drone in the Burj attack."

"Has to be," Rogers says. "The prototypes have been out there for years. We don't have hard evidence they worked, or if they were used at Mecca or Burj. We don't know if there was continued CIA involvement, or whether they are in only private hands. Suppose someone took the models and improved them, or mass produced them? We have many more open questions than we did before."

"It's not even that things are now more dangerous," Mac says, "it's just that we finally know about it. This material has been floating around a long time. Maybe the RossTech device caused the Burj or Mecca attacks, but also—maybe not."

They sit silently for a moment. Rogers closes his eyes.

The absence of terrorists in the cockpit at Burj points to some form of remote control, and the Drone is the only reference to remote control they have seen.

"You alright? Need some coffee?" Mac asks. Rogers waves him off. The lack of sleep makes his body feel dirty and the space behind his eyes is grainy.

"Why shut off the radio?" Mac asks. "Operational security, to prevent knowledge of the Drone from leaking out?"

"Political security, my guess. To prevent the public from knowing that the government was the one that turned off control of the airplane." Nothing in the Deadbolt minutes or RossTech files spoke to the question of radio silence, but Rogers worked it through returning to Washington. "The government priority, if they ever used the Drone, was going to be people on the ground and not people on the plane. You couldn't just crash the plane the moment you take control, because it might be in a city. But there was no guarantee you'd get a chance to land it."

Mac concurs. "You stop the plane from becoming a weapon, but the passengers become expendable. Not something politicians would want to advertise. Not much different from just shooting it down."

Rogers nods. "Right. Unless you're lucky, once a hijack starts everyone on the plane dies. That's built in."

"That's why the CIA abandoned it."

"I hope they abandoned it. I hope that's why," Rogers says. His voice rises. His outrage isn't for himself, but a righteous anger over slaughtered innocents. "The Drone might be a thread the CIA doesn't want anyone to pull on, because it will expose something else."

"If the CIA even knows. This could have been Abbott, solo."

"If someone higher up in CIA approved this, they'll want it buried," Rogers says with a grim certainty. "Ross sent a check back to Cain after the Burj, then ran his car into a bridge abutment. I can't prove it, but I think Ross knew the Drone he had designed killed thousands. His brother died in the Twin Towers and for Ross that must have been beyond what he could bear."

"Independent development of a Drone by someone else seems like a long-shot," Mac says.

"That's right." It was the conclusion Rogers had reached, flying back from Seattle, and he sees his friend has made it as well. "We're on a collision course with the CIA. You thought they were acting hinky when you brought me in, and this could explain why."

Mac says, "I'm meeting Thorpe in a few hours. I'll bring him up to date on all this. He won't bury this on the CIA's behalf. Probably turn Abbott's name over to the FBI for a full-blown counterintelligence investigation. Even if the CIA had nothing to do with the attacks, the questions are going to be painful."

"I'm sorry to drop this in your lap," Roger says.

"No you're not. You want in."

"If Americans took part in the attacks, yes. My country is better than that."

"You never miss a chance to punch above your weight, take a swing at a bully," Mac says. He pauses a second and then asks, "Think you can get a semester off with the Academy, work full-time at the BAG while we solve this? Someone's going to have to do it."

"Dub's not going to like it."

"If she says no, then don't do it."

Rogers stays silent.

They leave the RossTech material in Mac's office, in a safe.

Rogers' flight home won't leave Reagan Airport for several hours. He takes a cab to Capitol Mall, to walk around the Lincoln Memorial and the Wall at the Vietnam Memorial. The day is unseasonably cool, with low humidity. Tourists swarm the area. Being untethered from work, even briefly, lets Rogers appreciate the simple human moments around him: Children begging for treats from vendors and parents indulging; strangers taking group photos for one another; office workers briefly escaping for a lunch hour.

Rogers walks the path next to the Wall, seeing without reading the names of men from his father's generation. No name is greater or lesser. There is nothing to note whether the departed's last moments had been brave or spent in fear; whether the mission that led to death in uniform had been successful, or failed, or been a mistake; whether death had come fast or slow; whether the soldier had been popular or friendless; whether the life that ended had been happy or sad; whether the end had come at night or in the day. In death, each life had been rendered truly equal.

Across from the Wall, he sees a black man with salt-and-pepper hair, dressed for business in a dark suit and somber tie, staring straight ahead at the inscribed names. As Rogers passes, the man salutes, a gesture Rogers returns. On his way back from the WWII Memorial, Rogers sees the man is still there.

Their eyes meet and they exchange a cordial nod. "Friends?" Rogers asks, with a glance to the Wall.

"Yes sir. The memory of old friends," he replies. "Long gone." They share a quiet moment.

"Iraq for me," Rogers says.

"Life's different for people who didn't spend time outside the wire," the man says. "Still in?"

"Pentagon consultant," Rogers says.

The man gives a negative shake of his head. "Too many REMFs there. You drawing up orders to get people killed?" the man asks.

"No, trying to keep people alive," Rogers says.

"I hope you do," the man says. "I hope you do. It's not a numbers game." He gestures toward the 58,000 names carved into the Wall. "One by one. They depart this world, soul by soul."

-o-

INTERLUDE—PROJECT DEADBOLT
Project Deadbolt: D.C. Cain

February 2007
Reston, Virginia

Seated along the wall in the hotel ballroom at Table 15, a spot where ignoring the speakers is sufficiently inconspicuous to allow them to talk, Thomas Cutler is in deep conversation with the CFO of Cain Industries, Micah Pfennig. They are talking about money—specifically, campaign contributions to Sen. Mason, for whom Cutler serves as chief of staff.

The convention's sponsor, D. C. Cain, has appointed himself luncheon speaker. The other speakers are politicians seeking his favor and cash, and the chance to speak in front of committed partisans. From the elevated podium, Cain looks down at attendees cutting into their breaded chicken.

"Implicit in the message of the terrorists is this: 'Your existence in the West offends us, so much that we will use our time, energy, money, and lives to harm you.' Jealous of the West, incapable of improving their meager and primitive way of life, they'll settle for making our lives worse."

For Cutler and Pfennig, Cain's speech is white noise to their conversation, like a radio broadcast baseball game playing in the background at a barbecue.

Pfennig leans in. "The senator's not going to get squishy on us, is he?"

Cutler hesitates for an eye-blink. "On what, specifically?"

"Immigration."

"I don't think he has come out formally either way. But there are big problems..." Cutler starts to say.

"Stop. Change immigration and you re-write the advantage we got from LBJ in '65. We own the South. We're not putting it back up for grabs."

"The plan's plus/minus. Some good, some problems," Cutler begins.

"Well, that's why we're talking. You and I will talk over how the Senator is doing his math. We think the immigration proposal is a minus. We aren't asking the senator to lead the charge against. We think it'll die by itself. Just....no need to nurture the president with false hope," Pfennig says.

"Certainly, I am going to pass along to Sen. Mason your views."

"Strongly held views."

"Right."

"Look, we're both on the same side," Pfennig says. "Don't over-read this. This is an opportunity for the senator when there's more money to be spread around. No one is asking for Mason to put a knife into Bush."

"You found someone else to be Brutus?" Cutler asks.

"Right. Mason just needs to be standing around watching when it happens."

"A lot of our constituents are aligned with your advice already," Cutler says.

"They are. Georgia was the heart of Dixie. On everything else, we're good with the senator," Pfennig says.

"If civil liberties get mussed up a little, it is a small sacrifice for survival of our way of life. Like they say, the Constitution is not a suicide pact. We don't have to live up to it at the cost of our lives and our culture."

"I wanted us to come down here so you could hear Cain directly,"

Pfennig says. "He believes in strength. And he doesn't take shit from anyone who threatens America."

"I gathered that."

"It's personal, too. He lost his oldest son on 9/11."

"Oh," says Cutler.

"There'll be cash moving off the sidelines soon, for people he thinks will help his goals, be on his side. Cain wants to make his side bigger," Pfennig says. "If Mason is vocally in support on our issues, and helps grow the side, that's helping us. And if he's neutral and stays out of the way on things that we think are bad, like immigration, we're big boys and we don't hold it against him. He doesn't score extra points with us either, but the math is simple."

"Sure. In the end, there's only so much cash Cain can spend under election law."

"Not all the money has to be direct," Pfennig says. "It doesn't all have to go to candidates, and it doesn't all have to be spent on a campaign. Sometimes people write books and need someone to buy them. Sometimes someone has a foundation that supports what we support. We're building infrastructure here. And if the campaign laws change, well, then the donation spigot opens up, too. For our friends."

"They are like cancer cells. Cancer lives inside a body, but it declares war on the body that it lives in. So we have to treat them like cancer. You don't get rid of most of the cancer in a body. You get rid of all of it that you can find, and if it comes back, you kill it again. The cancer is always a threat to the body and you always have to work to destroy it utterly, and that is what we must do to the terrorists. Healthy cells are sacrificed to prevent the cancer from being able to spread further. And we, as a society, have to be willing to take those steps against the terrorists."

"Now, one other thing," says Pfennig. "There's an item in the appropriations bill that we think deserves support, maybe a co-sponsor. We think that it is good, strong, pro-American legislation, if the senator could work to get that in and help get it through." Pfennig took a folded copy of the proposed legislation from his pocket, and slid it to Cutler.

"'Electronic Prevention of Airline Weaponization.' Sounds 9/11-ish. Who could be against it?" Cutler says.

"Exactly. We already have other support we expect to see. There's a skunk works project to demonstrate proof of concept, and now's time to roll it out. Good stuff."

"Specifics?" asks Cutler.

"The CIA knows. Specifics will be discussed in a classified briefing; the senator may even want you to go. The right people know already. The important details are that we're not going to have another goddam airplane hit an American building again."

"Price tag?"

"Not line item. Black budget. But cheaper than a war, I'll tell you that. Cheaper than a knocked-down skyscraper," Pfennig says.

"I don't see a problem here."

"Cain is grateful for the help."

Coffee service. They stop talking while the servers clear the plates.

"If civilians harbor terrorists and get blown up when we attack them, well, healthy cells near a tumor get damaged in chemotherapy. If innocents are suspected of being terrorists, and are killed or jailed, that is too bad for them, but we have one goal, to root out the terror cells. There are no neutrals in this war."

" 'Beware, in fighting monsters, lest ye become one,' " says Cutler.

"What?" Pfennig asks.

"It's from Nietzsche. German philosopher? 'When you gaze into the abyss, the abyss also gazes into you'?"

"Yeah, you went to Harvard, not me." Pfennig stands. "Tom, great as always to have the chance to talk. I'll send details."

Pfennig leaves. Cutler stays for the end of Cain's speech.

Every terrorist should fall asleep at night with one thought and one thought only: "The reason I lived through this day is that the United States military hasn't found me and killed me yet, and when they do find me, they will kill me. My lousy little terrorist life is in their hands and I live at their sufferance."

I am a little too old to pick up a rifle, but I'll defend this country by using my money to hold conferences like these, to unite the real Americans against the weak, cowardly politicians who don't have the backbone to do the things that have to be done, and who don't love this country enough to go out and do them. Join me, join me, and God bless America.

The applause for Cain is polite, not rousing. Cutler looks around the room. The expressions are earnest. Audience members are serious, neither dismissive of Cain nor ready to join his crusade. None of which is important to Cutler, so long as the checks clear.

Later, Cutler briefs the Senator, who bluntly asks what Cain wants.

"He wants to kill terrorists. Or Muslims. *Potayto, potahto.*"

"Well," says Mason. "You can't fault a man for that. Anything else?"

"He's looking for you to be silent on the immigration plan. He wants it dead, but understands you have reasons not to be an active part of killing it. He'll settle for neutrality rather than advocacy."

"What numbers?"

"We talked about $2 million, maybe even up to $5 million, about $1 million direct to the campaign and PAC, the rest bundled."

"God bless one-stop shopping," the senator says.

"He also wants you to back a CIA project line item—hijack prevention. Hennings is introducing the bill in the Senate, Nadeau in the House."

"Hmmm. Usually when a donor asks for two things, there's the one he wants and there's the distraction. I wonder which is which here."

Cutler shrugs. "If they bring it up, they want it. Cain's not a horse-trading kind of guy, is my read on him."

"Well, I have no problem with Hennings, so the terror bill is okay. And I can't touch immigration. Half my constituents are farmers who need migrants to pick crops, because the other half are rednecks who won't do the work. I can't be in the middle of a bill that loses me half my voters no matter which way I go."

Mason looks at his chief of staff. "I'm being offered $2 million to do what I was going to do anyway. As much as that pleases me, it makes me think Cain's real ask is going to come later. Keep tabs on that for me, will you?"

-o-

Project Deadbolt: Jared Cain

April 2012
New York City

Jared Cain is poison on Wall Street. Jared's former employer, Guaranty National Trust, left his name out of the press release on GNT's $800 million loss, but everybody knows Jared was responsible. Securities traders in New York are a tiny, wealthy village, wrapped inside a major city, and as in any village, rumors travel.

GNT stock is down hard. Jared single-handedly knocked $18 billion off the bank's market value, nearly 20%. The bank's CFO lost his job. "Failure to properly supervise the trading department," in PR-speak. The CEO is barely hanging on. Jared would never work again in a bank finance department.

It all strikes Jared as exceptionally unfair. Yes, he entered into trades in the bank's proprietary trading account in 2011, and generated losses of about $200 million in one quarter on a currency trade. But the loss wasn't arbitrary, it wasn't random. He'd calculated, he'd looked at the markets, and he was convinced he had spotted a money-making opportunity. He'd done the work. There was uncertainty in investing, always. The trade was a risk, but not a gamble.

And yes, Jared concealed the loss by falsifying his internal reports. He'd doubled down on the initial investment position, and recorded all the amounts as ultimately collectible. He'd had to do it, he rationalized: He was buying time to have the whole trade work out. And then, after he was wrong again and hid the problem, he doubled down again and the whole trade blew up. The bank ate the loss.

Jared is aggrieved. They hired me to look at risk/reward situations, and I got unlucky, he sulked. Any monkey could buy T-bills. He'd been hired to take risks. Why was he the one who had to take the blame when something didn't work out?

When Hugh Abbott calls, Jared doesn't recognize the number. Washington area code. He picks it up on a whim rather than let the call roll to voicemail. Jared is in sporadic touch with his former fraternity brother over the years, but they aren't close. He knows Abbott went into the CIA, but no details.

"I heard the news," Abbott says.

"Whatever you heard, it was one side of the story, probably bullshit," Jared says.

"Well, it's hard to take stories at face value," Abbott says. "I should know."

"Are you still with the Agency?" Abbott isn't suave enough to be James Bond, that much Jared knows.

"It's why I'm calling."

"Schedule's open right now. I'm available to spy on the Chinese if that's what you're after."

"I'm about to handle some Agency business that requires me to have a financial middleman I trust, and I thought of you," Abbott says.

"What are you looking for?"

"I need someone to set up a hedge fund in New York that I can use to route payments around the world. Something that looks like a bona fide business. Actually, something that is a bona fide business, but just happens to have a side business running occasional payments for the CIA. Just a few. Run by someone with credentials, solid background. You," Abbott says.

Jared brightens. Another door opens, he thinks.

"Is all of this legal?" Jared asks.

"It has to be. It only works if it's a legitimate business," Abbott says. "It's hard to set this up from scratch, you need someone solid at the center of it. Those kinds of people are hard to come by."

"Where are you getting the money to set up the fund?"

"Someone who can call in favors, pull together a couple hundred million for you to start with. After that you just have to make the money yourself, and handle payments on the side," Abbott says.

"What's the catch?" Jared says. "I mean, it sounds great. Investment management has always been my dream job. I just have a natural talent for it. And I was worried I might not get a chance. But since this sounds too good to be true, I need to know what the problem is."

"I find you money, you help me make payments, and that's it. Once the cash is in, you run the investments. Just you. Not the CIA, no outside board of directors, unless you want one. No catch," says Abbott.

"CIA money?"

"Private," says Abbott.

"Anyone I know? Because investment business is all about personal contacts," Jared says. The more Abbott tries to be cagey about his backer, the more Jared wants to know.

"Yeah," Abbott says finally. "It's your dad." For a moment there is silence on the line.

"You said there was no catch," Jared says.

"There isn't," Abbott says. "I know you and your dad are on the outs. But I told him the CIA needed this. He said he won't use his own money, but he'll have people he knows invest enough to get it going. And if you were involved, they'd probably think they were doing him a favor."

"So my dad won't help me, but he'll help the CIA," Jared says. "What a fucking asshole. The answer is no, I don't want anything he touches, and you're an asshole for getting him involved and acting like this is all just good patriotic bullshit."

"No, it's..." starts Abbott.

"USA, USA, let's just chant and it's all cool, right?" Jared says. "Fuck you." He hangs up.

-o-

Project Deadbolt: Cain Industries

June-September 2012
Washington, D.C. and New York

D.C. Cain's night vision is weaker than in years gone by, and driving in Washington is like navigating a maze even during the daytime. A little wine at dinner, but Cain believes he is fine to drive. As he pulls out of the garage onto a north-bound numbered street, he hesitates, trying to pick between the east-west lettered street and the diagonal street named for a state. Then the drug suspect the cops are chasing rips through the intersection at 65 mph and plows a stolen BMW sedan into the rear driver's side door of Cain's car.

Cain's car spins almost completely around and rolls twice. The air bags pop. Four feet closer to the driver's door and Cain would have been dead.

EMTs remove Cain, unconscious. When Cain wakes in the emergency room, doctors tell him he'll need implants to his damaged right shoulder and hip.

The months he loses to rehab, along with his diminished strength and energy, force him to set new priorities.

Cain hands day-to-day operation of Cain Industries to Pfennig. He dictates a few details—purchase of an annuity to pay Cain $10 million per year for life for living expenses, and veto over things he doesn't like. But Cain Industries is a private company and he is sole shareholder, and so long as the banks are satisfied with the company's ability to repay principal and interest on its loans, Cain can do as he pleases.

Cain Industries funds pet Cain projects like the Center for Common Sense on the Middle East, and channels additional cash to the hedge fund Herakles, to be disbursed only as the senior Cain directs.

An obedient soldier, Pfennig does as he is told, with no questions. Ownership of the company is placed in a trust, Cain as trustee. On Cain's death, control of the trust—and therefore the company—goes to Pfennig, or trustees Pfennig names, but in no case will Jared Cain be a trustee, nor his wife nor any offspring. Cain doesn't care who winds up controlling the company once he is gone, as long as it isn't Jared.

-o-

Project Deadbolt: The Ports

January
New York
(Four months before Mecca)

D.C. Cain reviews the term sheet—Port restoration work in the Iranian cities of Anzali and Noshahr will be as big as any project Cain Industries has ever undertaken. Bigger. And international, worth billions. Cain's would-be business partner, Ivan Zaroff, claims to be a major international player in industrial construction, but Cain knows the truth. Zaroff's companies used to do large-scale projects. Now Zaroff's over-leveraged position means Cain Industries will provide both the financial stability to secure the agreement and, in the early stages, the bulk of the performance.

The financial and logistical planning for the Ports proposal took years from the time the Iranian transportation minister first suggested the project would be available to Cain, for a price. Cain used the time to establish companies and partnerships to evade U.S. restrictions on business with Iran.

Zaroff wants to front-end the profits and cash flow in his favor, probably because he needs the money. This doesn't bother Cain, who sees it as the normal give and take in negotiation. Zaroff's numbers either will work or they won't.

Hugh Abbott sees himself as a promoter, who brought Cain's solid financial presence to help Zaroff win a major project to restore his fortunes. Abbott likes to think he introduced Zaroff to Cain, but the two men had known of one another for years and met once or twice around the turn of the millennium. On many matters, the Russian and the American might be opposed, but the hunger for money and their shared indifference to morality in the pursuit of it binds them.

Cain does not believe Abbott's objective is the selfless enactment of CIA policy. Ambitious men have been trying to separate Cain from his money for decades. Cain believes he is adept at spotting them and, on occasion, turning their ambitions to serve Cain's purposes.

Abbott brought Zaroff; Zaroff brought the Iranians. Abbott wanted money. Zaroff wanted money. The Iranians wanted money. Cain doesn't like these men but Cain knows he controls them through their appetites: All of them can have the money they're after, he thinks, but have terms too, and to get their money, they'll have to deliver what I want.

-o-

Project Deadbolt: Herakles

March 18
New York City
(Six weeks before Mecca)

Jared wants to put off the meeting with Mrs. Van Dyne. He has too much going on this morning to give her his full attention, and the meeting will give him no satisfaction. But she arrives nonetheless.

"It's very simple, madam. Under the terms of your investment, you can pull your money out only once a year. You have to give me a notice between November 1 and November 30, and then I arrange to pay you, based on your year-end value, after January 15. That's the process. That's the way it works," Jared says.

"But you didn't give out refunds this year, even to people who gave you notices in November." The white-haired Mrs. Van Dyne is elderly, but sturdy, elegantly dressed, and possessed of decades of life experience in browbeating tradesmen and other social inferiors. She has a strong voice and is not tender in speaking to Jared.

"I'm in a dispute with investors and I can't talk about pending litigation," Jared says.

"It's my sister and she and a bunch of others got together and wrote to the SEC and to the Attorney General. Don't tell me you can't talk about it. I know about it."

"Pending litigation," Jared repeats.

"That's nonsense, and I don't want to do business with you any longer."

"Listen, you gave me money. Under the contract, I do with it whatever I want, to generate a return for you. And you get your money back once a year. Period." Jared's impatience is getting the better of him. "So I don't care what you have to say. If your account balance is positive in November, you're going to stay, no matter what you tell me now. The contract is written to keep you people from bothering me during the year, so I can do my job."

" 'You people'?"

"Yeah, you people, the investors. Your role in this fund, once you give me money, is to shut up and take your dividends and leave me the hell alone. That's the way it works."

"I'll be sending my own letter to the authorities," she says.

"Please do. Don't forget to send me a copy so I can throw it away." Jared sees his attorney Bob Stewart outside the office glass. Abbott is with him. "My other morning meeting is here, we have to cut this short. Please be sure to call me in November."

Van Dyne stalks out of the room, turning sideways to get through the door as the two men enter.

"Another satisfied customer," Jared explains, as she walks by.

Abbott and Stewart sit at the table Van Dyne had just abandoned. "We have a prosecution standstill agreement," Stewart says. "You provide confirmation that you have paid off the withdrawing asset holders, and either make enough money or have permanent subordinated investment by the end of the year to pay off the $23 million you took down as a bridge loan, and the Attorney General will not prosecute."

"Not prosecute for a year? Or ever?"

"Not prosecute during the year, if you confirm you have made the payoffs to the investors who left. Not prosecute ever if you bring the new capital in."

"And they agree to keep everything confidential," Abbott says. "No comment is the most they'll say, unless the CIA gives permission to say something else, and we aren't going to."

"Okay. And the records they grabbed in the raid?" Jared asks.

"They hold on to those for a year. If you get the new capital in faster than that—which I recommend you do—we ask for the records back."

"The good news is that they're willing to work with us," says Abbott. "So we just have to get the new cash in, and everything goes back to the way it was."

"I don't like having the records in their hands," Jared says.

"We made a run at it, but they didn't want to hand them back until they were sure everything was settled," says Stewart.

"I had next year's withdrawal in here just before you came." Jared nods at the door Mrs. van Dyne recently exited.

"There's an agreement between the fund and the Attorney General, and another between the AG and the CIA on confidentiality. The AG's office didn't like it, but they weren't going to say 'no' to the CIA," says Stewart.

Stewart stares at Jared. "In practical terms, Herakles needs to replace that loan a lot faster than the one year. Permanent funding needs to be in place well before the deadline, to be certified to the AG by the independent accountants. Otherwise the investigation isn't closed, and we lose the cooperation and confidentiality agreement provisions."

Stewart was retained after the hedge fund was raided by the New York Attorney General under the Martin Act. The investors had the right to take out their money at a specified time under the fund contract, but received instead delays, excuses, evasions, and ultimately bad checks. The investors went to the AG, and the AG moved quickly because problems with investment funds tend to get worse, rather than better. No one wanted to ignore another Bernie Madoff, although the SEC had gotten the same letter from investors and done nothing.

"So what'd you do to them? You screw somebody's sister?" Abbott asks. Jared is offended that Abbott thinks Jared's problems are amusing.

"What do you mean?"

"They hate you. The AG."

"Why? What did they say?" Even though Jared tends to bluster, he is sensitive to slights, whether they are small or large.

"Something about you having other people come behind you to shovel up the shit you leave. Sounds like you have a long history with the Manhattan DA. The lawyer said you had a problem borrowing an ex-girlfriend's Mercedes a few years back."

"That bitch Connie. I told her the car was stolen."

"The lawyer's words were, 'burned to a crisp and dumped in the river by the Meat Packing District.' I told her I didn't know anything about it," Abbott says.

"That's why I paid Connie off, to shut her up. That shit could happen to anybody," Jared says.

Abbott and Stewart don't respond. The room is quiet for a few seconds.

"Yeah, look," says Abbott, "on the fund, you need to hang tight. You'll have the money, because I need you to have the money. But you have got to stay on the fucking reservation, not wander off on your own."

"I don't like not getting the records back until I put in more money," Jared says. "Where am I going to get it?"

Abbott says softly, "Your trades put you in trouble, and that put a CIA operation in trouble. We needed to bail you out with the AG, and we did. But now we need you to work with us. Don't do things to increase the risk."

"That trade is right," Jared says. "Going against the dollar side of that trade is the right thing to do. That trade is going to pay off and pay off big. I got in too early, but I am absolutely right on this."

"Your problem is that it's still early," Abbott says. "You got in, lost, doubled down, and doubled down again, and now you don't have the cash to keep trying."

"You should listen to me, and we'll make the cash back," says Jared.

Abbott's tone is patronizing. "Jared, Jared, Jared. The money will come. It will take time. Everybody thinks you're doing a terrific job."

-o-

Project Deadbolt: "The Price Is Just The Price"

March 25

London

(Five weeks before Mecca)

Abbott walks through the bright raw springtime from his hotel to Zaroff's home. Zaroff, in an overcoat, is already outdoors at the corner to meet him. It is late afternoon. They pass through the nearby park. The trees are bare. It is the best area to meet. In the clear lines of sight, Zaroff scans for observers.

Zaroff is worried about D.C. Cain's volatile demeanor. Cain is not always able to compose his thoughts, and Zaroff limits his calls to the mornings, New York time, because Cain is sometimes nearly incoherent when he is tired. "I've tried to deal with Pfennig, but he's no better than a clerk," Zaroff tells Abbott.

The year of negotiations between Zaroff and the Iranian transportation minister, Sanjani, is about to yield a detailed Letter of Intent, a meaningful milestone. The contract will contain more complete engineering specifications and confirm the pricing, but the Letter of Intent is the task before them.

"The work should last five years. Dredging the Ports, creating docks and modern crane systems. We might get to bid on the work to modernize the roadways away from the Ports too." Zaroff looks at Abbott. "We might be able to leave Cain out of that later work, keep it ourselves."

Abbott resists Zaroff's transparent attempt to flatter him by referring to him as a business partner. They still have no arrangement for Abbott to be paid or take part in Zaroff's business, and Abbott is still waiting for his chance to make big money.

This is, in fact, Abbott's chief worry. In Abbott's thinking, he'd been the entrepreneur, bringing Cain to the Drone, and then later bringing Zaroff and Sanjani to Cain, but he's only gotten a middleman's commission, rather than being a full partner.

"Cain is making difficulties. He's making demands," Zaroff tells Abbott.

"Yes?"

"He said that he's had the Deadbolt material for years, it's time to take action, and he wants it used."

That's out of the blue. "What's he after?"

"I promised to install the mechanism in planes running routes in the Middle East. KLM runs through Iran and Saudi Arabia and around the Gulf. That part is done. I have the ID numbers on the planes. They can be tracked, and so...it's just a case of deciding when. And where."

"So, Cain's gone crazy, is that what you're saying?"

"He says he'll back out of the Ports deal without it."

"He can't do that! There are billions on the line!"

Zaroff shrugs. "He turned over his company to Pfennig. The money no longer motivates him in the same way."

"Then we should bypass him and go straight to Pfennig. Pfennig still likes money."

"I've tried," says Zaroff. "As I said, Pfennig's a clerk, he won't cross Cain."

"Without Cain, we have no cash and we have no Letter of Intent, much less a contract. Is this personal, because you bailed out Jared?"

"Cain recognizes that I am at a moment of financial weakness, and that he can dictate terms. Part of him remains lucid, and then the old pirate in him comes out."

"Businessmen are pricks," says Abbott.

"You need to understand, there is a positive side to things. I have spoken to Sanjani," Zaroff says. "I have a way for him to make maximum advantage of this situation. Sanjani will be able to consolidate power within the regime, if he prepares in advance and casts blame on his opponents as being in league with terrorists. As he gains power within the regime, our project becomes even more secure."

"Would he do that?"

"Yes, he wants to do it. It increases his willingness to work with us."

"Well," says Abbott. "You have the control software, I guess you should do what you have to do."

They had walked to the end of the park and were about to start back. Zaroff turned but didn't move.

"No, my friend. You have the software as well, and my judgment is that you have to control the plane," Zaroff says.

"Me? Why?"

"You may in fact be the greedy man that you have always told me you are. But I have recruited many spies in my time, always for the benefit of my superiors. You came to me, and you claim your superiors wanted me to draw in Sanjani, but everything else with Cain is your own idea. Now you can prove it. This will put you outside the CIA forever. Once that happens, then I have a guarantee you can be trusted," Zaroff says.

"You don't trust me? How do I know I can trust you?" Abbott asks.

"When we first got started, you were able to get me a million dollars from the CIA, just on my request," Zaroff says. "At first, that made me think that the CIA, not you personally, had use to make of me. Then you started paying me through Herakles in small amounts that you siphoned off, which makes me want to believe you, that you are now acting on your own. But I must confirm that fact, for my own safety." Zaroff's breath frosts in the air before him.

"As for trusting me," Zaroff says. "I have nowhere else to turn. I have put up nearly all my free cash on your word. You know my financial position. There is no one more desperate than a man who is in debt but pretending to be rich. It is why I am vulnerable to exploitation by Cain. It is your time to put something on the line."

"Can we talk him out of it?" Abbott asks.

"He is fixated." They are returning in the direction of Zaroff's home. "You can't walk away, Abbott."

They stride in silence.

"You can only move forward," says Zaroff. "We can arrange for the plane not to hit the Grand Mosque without telling Cain. Hitting the mosque would risk a regional war, very bad for business."

The setting sun is to their backs. The shadows of bare trees grow longer before them.

"Cain told me that you gave him a price of $40 million to pay Sanjani for the Letter of Intent. You're planning to keep the other $5 million for yourself, aren't you?" Zaroff says.

Abbott is silent.

"Don't misunderstand," says Zaroff. "You didn't tell me. You were planning for your own benefit. I don't judge this. If you steal from Cain, that's not my business. You were wise, not to try to steal from me. But now we are at this moment."

"There has to be something else he'll take," says Abbott.

"I've talked this all the way to the end of the negotiation. Now the negotiation is complete, and there is only the question of whether there is an agreement. As you Americans say, this is when the shit gets real."

"Jesus," says Abbott.

"Sometimes," Zaroff says, "the price is just the price."

-o-

Project Deadbolt: Hugh Abbott

May 15

Arlington, Virginia
(Two weeks after Mecca)

His furnished one-room apartment provides Abbott a place to flop at the end of the day and to play video games or watch TV when he isn't working. The apartment didn't start shabby but two years of occupation by Abbott have made it a hovel. There is no art on the wall. There are no pictures, no books. He sporadically clears take-out food boxes off surfaces after enough cardboard has accumulated to bother him. Abbott maintains sufficient personal hygiene to be presentable in the workplace, but otherwise lives in squalor.

For two weeks, TV has shown only coverage of the downed airliner near Mecca. Abbott's routine is to sleep by downing half a bottle of vodka in the evening, or to skip sleep altogether.

The $40 million from Cain has finally arrived at Herakles. Through his Tamerlane email, he'll provide Jared the routing instructions in the morning: $35 million to Sanjani, $5 million to Abacus.

The upper levels of the Agency support his work on the Zaroff/Sanjani intelligence operation, but Abbott recognizes that among his peers he is at best politely appreciated, not perceived as a key player. He is not on the fast track. Only in his secret life siphoning money to hidden accounts does Abbott have a sense of accomplishment.

Abbott wrote up the Iranian claims that the Mecca attack was the work of terrorists who were quickly suppressed by Sanjani. Abbott knew Sanjani's boastful account of his complete victory over forces of terror was utter bullshit for consumption by other Iranian government officials. Abbott didn't want Sanjani's claims subjected to closer questions within the Agency—he described them as "unlikely" and "not susceptible of confirmation."

Zaroff became rich through a combination of wit, skill, tradecraft, and dishonesty, but Abbott finds his own progress toward that goal to be frustratingly slow. It has taken him six years to accumulate two million dollars, siphoning off cash each month from the payments he directs to others. The skim to Abacus has gone unnoticed, a trickle diverted from the river of money going out in bribes and payments.

Once Sanjani gets Cain's $35 million he'll sign the Letter of Intent for the Ports deal. There will be another bribe payment due when the contract is signed, from which Abbott can commandeer a second $5 million. Once he has the $12 million in hand, Abbott will think about what he wants to do next.

In the meantime, the money has not smoothed out his mood. He powers up his gaming system, and finds another player has sent him a message:

AAardvark: Score's down, bro. Sux 2 B U.

Abbott stands mid-tier in the rankings on the multiplayer first-person shooter games he favors. In the game message boards, he is baiting, barbed, constantly on attack. He taunts fellow players as fools, cowards, faggots, castratos, geldings, eunuchs, and members of an inferior race. He traffics freely in the language and images of fascism in his taunts. Aardvark's trash talk is weak, but Abbott (using his electronic nom de guerre "Tamerlane") is behind him in the standings.

Money and the thrill of the electronic hunt are Abbott's two passions. He spends his vacations at the console in 14-hour chunks which are broken only so he can eat, use the bathroom, stretch occasionally on his balcony, and taunt others on the message boards. Away from work he is immersed in the games by day; at night, his dreams consist of blasting away his enemies.

The gaming world suits him, an environment he can control. Mock Darwinian battle in which success is rewarded, but where the downside is not real-world extinction, merely temporary shame within a small circle of gamers.

Today, Abbott stews. Edgy over the Ports deal, he tells himself, not the idiot taunt from another gamer. Not anything else. Abbott switches from games to the TV. Overhead shots again of the downed airliner near Mecca. The caption reads "177 passengers, six crew aboard."

As with any major transaction, last-minute problems keep cropping up with the Ports. Events are moving. Abbott is consumed by the urgency to make his money now. There will be no better chance, no second chance, and he can't let this one slip away. He hates that the deal could fall apart because of a last-minute slip by someone else. He has been a sneak thief all his life, stealing small, and now he can move up. Steal big.

Mecca had to happen to keep Cain on board. Abbott did what he could to contain the damage, to keep it from being a world disaster. Now Zaroff has a new financial problem. The crucial moments are approaching. Only two months ago Zaroff's cash had plugged a $23 million leak in Herakles, but now Zaroff says he might spring a leak himself.

Abbott keeps the bottle of vodka next to the chair with his game remotes. He stays out of the quick reflex games when he is drinking, and goes to the chatrooms instead. Then he drinks from the bottle like he is swigging Coca-Cola.

Online, Abbott has been playing less in recent weeks and his scores are down. He is less strategic when he plays, less efficient. He lingers over the chance to fire extra rounds into his online victims.

His commentary in the online chats has changed too, from his former faux teenage macho to mere bitterness. He settles on the reply message to his fellow gamer:

Tamerlane: Fuck you...

Abbott is seething. It is like road rage, but in his living room. There is a lot of money on the line. He tells himself to be cool, to stay in control.

-o-

Project Deadbolt: Ivan Zaroff

May 15
London
(Two weeks after Mecca)

Zaroff still owns a home in Prague but prefers London. Across the street is a park, green with spring. He isn't obligated to live in Russia and doesn't want to. He is not sentimental about his native land. He grew up impoverished in St. Petersburg as the son of a one-time tank commander, a hero of the Great Patriotic War, whose sole reward had been...well, nothing, in Zaroff's eyes.

Zaroff uses old KGB tradecraft to manipulate his banker into looking the other way on initiating collection, even though the loan with Deutschebank has been in default for half a year. When the banker calls to announce he will no longer be on the account, Zaroff knows the replacement will pull the loan before the Ports deal can come through.

Zaroff has $75 million in the bank, and $400 million of debts. He's been selling off villas and commercial real estate, very quietly, for five years. He still holds income properties and assets that throw off cash to pay minimum interest to the banks, but he spends more than he takes in. He appears rich but is living on credit.

In the KGB, he was a lean and aggressive agent. Now, a quarter of a century after his knowledge and tradecraft gave him control over a shipping and construction fortune, he recognizes that too much of the good life has dulled his edge. He is in decent physical condition, but he has been too rich for too long and taken it all for granted. Now everything he owns is in hock to one bank or another.

"It's a great life, if you don't weaken," Zaroff says aloud. Zaroff remembers the British agent who had first said that to him. He can't recall the man's face any longer, only his voice. The round English public school tones. He killed the man in East Berlin in 1988, and then a year later the Wall fell. Did that render the Englishman's life and service meaningless? Who knew?

The collapse of the Soviet Union ended the terrifying power of the state, and let loose the terrifying power of greed and amoral hunger, as former bureaucrats, including Zaroff, looted the state-owned industries. He'd gained control over a commercial shipping and construction concern operating in the Black Sea and Caspian Sea as crumbs fell off the golden table in KGB's scramble to seize ownership of state assets. Perhaps a small prize compared to the oil companies, banks, and manufacturing enterprises his more nimble colleagues obtained. But shipping connected to smuggling and money laundering, allowing Zaroff to remain close to his old line of work.

Political freedom never interested Zaroff. He savored the freedom of a voluptuary to gorge on fine food and wine, and to purchase worldly goods or experiences as he willed. For a quarter of a century, that freedom has been his, but business reverses—many of them caused by his own inattention—now have placed Zaroff's fortunes in decline.

With a bit more time, Zaroff will be wealthy again. His arrangement to be the CIA's point person for Sanjani is working out well. The CIA claims it wants to leave no fingerprints on its relationship with Sanjani, and uses Zaroff. Zaroff knows this is a ploy—the CIA is trying either to recruit him or compromise him. He's dangled too many enticements before others to believe otherwise.

He notified the SVR (Russia's foreign intelligence service, successor to the KGB's foreign operations) of the approach, and of his intention to take the American money. If the SVR didn't want to pay him, and the Americans did, then he would go where the money was. He'd used the CIA's money to cultivate Sanjani, and reported religiously and accurately to the SVR whatever Iranian intelligence he had learned and passed on to the CIA. He had provided the information to the SVR gratis. All of that was self-protection. He never wanted to be on their bad side.

Zaroff also gave the SVR any information on U.S. intelligence he gleaned from Abbott. A slim harvest: Abbott is inept as a spy, but generally good at keeping silent. Zaroff had pushed for extra money from the cash used to compromise Sanjani, but Abbott got it only once. Occasionally Abbott offers him information, which Zaroff expects is being planted by the CIA. He passes that information on to the SVR, too, with disclaimers. SVR has been waiting for Abbott to volunteer himself to be a recruited as a Russian asset, and the CIA, for its part, is undoubtedly waiting for the same from him. What neither the SVR nor

CIA expected was that Zaroff and Abbott would strike their own separate deal.

Zaroff told no one he needed to guarantee Sanjani's advancement within the regime in order to obtain the Ports deal, or that the Drone gave him the tool to achieve it. Zaroff had finally leveraged the Sanjani and Cain relationships into a shot at making billions of dollars—revenue to restore Zaroff's businesses to profitability. Zaroff could be back on top in a year or two—if he can get through the next several months.

In the immediate term, Zaroff needs to get his $23 million back from the American, quickly. His cash is tied up keeping Herakles afloat. The banks will love him once the Ports deal is in hand, but right now his bankers are governed by their fear and it takes all of his tradecraft to delay them from calling his loans and destroying the Ports deal: Even bribed, Sanjani could not give the deal to an insolvent company.

Zaroff is pleased he'd taken a quick two million dollars in the American stock market after Mecca by starting a small panic in the airline stock index. He knows another profitable trade will return him to the path to solvency.

-o-

Project Deadbolt: "Bling, Bling"

July 2
New York City
(One day after the Burj)

Jared Cain uses his wife's computer to set up the brokerage account. The address on the account is fake, the Social Security number is fake, the email attached to the account is a dummy and the name was copied from a Mel Brooks movie. He transfers cash from Herakles and buys put options on Boeing.

After the plane hits the Burj, Jared is in the money. He'll make a quick million bucks if Boeing falls by seven percent at market open. He is hoping the price will fall more, like ten percent.

Jared knew something big was coming. Abbott asked for $6 million of the Herakles Fund's money, promising that the fund would make enough to satisfy the New York Attorney General. Jared copied the trade when he saw a $6 million spike in the put options on Boeing. The option expirations were all mid-July, giving Jared an idea of the timing. Jared didn't know what Abbott was doing, but he wanted to make money.

Jared starts singing tunelessly, attempting to make up a rap song. The only words he finds are "bling, bling, bitch." He's scoring a double payoff. It is a fast win on the cash, and he's putting one over on Abbott. Jared wants a little payback: Abbott needs Jared's financial contacts, but constantly talks down to him, even though they'd been at Yale together. Jared took enough of that crap from his brother, back when he'd been alive.

Jared will cash out when the market opens. He needs the million to pay off debts and then to treat himself. He didn't know if the market would keep falling. He might be leaving money on the table. But taking a sure profit and then putting the original cash back into the fund's account was the way to go. Nobody would be any the wiser. He is pleased with how clever he is.

-o-

PROLOGUE TO PART II

Fallujah
2004

HASSAN LEAVES *Youseff in the alley and enters the street. Youseff told him the bomb switch would become active once Youseff was safely away.*

The Americans are ahead and Hassan's steps are halting. The closer he comes to the American troops, the sooner the end will arrive. He reaches the center of the street. He begins to speak. As he does, townspeople scatter.

"I am not a rich man, or a mighty one," Hassan shouts.

Hassan sees Youseff observing from a side street, making sure that he is doing what he had promised. Hassan holds a dead-man's switch in his left hand for the explosive vest beneath his cloak. He clenches it so hard his hand aches. Youseff explained that the bomb will go off when Hassan releases the switch.

"I welcome the stranger as a guest. I tend to my family. To be good for the sake of good alone—that, I have done."

"Don't move," shouts one of the Americans in Arabic. "If you are in danger, we can help."

Hassan had not planned out his final words. It is an impulse. He doesn't know why he's compelled to speak. The words are not an explanation. The words will not change what is to come, nor will anyone tell of what he said as he met his end.

"Then the war came to me. All I have done, and sought to do? Gone. Washed away by the war, like a storm."

Hassan looks downward. As he lifts his head, he sees the eyes of the American who told him to stand still. The bomb vest beneath his cloak is visible.

"Don't be angry..." he begins. Mac's bullet spins him partway around. Hassan falls face down. The vest does not go off. The dead-man's switch is a fake.

Silence claims the street. No one moves or speaks.

Rogers and the rest of the patrol are alert for reactions, checking all directions: Snipers, bombers, whatever. They can't know—the bomber might be a diversion for the real action. Seconds pass. Blood pools from the head wound.

The world begins to move again. Rogers, partially shielded by the open door of the Humvee, starts to step down. Rogers' eyes keep on Hassan but sweep the street. Leinheimer rises. Rogers' foot reaches the dusty street. Leinheimer is fully standing, his upper body exposed.

Youseff hoped the Americans would rush Hassan's body, to create a higher casualty count. Instead they delayed, and Youseff loses patience. He uses the radio control to activate the vest.

Half of the bomb is on the ground pinned beneath Hassan. In the explosion, that half throws shrapnel on a low angle, daisy-cutter style. It strikes Rogers in the left shin, disintegrating bone and flesh for five inches below his knee. Rogers tumbles to the ground.

Shrapnel from the portion of the bomb on top of Hassan's body flies randomly. One piece ricochets off a building and hits Leinheimer in the neck, severing the carotid artery.

Half of the American squad rushes to aid the two men. The other half covers the street. "Need back up immediately," Mac radios to base.

Rogers gets a tourniquet, while the medic turns to Leinheimer. The *medic puts his hand over the wound. The blood pulses warm and bright red and thick through his fingers. There is a smell of rust. The medic works until Leinheimer's heart stops and the gouts of blood end, a matter of minutes.*

"It was too big," the medic says to no one in particular. "We couldn't have saved him. Even the hospital..." he starts to say, and trails off.

The medic then turns to Rogers, who is ten feet away and had watched Leinheimer bleed out. Rogers already has morphine. The medic examines the wound. The leg is severed. The body above the injury is intact, other than perhaps knee cartilage and ligament strain or tear from the impact. The bone and muscle of Rogers' foot, ankle, and lower leg look like debris from the butcher shop. There is nothing to save. They need to get him to base hospital, either to amputate more of the leg there or, if he can be stabilized, to move him to a rear hospital.

The medic is unable to tell if Rogers has sustained a concussion, but certainly he is in shock.

There are no other injuries in the patrol.

Long minutes pass. Slowly, support rolls in toward the patrol. Forward scouts for the support were sapping for IEDs. The enemy had taken to planting IEDs along the route rescuers would take, so that soldiers rushing to their fellow Americans could be slaughtered. Once the military caught on, the protocol to address the risk was to move carefully. That meant no quick rescues, only systematic movements to prevent contributing to the body count.

Rogers finally is placed in a field ambulance and moved to treatment. What little remains of Hassan is placed in a bomb disposal container.

-o-

PART II
BASED ON TRUE EVENTS

August 13
McLean, Virginia

Mac is on time for his meeting in Thorpe's office, but then Thorpe is called down the hall and Mac must wait. Mac spots the bowl of wrapped hard candies on the coffee table between the couch where he is sitting and Thorpe's chair. Thorpe has already picked out all the blueberry ones. Just as well. No need for empty calories.

When Thorpe returns, Mac begins his briefing on Rogers' trip to Seattle with a preamble full of the qualifications and cautions he would have provided to General Smith.

Thorpe interrupts him mid-disclaimer. "Colonel, I'm a hell of a lot less interested in what you don't know, than I am in what it is that you do know."

Mac promptly summarizes the news from RossTech: The Drone used seemingly abandoned CIA technology, D.C. Cain financed the Drone's development, and Cain took delivery of three prototypes.

"Delivery suggests that the prototypes were functional," Thorpe says.

"In the lab, according to the files. No information on field testing."

Thorpe leans forward. "Yes, well, Mecca and Burj might have been the field tests. Any names attached to the CIA involvement?"

"A guy named Abbott. We don't know who has the email name Tamerlane. Those were the ones Rogers mentioned."

Mac notices Thorpe's reaction. Thorpe already seems familiar with Cain and expresses no surprise at the new names. Perhaps this is all old news to him.

Thorpe leans back in his chair. "Col. McCaulley, so far in this investigation, your name comes up when there are new developments. I plan to ask your superiors to keep you involved as acting head of the DIA while we work this thing out. I'd also like your continued participation in the BAG. Will that be all right with you?"

"I would be grateful if you did that, sir." Mac is pleased by the vote of confidence.

"The CIA has been quieter than I would have expected in the BAG meetings. But if they were part of creating this item, they may not want to brag about it."

"I brought in my colleague from the outside, originally because I also had reservations about the CIA's contributions." Mac gave Thorpe a quick overview of Rogers' background.

"Does Rogers agree with you? That the CIA might be an issue?"

"Based on the files and the BAG minutes, he suspects CIA is avoiding the release of information that might reveal a human intel source somewhere in the Middle East. Just his hunch, but I brought him in because he's got good instincts. CIA's concern may not even be connected to the main question of who attacked Mecca and Burj. But the more we look at the Drone, we have to decide if anyone at CIA other than Abbott knows about it."

"Do you plan to keep Rogers involved?" Thorpe asks.

"He's a consultant. I'd like to have him full-time for this if he'll do it." If Rogers takes point on the Burj, it'll buy time for Mac to learn the rest of the DIA portfolio.

"Hmmm. You may ruffle some feathers in the regular DIA staff with that," Thorpe says. "But you should do what you think works best. In the meantime, keep news of the prototype, Abbott, and Cain compartmented until the FBI has had a chance to run the details to ground. The CIA and FBI need to add the search for saboteurs to their searches for terrorists."

Thorpe knows the FBI counter-intelligence investigation of Abbott has been in place for weeks. Abbott showing up in two separate lines of investigation surrounding the Burj suggests to Thorpe that the inquiries will eventually connect. As Mac doesn't need to know about the insider trading probe in order to pursue the sabotage angle, the ever-cautious Thorpe elects not to share the additional details with Mac.

-o-

August 14
Langley, Virginia

Thorpe travels to Langley to meet Nadeau on Nadeau's home turf. The relationship needs tending, but Thorpe also needs to take an in-person read of the man. The Drone discovery means Thorpe must engage the CIA along a new front in the Burj investigation.

Over coffee in an Agency SCIF, Nadeau expresses concern that Thorpe is limiting his, and by extension, the CIA's, exposure to national security information. "We don't need a return to the bad old days when agencies didn't coordinate," Nadeau says. Thorpe agrees, but issues relating to Abbott need to be vetted outside the CIA to ensure an unbiased view.

"We're hands-off," Nadeau assures him. Nadeau says Abbott runs an intelligence asset in Iran with Herakles as the payment conduit, but Nadeau personally knows no other details. Abbott reports directly to the Regional Director for Mideast Operations, who finds nothing out of place. Nadeau offers full Agency cooperation, and Thorpe accepts that he's sincere. For the time being, Thorpe says, it's vital to keep Abbott in place without knowing he is the target of an investigation.

"If Abbott is holding something back, his superior hasn't spotted it," Nadeau says. "As I understand, he runs a human intel source in Iran with details that are kept coded. His material is coming through normal workflow. Other Agency sources for known terror groups keep coming back empty on who did the attacks. It looks like State is experiencing the same."

Thorpe asks Nadeau to have OTS generate an assessment of nations that have the expertise to create an autopilot over-ride. Thorpe doesn't mention the Burj—the subject matter speaks for itself. Thorpe treats the new request like a matter separate from questions on Herakles and Abbott, although he knows they are linked.

Back in his office, Thorpe reads the FBI's status report on the men in the trading inquiry. The backgrounds of Abbott, Zaroff, and Jared Cain don't enhance Thorpe's understanding of their connection to one another, or to the attacks.

The three men have not been in communication with one another since the FISA surveillance began. The FBI, with a warrant for black bag searches, located three burner phones for Abbott, two in his apartment and one in his upper right desk drawer at Langley. FBI modified them all, so if Abbott uses one, the FBI will listen in. Thorpe doesn't know how the conspirators manage to work together, but he is determined to bring them all down.

-o-

August 15-16
Hudson River Valley; Washington, D.C.

Rogers waits until he is back home in the living room and sitting with Dub to break the news to her that the DIA wants him to take a leave from West Point in the fall to keep consulting. It is late afternoon, and their son is playing with friends. Rogers is travel-worn after the flight from Washington and the drive from New York. But he can't delay.

Thorpe has to track all national intelligence issues, Rogers explains, and Mac has to track all DIA issues, so Rogers would be the person in the Defense Department whose sole focus is figuring out what happened at Mecca and the Burj. A contract through the end of the year, even if the work wraps up early, with pay at 150% of his teaching salary.

"And you want to do this without talking to me," Dub says.

"We're talking now."

"After you've already lined up all the arrangements."

"I needed to gather the facts."

"For a role with one hundred percent of the responsibility, and no authority." Dub gives him her 'disappointed parent' look. "You know better than that."

"That's cruel," Rogers says. "Accurate. But cruel."

"You're talking about more time away from family, and reneging on our summer plans, including the trip to see your father."

"You know I wouldn't do that lightly." She is examining him, looking for emotional weariness beneath the physical strain, and she is dubious about the economics of the deal—a few months of bumped-up salary is a bad exchange if it puts his teaching career at risk.

She stands and Rogers rises beside her and takes her hand. "When you say 'take a leave,' I worry Klamber thinks you're telling him you have one foot out the door."

"Klamber's a wild card," Rogers says. "He accepted my paper with no comment other than saying it looked complete. He says being tapped to work a high-profile terrorist investigation 'reflected well on the department.' He could be lying to me while measuring my grave, but I can't know."

"Consulting's not the life I expected," she says. "It's not the life we expected. So why do it?"

"I've already found some things in the investigation. It's serious and it's complicated." Rogers pauses. "I...just have a duty."

"Why? What duty? I don't get that. This isn't your fight. The attacks were in the Middle East. The planes were in the Middle East. Americans didn't take over the planes. Americans didn't..." She stops. He is trying to keep his expression impassive but she can read his face. She knows.

"Oh, shit," she says.

"You know I can't talk about it."

"So you have to take it." Rogers sees her shift gears, channeling her wariness, frustration, and anger into a plan of action. "Left to yourself you'd put duty ahead of your health. Stay on program. Keep meds with you."

"I haven't had a panic attack in years."

"Better to be safe," she says. "If you start finding sleep disorders, stress behaviors, don't be reluctant to back away from the whole project. I care about the rest of the world, but I care about you the most."

"This thing could come together in a week and be done, for all I know. Maybe months at the longest. Then we can take a make-up vacation," Rogers says.

"You've run up a big tab with me already. Stay healthy and pay it off. I don't want this to trigger new years of struggling back to even. We already did that." Rogers nods, and they hold one another. "I really don't want to do it again."

They look silently around at the home they'd made with the life they'd built. "I didn't tell you the news about Jerry Howard," Dub says.

"I'm supposed to cover his spring classes."

"He overdosed last week. Prescription opioids."

"Damn."

"Accidental, they say. But..." She leaves the rest of the sentence unsaid.

"Yeah."

Rogers will be in Washington the day of the memorial service. He recognizes the death gives Klamber a new chance to diminish and undermine Rogers at the Academy, by shifting him into additional introductory classes. It's a problem for later. It's selfish to react that way to Jerry's passing, but Rogers had learned on the battlefield to keep evaluating tactical dangers when a buddy fell; grieving sometimes had to wait.

On his return to Washington, Rogers learns Mac has reassigned staff to route investigation-related reports through him. Thorpe's forecast of staff dissention over Rogers's role is quickly borne out.

Lillian Charles, an NSA employee on temporary assignment to assist the DIA investigation, seeks an audience with Rogers. She wears a breast cancer awareness pin but no other jewelry. She's been at NSA for 15 years, has a master's degree in computer science, and radiates focus and intensity. She works with signals intelligence and computer programming. She has been monitoring reports from the NSA, the DOD's reports, and reports from other assets on developments in the Middle East since the Mecca and Burj attacks. Like Mac, she had previously been reporting directly to General Smith.

"I want to introduce myself, and become familiar with your background and knowledge, so that I know what information I'll need to prepare for you and the BAG," she says.

It's a nice, crisp professional request. Rogers also gets the impression she asked for the meeting to take his measure. Mac dropped a white male into the DIA investigation ahead of a qualified woman of color, Rogers doesn't blame her for wanting to see whether he is the real deal, or is there because Mac is playing favorites.

"I was Mac's intelligence officer when we served together in Iraq. He saved my life more than once. I'd give you the actual number, but I lost track. He and I know how one another work. With him in a new position, in a time-critical investigation, he wants someone that he didn't have to break in to act as lead. I'm quite sure my role came about because of exigent circumstances and is not a negative reflection on the skills of anyone else in the department, including you," says Rogers.

"As for my background, I teach history and modern Middle Eastern developments at West Point, along with language. That means that I have a good grounding in current Middle East military, economic, and cultural situations, and that you can pass along information to me in summary form, because I am going to already know who a lot of the key players are and what a lot of the key issues are. How's that?"

"That's fine." Lillian starts to rise from her chair. Lillian's expression doesn't change but Rogers intuits she's still bothered.

"Look, I'm here on a temporary basis. You were used to dealing directly with General Smith?"

"Yes."

"Are you worried my presence is going to set you back in career terms?"

"It's always a good idea to stay alert to downside risk," Lillian says.

"Fair enough. I recommend you speak directly to Col. McCaulley about any concerns you have with the reporting structure, and tell him that you're doing so on my recommendation."

"I'll think about it."

-o-

August 16
Washington, D.C.

Just back from the Hamptons, John Dallas is in pain. The skin on his back and legs is the color of radishes and radiates heat, while his face is still nearly pale. The day before, on their last vacation day, his wife Maureen had gone off to late-morning yoga while John took some sun. They'd partied until 3 a.m., Maureen drinking club soda from midnight on, and John not. Then John slept away the rest of the morning and the noon hour face down on a chaise in swim trunks.

Their trip was vacation/work. The work part was seeing and being seen, to gather social credit for the autumn season of Washington parties where so much of their real work is done, of connecting to sources and tracking the town's ever-shifting power structure. The sunburn story would carry them through the first two or three of the fall's soirees and provide opportunities to name drop celebrities and financiers they'd met over the summer.

Maureen got a more immediate pay-off, a rumor about who tipped the Saudis about the attack at Mecca. She is planning interviews for her return to the office, to check whether it really was Israel helping the Saudis. The Odd Couple.

At home recuperating from the trip, house empty with Mikey in his final week at camp, Maureen tends to John's wounds in their bedroom. With the TV on, sound at zero, John sits on the edge of the bed. Maureen sits behind him with her legs wrapped around as she applies zinc ointment to his back. They plan to split a simple dinner of pasta and a bottle of wine, then stream a movie they had missed from a year before.

"Why don't you ask Rogers if he'll help confirm the tip about the Saudis?" asks John.

Maureen hisses. "He's a dear friend, but tight as a clam. He'll talk theory, but if he actually knows something he won't say a word."

"His name came up at the party—new job at the Pentagon. Heard it from a Treasury guy working the insider trading angle on the Burj attack. He is telling me there was some money laundering too."

They look up at the quiet television. It is a local current affairs program. They see Cutler on screen, debating a young woman with Middle Eastern looks. She has a scar near one eye. "I know him," John says. "Interviewed him years ago. Campaign bagman for some senator, now an anti-Muslim propagandist for D.C. Cain. Pushing—I don't know what you'd call it—genocide-lite."

"Yeah?"

"Really full of himself. And not as smart as he thinks."

"You're kidding. There's a guy in Washington who thinks he's wonderful, but doesn't have a clue what he's doing? That's news," Maureen teases. "You really are an ace reporter."

"You can stop."

"Pulitzer, maybe."

"You're free to stop, any time."

-o-

August 17
New York City

Ted Brooks guides Jared Cain into the interview room in the FBI's New York offices, turns him around to remove the handcuffs, then motions for him to sit at the table. Everything in the room is grey except the one-way mirror on the wall next to Andy Mayfair.

Brooks remains standing. "Mr. Cain, do you want your attorney present in this discussion?"

"Damn right. I had a deal to end the last investigation, and this is not going to end well for the FBI."

Brooks looks down at the defiant seated man. "Hmmm. Well, let's wait for your lawyer to get here. We'll make the call. Please give us the name and number."

"Wait, I should call, I get a phone call, right?"

"You have a right to a lawyer, not a phone call. The sooner you give us the lawyer's information, the sooner we can make the call for you," Brooks says.

The FBI men leave the room and Jared sits alone, monitored through the one-way glass by another agent. Jared is fidgety, like an ADD case. The FBI conducted simultaneous raids at both Jared's home and the Herakles office, with FBI personnel still quietly securing the cooperation of staff as they show for work. While Brooks and Mayfair wait for Jared's attorney, the agents at Herakles begin to look over fund files and report back to the interview room.

Jared's attorney, Bob Stewart, arrives after Jared has been in FBI custody for two hours. Brooks knows him from Stewart's time as Assistant U.S. Attorney in Manhattan. Brooks is by-the-book, scrupulous about the details whenever charges are brought in a case he works, and he knows his presence will signal to Stewart that something has gone seriously wrong for Jared.

Once Stewart is in the interview room Brooks begins.

"We want to let you know for starters that we have the Herakles Fund's files from the New York Attorney General's office, and we've had the chance to go through them."

Stewart holds up his hand immediately. "Okay. Before we go further, you need to tell me exactly how that happened. We had an understanding with the AG and other agencies that this material was to remain held in the AG's files, for reference, but that the AG investigation is suspended. Our agreement is that those files were not going to be disclosed or referred to any other investigative bodies or used in civil litigation."

"Without the CIA's consent. That's correct. That is what your prosecution deferral agreement said, and the AG is abiding by it."

"You're saying that you have the CIA's consent for the AG to turn over files to the FBI?" Stewart is asking for himself, for confirmation, but also to drive the point home to Jared.

Brooks slides the court order across the table. Attached to the order as an exhibit is the affidavit from the Director of the CIA in support of the court order, specifying the CIA's consent to release of the files.

"This is the first I've heard about it." Stewart examines the paper. "This is dated almost two weeks ago. Why don't I don't know anything about this?"

"That happens in national security investigations," Mayfair says.

Brooks watches Stewart. The cover the CIA had provided for Jared in the earlier investigation is gone. The words "national security" signal that the CIA relationship itself might even be part of Jared's problem. Stewart isn't prone to panic, having faced down tough situations in the U.S. Attorney's office, but he clearly doesn't like being thrown cold into whatever mess Jared has made.

"The FBI raided Herakles' offices at the same time we picked up your client. We already have an idea what to look for based on what we got from the AG." Like Stewart, Brooks is going step-by-step to make sure Jared understands what is happening.

"I don't think there's anything Jared can confirm about records sitting here in FBI offices, without conducting his own review of the files," Stewart says.

Brooks props up a tablet screen where Jared and his lawyer can see material the FBI had already prepared. "That's okay. A couple of things jump out at us. Here are some dates and dollar amounts of money coming in to Herakles from a separate account. Money goes out, money comes in, a net gain of $28 million to Herakles, all in a matter of weeks. What can you tell us about that?"

Jared shrugs. "I can't help it if I'm lucky. It's not a crime, right?"

Stewart jumps in. "He can't tell anything without the full records in front of him. Jared, I suggest that you just listen here. We find out what the FBI has to say, and then you and I can talk about whether there is anything to respond to."

Jared is sullen. He nods.

Brooks continues. "Here are the records you submitted to AG at the time of your standstill. They show a $23 million bridge loan from Nocturne, which is a condition of the settlement. We show you paying out $28 million to Nocturne, right after you made that big 'lucky' windfall. Your profits on that big windfall, all out the door to Nocturne. That looks like principal and very high interest on the loan to Nocturne."

Stewart waves Jared off and stays silent.

"Investors invest to make money," says Jared. Stewart's face shows aggravation. Jared can't resist chirping.

"We also see that your dad endorsed over a $2 million check to you, recently," Mayfair continues. "For a guy who was on the ropes a few months ago, you have a lot of money coming in and out of your fund."

Jared still has a bit of bravado. "The AG did a raid because they thought we didn't make enough money, now the FBI raids me because I made money. You guys should make up your mind."

"Your personal account also made an additional million on Boeing puts. You made big money on a bet placed just before a Boeing airliner hit the Burj. Who suggested that you should take a position that Boeing stock would fall?" Brooks asks.

Stewart jumps in. "Don't answer."

Brooks continues. "Now, you could have seen a lot of the short and put positions being established in the market and figured that there is a big move coming. Maybe you just copied other folks and maybe you just got lucky. Is that what happened?"

"Don't answer."

Brooks says, "Stew, when you tell your guy not to answer, is it because you know what the answer is and you know he should be pleading the Fifth, or are you just being cautious?"

"You've said you have a national security investigation that involves my client. I don't know what it is. You're asking questions about stock trading, which happens to be his business, and is not connected to national security. There's no reason for him to talk unless you put your cards on the table and let us know what you think he did to be arrested."

"Fair enough," says Brooks. He pulls a photo from the file and gives it to Jared and Stewart. "This is a picture of Lydia Marks. American tourist."

"Okay."

"We thought we'd show it to you."

"Because...?"

"She was killed when a Boeing 737 hit the Burj," Brooks says to Stewart. "She was killed when the shorts that Jared and Herakles had placed just before the attack suddenly became very valuable, because a plane built by Boeing, operated by a terrorist, hit the Burj."

Brooks turns to address Jared directly. "Now, you entered into those Boeing positions in your personal account before the terrorist attack, which made you a big score. That is your personal profit, made from the attacks on the Burj. Herakles needed money too, to pay off the bridge loan and make the New York AG happy. And there it is—$28 million Herakles made, also betting that the Boeing would hit the Burj."

Mayfair adds, "We don't think you got lucky. We think you bet on a sure thing. A sure thing that killed an American citizen, plus hundreds of other people."

Stewart says, "So you think this is insider trading by my client?"

Brooks shakes his head. "Securities violations are the least of your problems. I'm saying your client is complicit in a terrorist attack, the murder of an American citizen, and probably a few other crimes that we will get around to, once we know more."

A pale Jared asks to be excused for a bathroom break.

After Jared leaves under escort with FBI staff, Brooks turns to Stewart. "You know where we're going, right?"

"I see where you want to take it. Conspiracy to commit murder is going to take a lot more than what you've shown. And Jared may not be perfect, but...I don't see how you tie him in with a terrorist attack overseas."

"You know how it is. We're putting our cards on the table like you asked. But we're turning them over one at a time."

"Unless you're bluffing," says Stewart.

Brooks looks at his former colleague. "Stew, you worked with me way back, right?"

"Yeah." Brooks isn't bluffing. Without knowing what the FBI has, Stewart knows the FBI has something solid.

Stewart sighs. "Are you asking me if I'll recommend to him that he cooperate? I still have no idea what the entire picture is. I can't make a recommendation until I know what I'm dealing with. I'm guessing that you're after the CIA contact that gave him cover with the Attorney General."

Brooks nods. "For starters. If he had a tip about a terror attack, we need to know everything. Whoever's behind the bridge loan is also on the list. And Jared is going to have to be sequestered until we do it, get the other guys on the list. Not house arrest. Jail."

"You want him in solitary confinement with no trial? I don't think so," Stewart says.

"You don't think so?" Brooks says incredulously. "Your guy just helped this decade's version of Osama bin Laden kill hundreds of people —and the bad guy is still out there." Brooks stands. "I thought you were smart enough to get things by implication. But let me spell it out for you.

If Cain doesn't want to share a cell at Gitmo with the rest of the gang, here's what cooperation looks like: Whatever we ask, he says, 'Yes sir' and 'How else can I help you?'

"Also, just so you know," Brooks continues, "We have court-ordered taps on him. And on you. So no leaking. No obstruction of justice. No letting the bad guys know we're coming. When we do a national security investigation, we don't cut corners, and we don't fuck around."

Brooks observes Stewart calculating the difference between his client's best interests and Stewart's own. Stewart isn't part of Jared's scheme and clearly wants Jared's problems to belong to Jared alone.

"My communications with a client are confidential. That's the law."

Brooks' look to Stewart is poison. "Understood. But here's something else to keep in mind. We don't get to take chances. We have zero sympathy for people who help fly airplanes into buildings, and if you want to get pissy with us after the fact on privilege issues, go ahead, sue me. But our priority is stopping terrorists first and sweeping up broken eggshells later."

"How about a little presumption of innocence," Stewart says.

"Spare me the high school civics crap. Presumption of innocence is for the jury, and you're not in front of a jury. We want to make sure there isn't another attack. And from what we see, we presume your client is in on mass murder until we get evidence otherwise. Which we haven't."

Jared comes back into the room.

Stewart says, "May I talk privately with my client?"

"No, we're just getting started. You'll get private time later, but we have work to do right now." Brooks turns to Jared. "Mr. Cain, while you were out, my old colleague Mr. Stewart and I were talking about how deep the shit is that you happen to be in. Mr. Stewart at one point suggested that I was bluffing, and then I reminded him that he and I have a history. Mr. Stewart, please tell your client how likely you think it is that I am bluffing about having evidence to bring charges against him?"

"I don't know what they have. They are convinced that they have evidence to show that you were involved in the terror attack, somehow,"

Stewart tells Jared. "Right now, you should stay silent, for your own good, until we know where they want to take things. Okay?"

Jared keeps quiet.

Brooks says, "The big picture, Mr. Cain, is that the charges you face start at securities fraud and work their way up to treason, with a stop at murder along the way."

"That's a lot to prove," says Stewart.

"Yeah. Well, I guess we haven't turned over all our cards yet. But my point is—I'm not after you, Mr. Cain. At least, you're not my highest priority. I am going to want your help to go after Hugh Abbott."

Brooks and Mayfair have dealt before with arrogant and monied men who've lived a lifetime of bluster surrounded by yes-men. They expect that Jared will have too much to lose to fight the FBI for long. They exchange a glance as they watch Jared do the math: The FBI knows about the accounts. The FBI knows who Abbott is. The CIA pulled the protection Abbott set up for Jared with the AG, meaning the CIA has turned against Abbott as well. That means Abbott is already toast. The FBI wants to fill in the picture, confirm things they already have. So if he is going to strike a deal, he has to do it quickly.

"What are you offering?" Stewart asks.

"It will all depend on the level of cooperation, and the value of the information. We can't make any promises, because we don't know everything he did. But if he's straight with us and everything he says checks out, we'll get him the best deal he can under the facts. And you have an idea about the downside risk if he decides to stonewall us and refuse to cooperate."

"What are you looking for?" Jared asks.

Brooks is glad the conversation is taking this turn: Jared wants to help if there is something in it for him. They'll have to see whether he is actually a help over time.

"Complete, factual confession on everything. Timelines, names, and places. Any information on the source of the loan."

"You want me to help you get Abbott," Jared says. "I'll be happy to burn Abbott. This shit is all his fault, not mine. The Abacus account is Abbott. He used it when he skimmed money that came in all those years. He set those up, not me."

Brooks says, "See? That's helpful. It's what we suspected, but corroboration is good."

Jared tries as hard as he can to blame as much as he can on Abbott. It was Abbott who had set up Herakles to run CIA money in and out for years, and who set up the bridge loan, and it was Abbott who set up the overseas accounts that generated the $28 million to pay back the lender Jared had never met. Abbott didn't tell him an attack was coming, but Jared copied Abbott's trades.

The FBI men don't believe Jared was an innocent bystander. But they can start with the material he is giving them, and Brooks encourages him to keep talking.

"That's the kind of conversation we like to have about how the fund operates. One more thing. We may have you wear a wire the next time you talk with your dad."

This catches Jared off-guard.

"My dad?"

Brooks leans forward. "Yeah—That's one of those cards we haven't turned over yet."

Jared laughs contemptuously. "Well, good luck with that. That prick and I haven't talked in years."

"We're going to have to arrange a family reunion, then," says Brooks. "We've only been going over the books for an hour, but we found $40 million that came into Herakles from Cain Industries in mid-May. It wasn't an investment, and just went right back out the door, to overseas accounts. That money came into your fund two weeks after the attack on Mecca, and six weeks before the attack on the Burj. How do you explain that?"

Stewart silences Jared with a look. "If you don't know, don't speculate." Jared stays quiet.

"Literally," Brooks says, "we have only found this in the past hour. It's too soon to have any real theories about this payment. But you know what it looks like to me? It looks like your dad paid terrorists $40 million after they attacked Mecca and before they attacked the Burj, and you helped him do it."

-o-

August 18
Washington, D.C.

Rogers arrives at Mac's Pentagon office from his temporary space, several floors and sections away. The nameplate on Mac's desk displays his rank and full name, the one nobody uses. The space is cramped, windowless, and utilitarian, and Mac keeps a picture of his son on his credenza, next to a precariously stacked pile of papers and notebooks.

"What's the occasion?" Rogers asks.

"Thorpe says FBI counter-intelligence caught some chatter and he wants a face-to-face update with all BAG participants in two days, followed by a closed session with us, FBI and CIA."

"It's an ongoing investigation, we're not ready to go public with it," Rogers says. "I hate meeting just to meet."

"As I understand it, we should announce to BAG that we're looking into information that leads away from terrorism, but no more. Then Thorpe wants us to open the kimono to FBI and CIA leadership about the Drone—the voice record, Cutler, RossTech, the prototypes, the whole history."

"You want me to work up some talking points for you?" Rogers asks.

Mac looks abashed. "My superiors see this as insufficiently verified intelligence. They're telling me it should be your report and not mine."

"If I'm wrong, I'm expendable."

"I wouldn't put it that way myself," Mac says. "But...yeah. Thing is, I'm willing to do it. I'm comfortable with what we've got...."

"No need to explain," Rogers says. "We know the game. If we're wrong, the rent-a-guy takes the blame. If we're right they'll have plenty of time to claim credit for it later." Rogers is grateful Mac was at least embarrassed to make the ask and willing to own up to the underlying cynicism of superiors. They've both been there before.

"Fine," Mac says. "I have something else to run past you. Separate but related. These days I'm getting to see material General Smith didn't share with me. Right after Mecca, the Saudis and Iran agreed on an emergency basis to share specific military information to avoid a hot war, advance notice of troop and naval movements. Updates at least daily, so each side can confirm the other isn't doing something sneaky. Saudis say they're living up to their side of the deal and Iran is doing the same."

"And Saudis give us a copy so we can verify to them that Iran is telling the truth?"

Mac nods. "My contact at Saudi defense passes on what they get in advance from Iran. And I notice that when CIA reports to the BAG on troop movements, they never go beyond what DIA already has, and they never cite sources. But the CIA material is word for word the same as what Iran gives the Saudis," Mac said.

"Intercepted signals, maybe?"

"Fair point. It might be somebody swiping information off the radio. I'll ask Lillian to run an analysis of intercepted signal traffic. But you suspected CIA might have a high-level source inside Iran. I'm wondering if the Agency source is the defense minister."

Rogers weighs the question. "My pick in Iran for a CIA front is the interior minister, Sanjani. He used Mecca as a chance to eliminate his political opponents. A high-placed asset might leak reports from a different agency to deflect identification if something goes wrong. Their bureaucrats don't behave differently from ours."

-o-

August 20
Washington D.C.

Washington swelters under its fourth consecutive day of 90-degree-plus heat. The outside air, never dry, feels saturated. Even in the FBI's large and air-conditioned conference room many BAG meeting participants remove their suit jackets. Principals of all ten BAG agencies attend, bringing deputies and key staff.

CIA Director Nadeau is accompanied by Deputy Director Mundy and three subordinates. Mac introduces Rogers to them as the group mills around pre-meeting.

"Met your department chair at a conference last week," Mundy tells Rogers. "A bit desperate to make an impression. He dropped your name, some study on historic terrorism."

"It's set for publication in the winter," Rogers says.

"Huh." Mundy isn't trying to make conversation, and turns to speak to someone else.

Thorpe will direct the meeting and is already seated at the head of the table. Participants straggle in, surrendering electronic devices in the anteroom before entering. When the group is finally assembled, the only no-show is an ex officio member, the President's chief of staff Sangar Rainsford.

Junior representatives sit in chairs against the wall, with six feet of pathway to the table. The room is paneled in dark wood all around, windowless and cut off from the outside world—the isolated and solemn sort of room, Rogers thinks, that reinforces for those powerful enough to be in it that they are entitled to make choices for others.

The NSA representative asks to go first, out of order, citing a conflicting engagement. Review of signals data from May confirms Israel as a "day of" source to the Saudis of the imminent attack on Mecca. No confirmation on how Israel came by the information or whether Israel was the only provider of advance word to the Saudis. The NSA report is a data point, rather than an explanation of how the Saudi air force reacted so quickly that day.

When it is Rogers' turn, he announces there is information that, if confirmed, could contradict the prevailing assumption of terrorist involvement in Mecca and the Burj. The statement vanishes into the room with no perceptible ripple.

The FBI states it has nothing it can share at the moment. When the meeting breaks, seven men remain: Thorpe and two representatives each from Defense, CIA, and FBI.

Rogers begins by playing the partial recording from the Burj cockpit voice recorder. Faces around the table are grim—not only are these the last moments of innocent people, but the implications register immediately. Even in summary, Rogers takes twenty minutes to lay out the story of Project Deadbolt's creation, abandonment, and resurrection, and the delivery of three prototype Drone controls to D.C. Cain.

At Mac's insistence, Rogers is at pains to be clear about the limits of the DIA's information. Ross's letter to Cain said only that he was sending prototypes and software. DIA found no evidence of large-scale Drone manufacture, nor confirmation that the Drones worked outside of the lab, nor conclusive proof that the prototypes actually arrived in Cain's hands or were deployed. No DIA evidence implicates CIA involvement higher up than Abbott.

Rogers' presentation provokes an unstructured conversation around the table, which Thorpe does not interrupt.

Mundy, from the CIA, argues the recording is strong circumstantial evidence the pilots lost control to the autopilot, but there is no evidence the Deadbolt/Python prototype actually worked, much less that it produced the attacks. He finds it "unlikely but not impossible" that the Drone found its way from RossTech's workbench into the airliners at the Burj or Mecca.

Nadeau adds, "The Drone would be a handy way to explain the facts, but we can't let that drive our thinking. We know that terrorists exist, but a functioning Drone is hypothetical."

"I understand," says Rogers. "At the same time, I urge everyone to be careful about their motives for disbelieving the Drone information. Accepting that the Drone commandeered the planes forces you all to confront the possibility that a politically well-connected private citizen tried running his own foreign policy by facilitating terror attacks through sabotage."

The men at the table touch on the implications of the involvement of D.C. Cain. They are attuned to the political considerations and want to protect against the day a Cain crony claims bringing Cain's name into the matter arose from disagreement with his politics.

Had the FBI interviewed him? Did he still have the Drone prototypes? Were there explanations for his role that didn't involve him taking part in terrorism? Is the information verified tightly enough to withstand claims of political bias? Is evidence of his involvement incontrovertible? They want to be on record as stating that an investigation is not an accusation.

Rogers explains that many of the factors to support the explanation of terrorism are missing. "The folk saying is that when you have a hammer, every problem is a nail. In the research on cognitive errors, the term is 'confirmation bias'—the tendency to over-value information that supports your theory, and to dismiss contradictory or missing data. The whole world assumes the attacks were terrorism, and is under-valuing data showing the absence of terrorists."

Mundy fires back, "We can say the same regarding your contentions. The open questions about your Drone theory are too numerous for me to be convinced. You still don't have evidence to explain how a Drone device would have gotten into a plane."

"Are you saying, sir, that we should ignore the Drone idea completely until every element of the theory has been demonstrated?"

"Do you give students who hand in incomplete work an 'A' in your classes, professor?"

"I'm not claiming a conclusion, merely evidence to justify making additional inquiry,"

"Mr. Rogers," says Mundy, "you're not a full-time intelligence officer. Your thoughts are interesting, and I'm sure we all appreciate what you've discovered, but we can't take the chance that your opposition to the terrorism explanation is merely the musing of an academic pursuing his personal White Whale."

Rogers keeps his voice level. Whether Mundy is purposely baiting him with the "White Whale" comment, Rogers takes it as a personal insult. "Mr. Mundy, at this table, we need to arrive at the most accurate assessment that we can. Unlike Hollywood, it's not enough for our work to be 'based on true events.' When I encounter an honestly made criticism, intended in good faith to pursue truth, I encourage it, sir, to improve my analysis. As I am sure you do yourself. Appearances notwithstanding, sir, I am not Ahab."

Mac stands, a ploy to draw the room's attention and to keep Rogers from venturing into comments he'll regret. "Professor Rogers didn't oversell his information, and we ignore him at our peril."

"Is that the official Pentagon position?" Mundy asks.

"The official Pentagon position is that it's wise to make decisions after you have all the information, and not before."

Thorpe asks Robeson and Brooks to present the FBI's findings. Brooks describes the securities trading ahead of the Burj attack, including the money trail leading back to Zaroff, through Herakles and Jared Cain. "The name of Herakles Fund—which Mr. Rogers just mentioned in connection with the payments made for the Drone project—came up in connection with suspicious stock market activity ahead of the Burj attack. Jared Cain was part of that trading, but his father was not. Through the stock trading investigation, we found Ivan Zaroff, who is former KGB and now—supposedly—a private businessman. Zaroff's personal financial problems may be a driving force in the trading, and his presence in the money trail suggests Russian involvement in the attacks, or at least advance knowledge."

Brooks reveals the CIA's protection of Herakles Fund from the New York Attorney General, and describes Herakles' role as a payment processor for the Drone development and for CIA payments to Iran. Brooks notes the FBI uncovered that Herakles transferred another "significant" payment from Cain Industries to parties yet unknown but lacked details to provide the group.

"We're being cautious about what we can demonstrate, and what we can't. Herakles making payments for a CIA-authorized overseas source may be separate from any other activities. It's possible that Herakles is exclusively at fault, and not the CIA personnel." Brooks looks around the table.

"Nonetheless, the Drone and the trading investigations both independently lead to the Cain family. And while the trading and the Drone aren't necessarily connected, they have the same person in the middle, Hugh Abbott at the CIA." Brooks closes the folder holding his notes.

Sitting next to Mac, Rogers leans over to whisper, "That sounds like a White goddamn Whale to me." Mac keeps watching Mundy and without looking at Rogers motions for him to stay quiet.

Mundy glances at Nadeau and then faces Thorpe. "This is new to me and I'm not in a position to respond." Mundy's face holds a placidity that his speaking tone belies. "There were ways to bring this information to the CIA's attention earlier than this." Rogers' assessment is that Mundy is irritated that he personally was out of the loop on the Abbott investigation, rather than being angry on the CIA's behalf.

CIA Director Nadeau assures the room, "Director Thorpe and I are on the same page. There isn't an issue with the DNI. The counter-intelligence implications outweighed the need to share substantive information sooner." Nadeau looks at Mundy. "Not only within the intelligence community but also within the CIA itself."

"We don't know the identity or capabilities of whoever did the attacks. We're no closer to solving the problem. And typically my office coordinates details on a counter-intelligence operation," Mundy says.

"Well," says Thorpe quietly, "It is my request, and Director Nadeau agreed, that the information remain compartmented. My door is open if you'd like to talk to me about it after this meeting. It's some comfort, I suppose, that the FBI is quiet enough to remain undetected."

Nadeau says, "I have strong concerns over the Russian involvement. We can't ignore the fact that the Russians view the world differently than we do, and they sometimes act aggressively in what they view as their self-interest. We cannot underestimate the presence of the Russians."

Thorpe says, "Mr. Mundy, has Mr. Zaroff previously come to the attention of the CIA, so far as you know?"

"Almost certainly, just from your description of him. You can depend upon a former KGB agent to remain in touch with Russian intelligence, even one supposedly now in private life. I would need advance preparation to share specifics with the group what the Agency knows about Zaroff, but it certainly knows something."

Rogers says, "We have Russians, but we also have Cain. If there were three working prototypes of the Drone in Cain's hands, and two were used on Mecca and the Burj, there could still be one left. There's a reason to focus on eliminating Cain as a problem. If we don't, there could still be the potential for another attack."

This comment sparks a renewed discussion of Cain's presence in the investigation. Politicians throughout Washington had been beneficiaries of his campaign generosity, or had placed staffers or friends in patronage jobs at his think tanks and PACs. If Cain is exporting terrorist technology to the Middle East, there are ramifications in Washington as well.

Rogers brings the discussion back to a neglected point. "I have one other question, Mr. Nadeau. So far, we haven't discussed Abbott as an action item. Is he still in the Agency?"

"Deputy director for operations in Iran," Nadeau says.

Thorpe says, "Abbott needs to stay in place for the time being, as part of that counter-intelligence operation."

"Just thinking out loud," says Rogers, "But if Abbott needed a paymaster for an operation starting back a few years ago, the logical place for him to run an operation would have been in Iran, where his CIA duties are. And if you look at the only two people on the planet who benefited from Mecca, you'd probably pick Iran's defense and interior ministers, Azel and Sanjani, because they both wound up assuming greater authority inside Iran after the attack."

Seeing no reactions around the table, Rogers plows forward.

"When you think about it, nobody else really benefited at all from the attack on Mecca, other than those two guys. With the Burj you can point to a profit motive. But no one made money on Mecca. No terrorists came forward to take credit for Mecca. No nation saw its strategic position improve as a result of Mecca."

No one speaks.

"If Abbott is running an agent inside either of those ministries, and trying to promote that agent's advancement within the Iranian regime by using the attacks to consolidate power...Well, I'm just speculating," Rogers says.

"Just speculating," Rogers repeats. "But it's the only thing that makes sense to me."

"Nothing personal," says Mundy, "but any operation involving Abbott is above your pay grade."

"I thought we were all in this together," Rogers says.

Mundy offers a thin, humorless smile. His look is stern, territorial, and unforgiving. "Don't underestimate the kind of problem we have with Cain. And even in a setting as secure as this meeting, it's not our habit to speculate out loud on sources and methods of information without knowing whether they are classified."

"I'm exceedingly grateful for your guidance, sir," Rogers says.

With scheduled presentations over, the meeting breaks briefly. Participants rise and mill about, to talk together, or seek out coffee or restrooms. The agenda calls for discussion of action items next. An aide comes in and hands Thorpe a note.

"Very short break, everyone," Thorpe announces. "We have a change of schedule. A party calling itself the Lions of Jihad of Pakistan has stepped forward to claim credit for Mecca and the Burj and is making a new threat. The text reads:

"We have to date conducted attacks on those who have not shown proper devotion to Islam, or to Allah, or to the Prophet. If we attack those who fail in their devotion, we must also bring our battle to unbelievers. That must include the sites worshipped by the Crusaders and by the West, who continue their threats to the religion of the Prophet. Therefore, you must expect the greatest castle of the Crusaders, the Vatican, to be our next target."

Briefly in the room there is only the sound of papers rustling and the nervous movements of seated men absorbing shocking news.

Mundy quietly turns to Rogers and says, "This runs counter to your 'no terrorists' theory, professor. Unlike the hindsight of academic analysis, we're in the arena of choices made in real time with the best available facts." He pauses. "I think we professionals will be taking the lead from here."

-o-

August 20-21
Pentagon; Arlington, Virginia

Rogers spends a disconsolate afternoon in his Pentagon office unwinding from the presentation, letting the adrenaline subside, replaying the meeting mentally. Mac had remained behind to confer with Thorpe.

That evening Rogers joins Mac for dinner in a small private room at a Pentagon restaurant reserved for officers, one with tablecloths, cloth napkins, a menu, and a wine list. Rogers isn't sure of his appetite, despite having eaten only lightly for several days. Rogers orders scampi, richer than his stomach needs, but the scent of garlic, lemon, and shrimp wafting up soothes the fraying of his nerves. Mac attacks a veal chop with gusto. It is still early evening, but the sky is thick grey with churning rainclouds.

Rogers' voice is subdued and unemphatic. "The 'find terrorists' faction ignored everything we said."

"I'd say the folks prioritized the Lions over Abbott and the Drone," Mac says between bites. "The Lions gave them a good excuse to steer away from anything involving Cain. Nobody in that room wants to mix it up with a politically connected billionaire." Mac takes a sip of wine. "Except you."

Rogers scoffs. "Mundy accused me of being Ahab. But I was Quixote, going after windmills."

"You were telling people what they needed to hear, not what they wanted to hear. Against someone with political clout, none of them wants to strike first. Cain needs to be wounded before they'll pile on."

"Thorpe let us take all the incoming," Rogers says.

"He doesn't let us in on everything he knows," Mac says, "But he's not leaving us stranded."

"Thanks for standing up for me, literally."

"The FBI bailed us both out. Their data about the stock trading fit with what we knew about the Drone. But we couldn't connect the two, except through Abbott, and we couldn't connect any of it to the Lions."

Mac leans back in his chair. "Italy is circling fighter jets 24/7 over Rome. They're talking about shooting down airliners that come too close to the Vatican."

"Like the Saudis at Mecca," Rogers says.

"Italy complained the Saudis over-reacted at Mecca. Funny how things change."

Mac tells Rogers what he learned from speaking to Thorpe after the meeting. "Thorpe wants the DIA work to continue, because the Drone question needs to be resolved, regardless of whether it's connected to Mecca or the Burj or the new threat. The FBI counter-intelligence investigation is still ongoing. Thorpe also shared that Zaroff is connected to Abbott by more than the securities trading ahead of the Burj attack, and is connected to Cain through a seaport construction deal they made in Iran."

Rogers lifts his eyebrows. "That sounds relevant."

"Initially Abbott recruited Zaroff to cultivate an intelligence asset in Iran on behalf of the CIA, pitching to Zaroff that Iran is the sort of authoritarian system where he and Zaroff could aid the rise of a player to channel business to them—someone corruptible, yet capable of advancement within the system. Abbott also promised Zaroff a cut of the CIA's payments to the intelligence source."

"Why would CIA go along with having Abbott turn Zaroff into a sub-contractor to run the Iran relationship?" Rogers asks. "There's an angle to that we just aren't seeing right now. Maybe completely disconnected to the attacks."

Mac grimaces. "Not clear if the Agency approved Abbott's connection to Zaroff, or if that part was Abbott just freelancing to recruit Zaroff as a business partner, the way he recruited D.C. Cain to finance the Drone. However it sorts out, even though he looks rich, FBI tells Thorpe that Zaroff needs cash and only keeps up the appearance of wealth by massive borrowing. He was desperate to get that deal for port improvement work from Iran. Apparently, there's a letter of intent signed by interior minister Sanjani."

Rogers spears a shrimp and then twirls pasta over it on his fork. "If Sanjani signed the letter of intent, that might make him the agent Abbott and Zaroff were running."

"They also might have gotten the deal the old-fashioned way, through bribery," Mac says. "For the intel source, my money is still on Azel because we're getting so much military material. Either way, you got a rise out of Mundy talking about Sanjani and Azel at the meeting. Things got personal."

"I'll invite you to a faculty meeting sometime," Rogers says, downplaying the conflict. "Thorpe didn't do us any favors holding back the FBI information. I could have hammered harder on Abbott if I'd known he was also under investigation on the securities stuff. And Mundy's a predator. He found a weak point in the Drone theory and he worked it. How the device got into the plane isn't the key issue, but he used it to undermine all the other evidence we have in hand—the creation of the Drone, the black box, the financial connections to the Cain family. Once the message from the Lions came in, it all went out the window. Certainly we couldn't tie the Lions to Abbott and Zaroff."

Mac leans forward in a conspiratorial hunch. "I don't know all of Thorpe's reasons for things. But he's got 'em. For example, Thorpe's arranged a protective detail for you," he says in a low voice. "Undercover."

Rogers' eyes narrow. "What's that about?" As the news sinks in, Rogers's limbs tingle, body sending a slight jolt at the news of danger.

"He wouldn't say. I asked why you, specifically, and he said it's not just you. But he didn't say more."

Rogers looks around the room, empty except for the two of them. He looks back at Mac. "Russians? The crazy billionaire?"

Mac shakes his head. "No idea. Thorpe's looking at the whole picture, not just our piece of it. What I want to know is how would somebody even know who you are? Any of us?"

"We talked to Cutler. I talked to Ross' widow. FBI's been shaking a lot of trees. And we just told a roomful of people what we know." No obvious explanation presents itself. "Maybe it's just a precaution," Rogers says.

"Somebody's already killed a lot of people with those planes. You and me, they wouldn't even think twice." Mac raps his knuckles twice on the wooden tabletop. "We've been lucky so far. But I'm glad Thorpe's got our backs."

The waiter enters discreetly, tapping at the door first. He clears the plates and presents an after-dinner menu. Mac elects cheesecake and Rogers skips dessert. The men lean back in their seats.

Mac asks Rogers, "When Lillian Charles first started working with you, did you tell her to come in and see me about your qualifications for leading this investigation?"

"Yes."

"Is that because you couldn't handle that conversation yourself?"

"No."

"Then...?"

"I gave her an opportunity to talk to you face to face, and she took it. I know you wouldn't fraternize, but I figured you would benefit from meeting an intelligent, strong-willed woman who is wound as tight as you and who keeps the same hours. This investigation won't go on forever. Once she's out of the chain of command you can ask her for a drink," says Rogers.

"Damn," says Mac. "I knew it. You're worse than my sister."

Mac returns to his office and Rogers catches a cab to his temporary apartment, a small suite in Crystal City. He removes his suit and hangs it in the closet, then sits on the edge of the bed and removes his prosthesis. He doesn't think about the metal and leather and plastic any more than he thinks about shoes or socks. He makes no special note of the flesh that seals the stub where the rest of his leg had once been.

Away from Mac, he turns his anger about the day inward. He doubts the Lions are bona fide. But he's been a step behind all through the investigation, so why not? Damned little has been in his control, but it's no excuse. He should have done more with what he had. He turns on television news, which is dominated by the Vatican threat, and turns off the sound. Rogers has a nagging sense that he knows something about the Lions that he can't quite place.

He doesn't know why Thorpe ordered protection. He hates being left out of the loop, particularly on something as personal to him as his life. He also doesn't want to have to explain it to Dub. She didn't like the job to begin with, and if he's in actual danger....

He calls home to speak to Dub and Stevie. He listens to the details of Stevie's baseball game (the team lost but Stevie hit a single and scored a run) before Dub has him alone on the phone to ask what is going on.

"It was a bad day."

"No further news about when they would try to attack?"

"That's right. No ticking clock."

"If it's really terrorists, does your part wrap up now?" Dub asks.

"No idea. Maybe. I don't think what I have to say is welcome." He knows Dub can hear the discouragement in his voice. He can't put on a brave face. "You warned me."

Dub switches topics. "Did you talk to your brother?"

"It's late in Rome. I'll call him during the day tomorrow, his time."

"I went to the service for Jerry Howard. His wife looked like she'd had a burden lifted. Things must have been hard for a long time."

They exchange affections before ending the call, and Rogers resumes his sulking. He's worn but still wound up. He watches more news. The local broadcast features a story about a five-year-old boy in Baltimore, an orphan who adopted a stray dog as his dear companion, then found the dog dead, poisoned by an unknown vandal. The random and undiluted cruelty of the act leaves Rogers exhausted. He falls asleep.

Rogers wakes at 3 a.m. full of sudden dread. Outside, the sky has finally broken and he hears the heavy slap of rain on the glass door to the balcony. His first thought on waking is that his left foot has returned. Nerves registering pain in a limb that isn't there, like when he was first wounded. He tastes a soapy jet of vomit in his throat and chokes it back. Sweaty and trembling, Rogers remembers Chris Leinheimer's death, blood gushing in the dusty Fallujah street as Rogers helplessly watches. The images return unbidden, as do the old emotions, taking the form of black thoughts not fully arrived but that he can sense are coming nearer and nearer. The day's events have mapped onto a deep vein of shame and regret, one he thought he was past. The blame he'd assigned himself for failing to prevent Chris from bleeding out on a dusty street. The attack he survived and Chris did not.

He struggles to catch his breath. Despair is waiting for him to let it back in. Rogers can sense it. He knows it from how the feeling had gripped him so firmly for so long. He can't be certain to defeat it again if he allows it to return. He has a moment of sad and overwhelming clarity about a world full of horror—of murderers, and terrorists, and dog poisoners who go unpunished by man or God. It's not a law of nature that evil be vanquished, nor that Rogers be guaranteed his past despair will not return. The old emotions bloom in him again. The way he felt in the hospital in Germany recovering from the bomb, angry at present pain and grieving for the future he'd expected before it was stolen by the shrapnel.

He goes into the bathroom. From his bag, he takes out all his prescriptions. He counts the dozen tablets in the container.

He'd aimed high and risked more than he realized. He'd provoked contempt in Mundy, whose encounter with Klamber seems sinister now to Rogers, like a mob boss announcing, "I know where you live." Word of the BAG failure will seep back to West Point and what took years to rebuild will be washed away.

He tells himself, I wanted recovery to be real, even though it isn't. Wholeness to be here, although it's not. He thinks of Jerry, dead of an overdose, intended or not.

...found and lost again and again: and now, under conditions that seem unpropitious.

He needs air and cold. He knows his thoughts are exaggerated and dire. He puts on his prosthesis and opens the sliding glass door to the storm. A gust nearly blows him back into the room. Clad only in shorts, he steps onto the balcony, unaccommodated man. A white shard of lightning sizzles past, very close, and the immediate crack of thunder is like a bomb. The prosthesis is metal. If it draws lightning, I'll accept the judgment, he thinks. The rain isn't icy, but nonetheless the storm pulls the heat from his body. His speeding heart returns to its normal pace and he retreats inside.

He calls his brother in Rome, taking advantage of the time difference. It's breakfast time for James.

"I'm part of a Pentagon group looking for the people who did the attacks," Rogers says.

"It's why you separate church and state," James says. "Mixing politics with religion makes each of them worse."

"We don't know for certain that it's religious extremists. How are you doing?"

"I'm asking Sara and the kids to leave. It doesn't feel dangerous as much as it feels...unnerving, I guess. Living in a danger zone. Rome's a big city, and our apartment is miles from the Vatican. Not impending doom, but the chance of it. The Sword of Damocles. No need to take chances with the rest of the family," James says. "How about you?"

"You know how they say sometimes you can feel pain in a part of the body you've lost?"

"Yeah, ghost limb, phantom limb, something like that."

"I had that, first time since the war."

"Weird."

"It felt like an omen."

"Unless these guys get through to the Vatican, all the bad stuff's already happened," James says. "What does Dub think?"

"Haven't told her yet."

"You should."

Rogers ends the call with his brother and returns to the bathroom. He swallows a Xanax to buy a few hours of sleep.

He'd been guilty of believing his own theories after preaching against that fault in others. The world might need the truth, but it didn't need for him personally to be proven right. Not even that. The world doesn't need the truth, it can keep going without it.

He's been no real help. He needs to cut his losses. He decides to quit in the morning and leave for home.

At seven he is awakened by a persistent buzz from his phone. A message from Mac, already at work at the Pentagon.

It reads, "Abbott's dead."

-o-

PROLOGUE TO PART III

Hudson River Valley
2009

THERE IS A PICKED-OVER *plate of doughnuts next to the tin coffee urn on the folding table in the unadorned church basement. The frosted doughnuts went first. Rogers stands near the coffee, reading the news clipping from San Antonio, sent to Mac by a member of their squad from Fallujah.*

The Davy Crockett High School principal stopped valedictorian Fatima Abdullah from delivering her graduation speech. About to become a naturalized U.S. citizen, she emigrated with her family to America from Iraq in 2004 as a political refugee, after the local warlord tried to claim her as a child bride and then sliced her face with a knife when her family refused to go along. The principal demanded she remove comments about her father, who—she claimed—was killed for refusing the warlord's command to attack Americans in a bomb vest.

"Shack Wilson sent this to me," Mac says. "It sounds like the dude we met."

Rogers reads the clipping twice. He moves to the circle of folding chairs and sits down. The other vets from the group meeting are talking among themselves. Six paragraphs into the story Rogers finds the knife to the heart: "My father would always tell my sister and me, 'Don't be angry.' That was easy for him to say, because it was his nature to be calm and kind. My parents were raised on the border of Iran during the Iran-Iraq war, and my father would say war is like a giant storm, that could wash away everything and all you could do was survive it. Rescue what you can, and be brave and have faith you will survive, to move on with life when the storm has passed."

Rogers looks up at Mac, who is still standing. "It's him. The words are the same. It's the guy."

"She says he didn't attack. Maybe she didn't know, or she's lying. But it sounds like him," Mac says.

"Her dad blows up an American patrol so she can go to high school in Texas?"

"It's..."

"This is her story? This is her fucking high school graduation speech—about what a fucking hero her father is because he blew up a group of Americans?"

The rest of the group falls silent as Rogers' voice rises.

"It was you and Chris Leinheimer getting shot at behind that wall, Mac, when Shack and I pulled you out. And then a week later Chris bled out in the street. I saw it. I watched it. I remember it.

"Chris was the bravest kid....He bit his fucking lip, didn't say a fucking word, just held on and held on and held on. And then it didn't make any fucking difference...

"I mean...There's your story. There's your hero. Not the guy that killed him."

No one else speaks.

"Some asshole journalist wants to write a story about this girl who thinks the guy who killed Chris is the father of the year? Fuck that! That's just bullshit," Rogers says. "Chris had a kid too. Two years old when Chris bled out in the fucking street in that hellhole."

Worn from his tirade, Rogers ends in tears. "Two fucking years old."
Mac says softly, "My bad, man. I shouldn't have brought it up."

-o-

PART III
THE NAMELESS DEAD STAY NAMELESS

August 21 (morning)
Washington D.C.

Rogers maneuvers through Pentagon security, purchases coffee at the shop near the news and magazine stand, and glances at the main headlines in the newspapers on display. All morning he has stopped on the street and looked in store windows, hoping to find the reflection of his supposed guardians. He's spotted nothing, perhaps there is nothing. He hurries to Mac's office before going to his own desk.

Mac throws the Metro section of the newspaper onto the desk. "It's a dynamic world," Mac says.

"I don't believe it," Rogers says. "That's not possible."

"Police shoot-out."

Rogers takes the top off the coffee cup, sits back, and reads the story.

Man slain in police shoot-out

Arlington resident Hugh Abbott was killed last night at his apartment after confronting police with a weapon, according to police reports.

Police were investigating a complaint that Abbott had been stalking and making online threats to players of a popular multiplayer videogame. Police reported that they knocked on the door of Abbott's apartment, and that Abbott, after refusing to open the door, fired a shot through it. According to the reports, police believe Abbott had a small caliber handgun.

The reports describe Abbott as "extremely agitated" and "aggressive" and police believe Abbott may also have been drinking just prior to the encounter.

According to the reports, police broke down the apartment door, and Abbott fired at the first officer who entered. A second officer shot Abbott, who died at the scene. No officers were injured in the shootout.

Abbott is believed to be a federal employee. Police did not speak on the record or offer additional details.

Rogers puts the paper back on Mac's desk. "I decided overnight I need to quit."

"You look like someone who was up all night." Mac leaned forward and put his arms on the desk and stared at his friend. "Are you worried about personal danger? The protective detail?"

Rogers shakes his head. "How can I be? Look, Thorpe's a spook, he keeps secrets, I get that. But it means I don't have information to bring my own judgment to bear. Maybe there's a threat and maybe not."

"You're not a quitter. Why start now?" Mac says.

"I don't think I can add value to what you're doing."

"So you changed your mind? You think these Lions guys are legit?"

"No," says Rogers. "No, I'm quite sure that you and I and the FBI are right—Abbott and Cain used a Drone for the attacks. But if we don't get to see the whole picture, like Thorpe does, we can't win over the bureaucracy."

Mac nods. "I've spent the morning calling around. DNI already knows about Abbott. So does FBI, so does CIA. FBI sealed off his apartment to get evidence, CIA sealed off his office for the FBI team. FBI pulled Cain Junior into custody last week, very quietly."

Rogers attempts to take a sip of coffee. It is still too hot to drink, and he sets the cup back on Mac's desk. "Junior's hedge fund handled the money for the Drone, it handled the money to Abbott's Iranian contact, and it handled the stock trading ahead of the Burj attack."

"That's right," Mac says. "And since the CIA initially prevented New York state investigators from going after it, at least one of those activities is Agency-approved—the obvious candidate would be the payments to Iran. I don't think anyone explained yesterday how Zaroff found his way into the mix; whether that was Agency-directed, or just Abbott going into business for himself."

"Is someone overseas going to pick up Zaroff?" Rogers asks.

"You would think so. He may not want to be found."

Rogers is eyeing the coffee cup for another try. "And my FBI source told me they are going after Cain Senior, the company, and the company CEO today," Mac says. Rogers lifts his head quickly.

"Say again?" Rogers asks.

"FBI's moving on the billionaire and the financial players today, collecting evidence."

Rogers is quiet for a few seconds. "Abbott is at the center of all the money angles in this investigation. It's a bad time for him to turn up dead," Rogers says.

"You think an accomplice did this?"

Rogers shrugs. "I don't believe in coincidence." Rogers lifts the newspaper. "The FBI can now investigate Abbott openly within the CIA, which might speed things up." The coffee finally cools enough for Rogers to drink it. The men are again briefly silent. Rogers reaches for a memory he can't quite grasp, one triggered by Mac's comments about Zaroff and Iran.

Rogers stands and stretches his knotted muscles.

"Junior already had legal issues. Tackling him as a one-off wouldn't have signaled to the conspirators that FBI was after the whole group. But if the FBI is moving on Cain and the company today, it means planning for an FBI roundup has been in the works, even before the Vatican threat. Simultaneous raids take time to set up."

Mac says nothing. After a few moments, Rogers asks, "Does Thorpe buy into the Drone explanation?"

"He told the FAA and the airlines to create counter-measures. He said it was good prevention and he didn't need to wait for proof," Mac says. "Lots of alerts to maintenance crews to do double checks on autopilots, and a program with Boeing on diagnostics and hardening control systems against hacking."

"So Thorpe was making operational decisions, just from the material we gave him," Rogers says. "Even before bringing in the BAG. Maybe he's been making decisions on the search for terrorists too, and we don't know. But the Lions stuff is a curve ball for everyone. If Thorpe had plans before the BAG meeting, he's had to change them now. And he didn't call off the raids on Cain."

Rogers' tone begins to shift from sodden to animated. "Until yesterday Thorpe was the only one with the whole picture. FBI didn't know what we knew, and vice versa." He begins to pace. "We need the material behind the FBI's presentation, and the identity of Abbott's agent inside Iran. Depending on the answer, we might be able to connect Abbott and Zaroff to the Lions."

Mac's expression shows surprise. "How do you figure that?"

"State Department intel, from the time of the Mecca attack," Rogers says. "Not part of a public report, just background, raw data I saw early on and I remembered this morning. A Farsi website that was up for a few days and then disappeared."

"Farsi," Mac says. "As in Iran. As in, where Abbott is operating."

"Right. And Sanjani supposedly is cracking down on someone calling themselves the Lions of Jihad. I'll ask Lillian to start checking with NSA to see if anyone archived that original website material, to compare it to the new one. State's assessment then was that the crackdown was a thin excuse for Sanjani to eliminate political opposition, but if the Lions are back, we should take another look."

"I thought you said you couldn't add value," Mac says. Rogers ignores the comment. "If the Lions were a fiction created by Sanjani...well, if you can prove it, we can ignore them."

"You think my offer to resign is premature?" Rogers asks.

"Your offer to resign is rejected."

"I need the financial stuff, the Herakles bank statements to see how the money trail ties in," Rogers says. "Most important—get me on Thorpe's calendar ASAP. We can solve this, but we need to know what he knows."

-o-

August 21. (afternoon)

Pentagon

Rogers stops by the cubicle within the DIA offices assigned to Lillian Charles. It is unadorned by personalizing features, other than a calendar with pictures of the M.I.T. campus pinned to one grey side of the cloth half-walls.

She is immersed in her work, eyes focused on the computer screen, and she doesn't glance up at Rogers' approach. "I have a question about defeating the Drone," he says. She looks up from the keyboard and closes out of the story she'd been reading. Across the planet, no governments dismiss the Vatican threat, given the stakes. Travelers who had previously sworn that the discomforts of travel could never be worse learned that there was, in fact, another leg downward.

"We know from Ross' notes that the Drone connects to the autopilot and inputs a GPS coordinate, which the Drone either tells the autopilot to fly to, or to fly around it," Rogers begins.

"Okay."

"The Drone acts in response to a radio signal. The signal comes in on the same set of frequencies used in all air traffic control and airplane tracking."

Lillian waves her hand in a circle, to indicate that she's following, and wants him to pick up the pace.

"But would it be possible, if you know the code that accesses the Drone, to send a signal that reprograms it to do something different?"

"You want to hack the Drone?"

"Yes! Right. Exactly." Rogers is delighted she caught his drift so quickly.

"No."

"Why not?"

"Why not?" says Lillian.

"Yes, why not?"

"Mostly because I'm not Harry Potter, maybe? I'm just a computer and signals person. You need a magician."

"But computers get viruses all the time. Why can't we introduce one here?" Rogers asks.

"Unless you know the Drone programming and know of a trap door or way in that the inventor left open, all you can do is send a signal to turn the Drone on and tell it to go to or go around a fixed GPS spot," Lillian says. "Good luck looking for a trap door in a bajillion lines of code. But how about this? If you know the signal frequency the command goes out on—and you have to know that if you have the signal source—why not just take world aviation off that frequency until the crisis is over? And track anyone trying to transmit a signal on that frequency, if that's possible?"

"We can check that out. Odds are that Ross wanted the Drone transmit frequency to be one that isn't commonly used. You wouldn't want the devices set off accidentally."

Lillian still looks like someone who begrudges having her time wasted. "Yes, give it a shot. No harm to check. In the meantime, I have preliminary progress on the Lions website. After I sent out word that we were looking for preserved code from the original Lions site, we got several copies, one from Israel, one from the French, and one from the U.S. consulate in Iran. I'm going to check them all out, make sure they're legit. Then I'll run a comparison to the new Lions site to see if they are related, or if the new group are copycats. It may not tell us where they are, but it may tell us something about who they are."

-o-

August 21 (afternoon)
Westchester County, New York

Brooks' temper is foul. It's been hours since the start of the morning raid at the Cain estate, but the FBI entered the house one hour into Cain's in-home dialysis and the raid went to hell while they waited for the procedure to finish. There was no way to anticipate Cain would be in the middle of a medical treatment that would disrupt the FBI's timing. But the raid is botched, and it's Brooks' raid and it's Brooks' problem.

Cain used the delay to summon his legal team. Now Brooks can only monitor the phone negotiation between FBI legal and Cain's attorneys over the conditions under which Cain will be questioned. Brooks gets a text from his superiors that Cain's Washington allies are already letting the Bureau know they're watching. The pressure won't make a difference, but clearly Cain is calling in political favors.

Brooks stands six inches taller than anyone else in the house, and he is a massive man. Having a brooding giant in the living room clearly makes Cain's house staff nervous.

Agents on the search team are combing the premises for documents and electronic gear, in particular anything that ties to the Drone prototypes. The simultaneous raids at Cain Industries and the home of Micah Pfennig went smoothly and Mayfair relays updates to Brooks from reports on what the other agents are finding.

Cain's attorney Sullivan Downey insists Cain can't be moved without medical supervision and is too incapacitated to endure an interview with the FBI. Before noon, the dickering is settled. Downey will travel immediately to the house, and the interrogation will occur there in his presence, videotaped, where Cain has on-site nursing care. Cain's medical status—and almost certainly, his wealth—bought him concessions from the FBI.

Downey is a white-collar criminal defense lawyer who tells Brooks his default position is to have Cain to say little or nothing, since he doesn't know where any statement by Cain might lead. The attorney is a graying, jowly man, dressed as if he is going to court. Brooks knows the type: Old enough and rich enough to retire, but afraid he'd be bored if he did.

"My client spends most of his day watching news on cable television. What help could he be to you?" Downey is still advocating for a truncated interview, while the videographer sets up. Cain's living room is spacious, and the window allows a broad green view of the estate's lawn and topiary. Furniture and appointments in the room were selected by the interior decorator for comfort and aesthetic balance and were arranged after Cain's accident to provide paths through the room wide enough for a walker or wheelchair. Careful thought had been given to the soothing woodland and pastel colors used throughout. Nonetheless, with minimal house staff and Cain's limited movement, the room is rarely used, and seems more like a museum display than part of a home.

"If the man is senile it'll show up in the interview and we'll stop wasting everyone's time," Brooks says. Word comes from the team at the Cain Industries raid that the CFO, Micah Pfennig, is talking but unhelpful, particularly in his insistence that the $40 million payment was initiated by Cain but is completely legitimate because Cain said it was contractually required and Cain is a man of untarnished integrity.

The FBI knows from the records what Cain did. Brooks and Mayfair want to ask Cain why he did it and what else is coming.

When the video equipment is in place, Brooks explains the background to Downey. "We have evidence that material used in the airliner attacks on Mecca and the Burj had been in Cain's possession, and that Cain paid off people connected to the attacks. And our team didn't find anything in the house this morning to reveal where that material went. So what Cain has to say might make the difference in whether terrorists blow up the Vatican or not. Just so you know the stakes."

Downey looks uncomfortable and uncertain. "You're putting me in a tough spot. I'm obligated to represent Cain's interest. I want to avoid prosecution based on what the client says in his interview with you, and the best way to do that is advise him to say nothing. Since I still have no idea if he faces charges or what those potential charges may be, that's all that I am prepared to do here."

Brooks says, "We can't force him to talk. We have the documents. We have enough to bring charges now on foreign bribery and aiding and abetting terrorism. But this interview is time-critical. If you think it's in his best interest to get zero credit for cooperation, plus piss off the prosecution—and take the chance of looking really, really bad after the fact if there's another attack that he could have prevented by speaking up —then by all means tell him to shut up."

"Would it be fair in such circumstances to say that the counselor here would also have blood on his hands?" Mayfair asks.

Brooks turns to Downey. "I don't know. What do you think, counselor?"

A shaken Downey retreats to his next line of defense. "Cain's mental capacity isn't perfect. Down the road I may argue inability to form criminal intent, if charges are filed. And I'll put all that on the record in advance."

"Whatever you need to do," Brooks says.

Cain's personal secretary, Petra Hedges, is a cordial twenty-something with hair dyed neon red. Her waist is as narrow as if she was wearing a corset, and she had put out sodas and snacks on the credenza as though everyone had come for a party.

She escorts the unsteady Cain into the room once all the seating arrangements are settled. He shuffles in on her arm, wearing dark socks and no shoes, carrying a cane in his right hand. He wears slacks and a polo shirt under a golf sweater, even though the day is warm.

Wizened by age, Cain hunches forward slightly. He is a foot shorter than Brooks and as he passes by Cain dismissively taps Brooks' leg with the cane even though Brooks is not in his way. Cain must lift his head slightly to look at Brooks directly. Under the folds of flesh over Cain's heavy lids peer hostile eyes filled with arrogant contempt.

This intrigues Brooks, who is accustomed to the FBI having the upper hand in interrogations. Over the years, he's questioned mobsters and white-collar criminals, and even the hardest of them come into FBI custody merely determined to endure the session, not to pick a fight.

Before questioning begins, Downey gives Cain the background. "These men are here to ask about the creation of a device to seize control of an airliner remotely, and whether that device was completed and used to attack Mecca and the Burj Khalifa. They're also going to question you about a $40 million transfer to Herakles by Cain Industries."

"They raided the company today, I already got word of that."

"I've told them that you can decline to talk, under the Fifth Amendment."

Cain turns to Brooks and says, "Oh, I want to talk."

Downey starts speaking into the camera for the record. "The FBI has been informed of Mr. Cain's medical condition and is nonetheless insisting on this interview at the present time. Nursing staff is standing by. If at any moment the interview is too taxing for Mr. Cain, we will call a halt to allow him to rest or even to end the interview."

"If we need to do this multiple times, we will, but we're going to get this done," says Brooks.

"Mr. Cain, I'm Ted Brooks, from the FBI, and this is my colleague, Andy Mayfair, also from the FBI. We're here to discuss financial matters about which you have information, and some related matters."

"If it's about my business, talk to Micah. He does everything now. I used to do it. But not anymore." Cain's voice quavers some, but his delivery is sure and emphatic. "Anything in writing you've already gathered up today, either from company headquarters or here in my house."

"We're here to talk about your personal activity, not your business per se. We want to start with your dealings with an individual named Daniel Ross. From Seattle, with a company called RossTech."

"Go ahead."

"Did you know him personally? Meet him?"

"A long time back. Yes. In Washington. Mostly we worked by phone or by email," says Cain. "He's Jewish, Ross. I mean, I don't care. But he is."

"And that is in connection with Project Deadbolt, with the CIA? Also called Python?" asks Brooks.

"Yes, Deadbolt and Python. Same thing, different names."

"What was Ross creating, as you understood it?" Brooks asks.

"He was working on an electronic box, that you could put in a plane, and prevent terrorists from taking it over. And then the CIA abandoned the project and asked me if I would put up the money to keep it going. Which I did. Gladly. As an American who loves his country."

"Do you know why the project was abandoned?"

"Change of policy, change of administrations, usual Washington BS. The first money that came in, from Congress, wasn't enough to get the whole thing done."

"What makes you say that?"

"I say that because they came to me for money to keep it going!" Cain says. "What a stupid question."

"Can you say who came to you?"

"Hugh Abbott. CIA. There was one other CIA contact early on, but I forget the name. He wasn't involved once the CIA dropped the project. Hugh is the one who told me I could keep it going, if I put up the money."

"Why did Abbott come to you?"

"I knew him. He went to Yale with my younger son. I thought it would be a good idea to have friends at the CIA, the way my money bought me friends everywhere else in Washington. I've been buying friends in Washington for 30 years. It was better before. You paid someone and he stayed fucking bought."

Brooks repeats the question about Abbott's approach, as Cain's answer meandered off the point. "I helped find him political supporters for the project, when Congress first funded it. Then after the public money ran out, we talked about how to keep things moving."

"What did he say he wanted to do?"

"He said that since the CIA didn't pay for the machine, they didn't own it, and we could go into business together to retrofit all the airplanes in the world with the box. He could get a CIA report written, and all the airlines would have to adopt the product. I didn't believe he had that kind of pull. Hugh wanted to get rich, but he was a government employee, he had no head for business. I liked the idea on the merits, though. Ahead of its time."

"Why did you use money from the Snake River subsidiary to pay Ross?"

"If I knew before, I don't remember now."

"What about changing the payments to go through Herakles Investments?"

"I don't know. There was probably a reason."

"Is this something Abbott wanted?"

"Probably."

Cain is suddenly using short answers. Brooks can't tell if it is discomfort with the line of questions, or true lack of memory, or something else.

"What can you tell us about what Ross finally produced?" Brooks asks.

"I can tell you it didn't work. Didn't you watch on the TV? Didn't you see? The box is supposed to stop a plane from flying into a building, the way bin Laden did to the U.S. on 9/11. Well, that didn't work out. All the pictures, from over in the Middle East! The plane flew into that skyscraper."

"Do you think the plane had one of the boxes in it that Ross had made?"

"If it did, it didn't work." Cain snorts. "Obviously."

Cain continues. "Now, to be honest, I didn't mind seeing that building come down. The Muslims need a dose of their own medicine, to see how they like it. So that's good. That's fine with me. I'm a little sorry for that girl, the one they show on TV all the time. You hate to see innocents suffer. But they started it. So the hell with them all, I say."

"Did Ross actually complete the boxes he was planning?"

"Years ago, he sent me three boxes. They were the size of a pack of cigarettes, with wires coming out. He said they were the prototypes. But that was the end of the project."

Brooks doubts Cain is being completely truthful, but corroborating the records from Ross is the most valuable thing he's said so far. "He sent them to you?"

"Right here. To the house."

"And where are they now?"

"I have no idea."

"You no longer have them?"

"No."

"What did you do with them?"

"I called Abbott to say I got 'em. He said he would have somebody pick them up."

"Is that what happened? Someone came by to pick them up?"

"Yes."

"But not Abbott?"

"No. Someone else."

"Any description? Anything that you remember? The car? Clothing?"

"No, that was a long time ago. He took the whole package, boxes and all."

"No memory at all? Maybe something he said? Did he have an accent?"

"No, it was years ago."

Brooks is exercising patience, but the line of questioning is going nowhere. "What did Abbott have to say?"

"About what?"

"About the boxes."

"He wanted to test them. But he didn't tell me how it worked out. We didn't go into the airplane business together, that much I know," Cain said.

"But you stayed in touch with Abbott," says Brooks.

"Yes, he is going to get business for my company overseas."

"What kind of business?" Brooks asks.

"My company—subsidiaries and partnerships actually—will get billions from refurbishing ports along the Caspian Sea," Cain says. "That project has been in the works for a long time, and there was a Letter of Intent signed in May. We're waiting for final signature, but the terms are all set."

"Is the overseas business the reason for the $40 million transfer to Herakles fund?" Brooks asks.

"You should ask Micah. He handles day-to-day operations," Cain says warily.

"We're asking you."

"Anything Micah did, it's for legitimate business expenses," says Cain. "I've known Micah for a long time. I can vouch for his honesty. I won't contradict him." For fifteen more minutes, Brooks asks questions about the $40 million, and Cain gives the same answer. Cain knows enough not to admit foreign bribery to the FBI.

Downey calls for the videographer to stop the taping. "It looks like Mr. Cain may be getting tired."

"Why haven't you mentioned that Abbott is dead?" Cain asks. "It was in the news in Washington. I already know. You're not going to trick me. And he's not around any more for you to talk to, is he?"

Cain doesn't look tired to Brooks.

Brooks says to Downey, "We don't have that many more questions. It's all pertinent to what we're investigating." Brooks conceals his true thinking: "Your client is lying, so let's get him on the record while we can and prosecute later."

Brooks turns to Cain. "Mr. Cain, why did Ross send you a large check recently?"

"I don't know anything about a check from Ross."

"A couple of months back? The check is for a little over $2 million."

"My son tried to send me a check for $2 million a few months ago. I don't know why. He's a fucking turd and I sent it back. But Ross—I haven't heard from him for years."

Mayfair takes a note to get a copy of the check.

"One last thing, Mr. Cain," says Brooks. "When you and Abbott and Ross talked about the boxes Ross was making, did you ever talk about using those controls for offense, rather than defense? To send planes into buildings?"

Cain's eyes bore in on Brooks. The contempt in them has returned—but also his temptation to speak. There is a hint of a smile on his lips. Brooks is certain the old man wants to brag.

"Talk about it?" Cain says. "No. That's not the sort of thing anyone would talk about."

"Do you think that would even be possible?" Brooks asks. The question is open-ended, to leave room for Cain to confess.

"We never talked about it. We didn't have to talk about it. We knew what the controls could do. There was a reporter who came to me, back when the legislation to approve the CIA project was in Congress. She said someone who was against the bill argued a control that could steer a plane away from buildings could also be used to steer a plane into them, and did I want to comment. Did I want to comment on being able to crash a plane into Muslim buildings, to pay them back for attacking ours? And I asked this reporter...I looked her in the eye. I said to her, 'Where's your proof?' I told her, 'You print that, and I'll sue you and your publisher and I will destroy you. You can't prove a damn thing.'"

Cain's gaze is fixed inward. To Brooks, it seems he relishes the memory of that encounter, the domination he exerted and the submission he extracted. Then he turns to Brooks and Mayfair, confident he is untouched and untouchable. "And neither can you."

Cain turns to his lawyer. "I'm done. I'm tired. I'm done talking to the fucking FBI."

"We're likely to have follow-up questions," Mayfair says. "We may decide you weren't completely forthcoming with us today."

Cain glares at the agents. "I don't give a damn what you think. I don't give a damn what you say. I only care what you can prove, and you can't prove a damn thing."

Brooks looks at the lawyer. "If we have to, we'll get a court order."

Cain points a skeletal finger at Brooks. "No. I'm done, done forever. Get a court order and I'll fight it for years, but I will never speak to the FBI again."

Cain glances first at Brooks, then Mayfair, and back to Brooks again.

"Who do you think will enforce your order?" he asks. "The judges and politicians who come to me begging for my support and money?"

Cain says to Brooks, "The laws protect me. They don't restrict me." Cain motions to his lawyer to help him to his feet. "I've been a wealthy man for more years than you've been alive."

-o-

August 22
Pentagon

The personnel in Mac's office follow his example of driving in early to avoid Beltway commute traffic. When a grinning Rogers arrives at Mac's desk with Lillian at 8:30 a.m., Mac was starting the third hour of his day.

"Check this out," Rogers says. Lillian holds out her phone, playing a video of Thorpe in a karaoke bar singing the Madonna song *Like A Virgin*. The bar's garish lights reflect off Thorpe's bald head as he prances and sings.

"What the hell is that?" Mac asks.

"No idea," Lillian says. "I don't even remember what I was searching for when I found it."

"You can't un-see it," Rogers says.

"It's like a car crash, you have to look," Mac says. Thorpe's voice drifts on- and off-key and his movements are robotic. "He's coming by here mid-morning for an update. You can ask him about it."

"You can," says Rogers. "I'll stick to business. I dug up that report from State that I saw before. It didn't prove the original Lions were fakes, but there was circumstantial evidence: Sanjani never mentioned the Lions again, the website vanished in days, and there was no independent evidence from the global intelligence community that the Lions ever were real."

Thorpe is barely seated for the scheduled meeting when Rogers peppers him with questions: "Why the protective detail? Who's Abbott's agent in Iran? And if the Lions are fake, shouldn't it mean the threat to the Vatican is fake?"

To Rogers, Thorpe doesn't look like someone who objects to the questions. More like a scholar whose students seem finally to be understanding the course.

"Protective detail is prudent, and necessary. We know how far the people we're up against are willing to go, and we don't know who they are or what they know about the investigation into the Drone." He looks at Rogers. "I do know that Betsy Ross called the FBI a week ago because an unknown person called her out of the blue and started asking about you and the Pentagon and RossTech. She told the FBI the accent was American, so I assume Abbott rather than Zaroff. But we don't know if Abbott has other allies."

Rogers' expression is grim as he takes in Thorpe's explanation. "My wife would get really pissed if I got killed," Rogers says. "So let's avoid that."

"Who is Abbott's agent in Iran? If it is Azel, is he the one who made the call to the Saudis ahead of Mecca? If it is Sanjani, how do the attacks and the Ports deal fit together?" Mac asks.

"I've been betting on Sanjani as a CIA asset, and Mac picked Azel," Rogers says. "But we both think the CIA is trying to hide from the intelligence community that the Agency is running a high-level agent in Iran."

Thorpe looks at both men and takes a long breath. "The CIA has long had a highly placed intelligence asset in Iran, defense minister Azel. Abbott recruited Sanjani later, with Zaroff as a go-between. So, both, actually." Mac and Rogers look at each other in surprise. "Did you guys have a bet?" Thorpe asks.

Rogers shakes his head. "Tying Sanjani to Abbott and Zaroff not only ties him into the Ports deal, it ties all of them into the new threat on the Vatican. The State Department reported Sanjani back in May claiming the Lions of Jihad were behind the Mecca attack. State didn't believe the Lions really existed, but the re-use of the name now may mean we're facing the same gang. Fake Lions should mean fake threat, right?"

"I understand your logic," Thorpe says, "but I'd prefer proof. The SEC says there's no advance off-color trading activity, so the Vatican threat isn't Burj 2.0. But it's one thing to know what this threat isn't—we still need to be prepared for what it is."

"The news on Sanjani is favorable," Rogers says.

Thorpe nods. "You're correct about the importance of the Ports transaction between Iran and Zaroff. Iran announced the deal in May, shortly after Mecca, although Cain's involvement wasn't part of the announcement. FBI first thought that the $40 million Cain Industries ran through Herakles was a direct payment to terrorists, but the revised thinking now is that it went to Sanjani as a bribe. Cain admitted his role in the deal but not a payoff." Thorpe turns to Rogers. "The FBI should get those financial files to you today."

"Abbott was the linchpin in the Drone development and was in the middle of the securities trading, too. The Ports deal puts Abbott, Cain, Sanjani, and Zaroff all one place: Cain got his Drone. Sanjani got his new job after Mecca. Zaroff got a multi-billion dollar deal, and shared it with Cain, and Abbott takes a skim when the money passes by," Rogers says.

"The FBI's counter-intelligence team worried that Zaroff recruited Abbott as a double agent when they found the two of them connected. Even though Abbott fancied himself a future international businessman, we can't ignore the fact that plenty of spies through history made money by just selling secrets," Thorpe says. "We know for certain that Abbott was running on two tracks—drawing CIA cash to run the Sanjani relationship, then brokering the Cain/Zaroff relationship, and skimming from both as the payments went by."

"Is there anyone in the Iranian government who doesn't work for the CIA?" Mac asks.

"I don't think the Prime Minister is on the payroll. I'm sure someone is working on it." Nothing in Thorpe's expression suggests he is joking. "Abbott finally broke his silence a few days ago, calling Zaroff on one of his burner phones that the FBI bugged. Abbott wanted to know when the Ports deal would be done, but Abbott also knew we were looking at autopilot questions, and he let Zaroff know."

Mac asks if Abbott and Zaroff resurrected the Lions as a ruse to divert the CIA away from its autopilot inquiry.

"I don't know. Abbott's call was the reason I called the BAG meeting," Thorpe says. "I also had asked the FBI to prepare to raid the suspects, but the Lions threat pulled in the timing. I've asked British intelligence to locate Zaroff in London and extradite him, but the man has yet to be found." Thorpe says.

Rogers says, "In the ordinary course, then, the FBI would have scooped up Abbott yesterday, along with Cain." Rogers looks at Thorpe, and pauses. Then he says, "Mr. Director, I have a question."

"Yes?"

"We haven't worked together long, but you strike me as being very organized and in control," Rogers begins.

"Don't flatter," Thorpe says. "It doesn't work, and you really aren't any good at it."

"Did you pull Abbott into Witness Protection?" Rogers asks.

After a pause, Thorpe gives Mac a slight smile. "You've got a nose for talent," Thorpe tells Mac. "Reports of Abbott's death have been exaggerated, primarily for Zaroff's benefit, if and when he tries to find his partner. We'd hoped to intercept more than just the one call between Zaroff and Abbott, in case they were in contact with anyone else, but it was time to end Abbott's role as an active participant once the Vatican threat was made."

Thorpe looks at Rogers. "In fact, the reason I'm here is to ask you to sit in on this afternoon's interrogation, which is about the Drone."

Rogers nods his agreement. "I'll have to hope our attempt at subterfuge works better on Zaroff than it did on you," Thorpe says as he turns to leave.

"One more thing," Rogers says. "Did you know there's a video of you online singing a Madonna song?"

"Yeah, *Papa Don't Preach*. I know about it."

"No, that wasn't the one I saw."

"*Vogue*?"

"How many of these videos are there, sir?" Mac asks.

"We do two staff updates a year, so...what? Maybe six?" Thorpe says.

"Very good, sir," Mac says.

-o-

August 22
Washington, D.C.

A black SUV with deeply tinted windows carries Rogers from the Pentagon into Washington, crossing the 18th Street Bridge and weaving through the city to the Marine Barracks on I Street. Rogers exits the car in a secure garage. On the drive, he is in the company of two agents wearing earpieces, FBI windbreakers, and stern expressions. No one talks.

Before leaving the Pentagon, Thorpe read Rogers in on the behind-the-scenes preparations. DNI staff had quietly queued up Witness Protection weeks earlier, against the possible need to haul someone in without the world knowing of the intelligence community's interest in them. The Arlington shootout was staged with police and FBI cooperation.

In the car, Rogers skims the background on Abbott and transcripts of the FBI's interrogations from the past two days. The material is supplemented with FBI commentary on evidence that sometimes confirms and sometimes contradicts Abbott's statements, such as financial records from Herakles or testimony from Cain. Rogers will sit behind one-way glass observing the interrogation team and feeding them questions to ask Abbott about the Drone, if he thinks the agents have missed issues of importance.

When Rogers arrives, he is greeted by the lead FBI counter-intelligence agent Ken Robeson, with an assistant, Grant Stockbridge. They bring Rogers up to date.

"Initially we restricted our questions to those actions of Sanjani, Zaroff, and Cain Junior that constituted CIA operations. Yesterday we added in the $40 million payment from Cain Industries cycled through Herakles, the one we now think is a bribe to Sanjani. Abbott left a lot of footprints, and he knows it," says Robeson.

"He's holding to the position that his only connections to Zaroff or Sanjani arise in a legitimate CIA operation, and that he is voluntarily cooperating with an internal de-briefing and examination," Stockbridge says. "That's been fine so far. We want him to talk to us, not resist us. He not only says that Zaroff is approved by the CIA, but that they paid $1 million to recruit him. He hasn't asked for a lawyer yet, but today we're going to get into the Drone, and the Burj."

"What happens when he asks for a lawyer?" asks Rogers.

"He's going to be unhappy with the answer," says Stockbridge grimly. Stockbridge hands Rogers the transcript of the Cain deposition. "Cain confirmed receipt of the three prototypes from Ross, but claimed to have turned them over to a mystery courier sent by Abbott. This still leaves hanging the question of how to account for all of the prototypes."

As the interrogation begins, Rogers watches from behind the one-way mirror. Robeson and Stockbridge sit on cushioned metal chairs on one side of a table in the stark interrogation room, and Abbott sits on the other.

Robeson asks if Abbott knows about the Vatican threat. He does. "It was in the news, just before you guys showed up at my apartment."

Robeson then says that the FBI had Cain's confession on the autopilot control device, and Abbott's role in its creation. Abbott does not react.

"We know that you, Zaroff, Cain, and Sanjani were behind the Mecca and Burj attacks," Stockbridge says. "We're going to spend the rest of the day talking about that. We're going to talk about the securities trading in connection with the attack on the Burj. We're going to talk about the money you made personally on the attack on the Burj. We're going to talk about Project Deadbolt and Project Python, and the whereabouts of the materials produced by Daniel Ross and RossTech that were sent to D.C. Cain. We're going to talk about whether that material is being used to threaten the Vatican," Stockbridge announces.

Abbott flares. "Have you idiots checked with the CIA about me? You need to go back to the Agency. You're messing with an Agency operation. You don't know what I'm involved in."

"Anyone in particular you'd like us to talk to?" asks Stockbridge.

"Yeah, I think you need to talk to my lawyer," Abbott says. "I've been cooperating for days, and you spring this crap on me. Until my lawyer arrives, I'll just shut up and let you figure out how you screwed up."

Stockbridge exchanges looks with his colleague. "I guess this is as good a time as any to break the news to you. You're in military custody as an enemy combatant, detained under military law, for assisting in terror attacks. You won't be seeing a lawyer for a long time."

"I'm a U.S. citizen," Abbott says.

"Even U.S. citizens can be detained as enemy combatants, when the circumstances require," Robeson says. "We know you helped kill a couple thousand people in two airliner attacks, including at least one American citizen, and we think you're part of an immediate threat to kill more. That's why you're here."

Stockbridge says, "We think you're a dangerous man, Mr. Abbott. We think you're involved with dangerous people. Are we wrong? Are you not a dangerous man?"

Abbott's belligerence fades. "You need to go back to the Agency. Quit messing with our work."

"It's not your work anymore," says Robeson. "You're out."

"That's not true...."

"You're in military custody as an enemy combatant, and you'll be detained for as long as we require. We need to know everything about the threat that you and Zaroff and everyone else you work with pose to this country and the world," says Robeson. "No one is coming to rescue you."

Abbott takes it in.

"The Agency knows you're dirty. Nadeau knows you're dirty," says Stockbridge. "Why do you think no one has come to help you already?"

Robeson leans back in his chair. "We've gone through your history. You came from money, and then your dad went broke. You were the smartest kid in the room when you were 14 years old. Then at Yale you were just another schmuck. And now you're one of those people waiting for the world to figure out you're an impostor. You lied your whole life and nobody cared, but now the risk is too big. You finally forced the world to care whether what you say is true or not."

"We've talked to Cain," says Stockbridge. "It looks like he expects you to take all the blame. This is your only chance to clear things up," Stockbridge says. "There's no one left to forgive you or put things right for you. We just need the truth."

Behind the glass Rogers watches Abbott's confrontational pose disappear. Abbott knows from the rush of details that he's been caught out, completely. Months of accumulated tension, waiting, anger, drinking, and lack of sleep finally take their toll. Visibly weary, Abbott asks for a glass of water. He gets one.

In the balance of the interrogation, the FBI builds question by question from what they already know, from the Deadbolt files, from the Herakles trading and financial records, from the payment history to RossTech, from the interrogation of Cain Senior, from the interrogation of Cain Junior. Rogers knows the record on the Drone and listens for inconsistencies in Abbott's answers. Abbott's replies are short and jibe with the record, until the end, when finally Rogers hears something new.

Abbott describes the physical appearance of the prototypes Cain sent to him by courier service. Three small plastic boxes, rectangular, each one about the size of a deck of cards, he says, with wires coming out. There was a computer disc associated with each box, the software controls.

Abbott originally was trying to keep Cain interested in the autopilot devices, to make a business out of retrofitting planes and selling to the government. But the multi-billion dollar Ports deal was much more attractive to Cain than a speculative, relatively low-dollar autopilot control business.

Abbott says Cain's deteriorating health made him moody, and one day on a call about the prototype Cain told him, "You and Zaroff want my money. But I want something too. I told Zaroff what I want, and it's a condition of my putting up money for the Ports deal. So you guys figure it out." Abbott says Zaroff told him Cain meant using the prototypes to send an airliner from a Muslim country into the Grand Mosque. Zaroff didn't want to do it. He kept stalling and putting things off, but he got the devices installed in a couple of planes. Then the Ports deal got closer, and Zaroff said Cain threatened to pull out.

"I met Zaroff in London just before Mecca," Abbott says. "I asked if we really had to go through with this. He just shrugged. He says to me, 'The price is just the price.' In the end, I set everything up. I set the plane up to circle the Mosque. I sent a link to Cain to activate the program. He just had to push a button. I...That was a step I couldn't take personally."

Zaroff didn't want to attack Mecca if there was no money in it for him. Sanjani wanted to become interior minister, and Zaroff came up with the plan to provoke a crisis that Sanjani could use to consolidate power—but only if Sanjani would commit publicly to giving Zaroff and Cain the Ports deal. Zaroff had his people set up the Lions of Jihad website as a false front to confirm everyone's expectations of terrorism, and to give Sanjani an excuse to round up his opposition.

On the day before the Mecca attack, Zaroff told his contacts in Israeli intelligence there was a pending attack in Saudi Arabia and to warn the Saudis. As far as Cain knew, the plane was headed for the Grand Mosque, just as he'd demanded. Blood and chaos on Muslim soil moved Cain to pay the bribe money to move the Ports deal forward.

When asked if Mecca was a trial run for the Burj, Abbott says it was not. The Burj was done strictly to raise emergency cash to prevent Zaroff from defaulting his bank loans. Purely an economic decision.

Finally, though, Abbott offers a ray of hope.

"Are you and Zaroff going to follow through on the threat against the Vatican?" Stockbridge asks.

"Zaroff just put that out there as a distraction," Abbott says. "The prototypes are all used up. Two for Mecca and the Burj. The first one got used on the real trial run—Remember that airliner from Jakarta that disappeared a few years back? That was the trial run. Zaroff set the autopilot for the middle of the Indian Ocean, and sent the plane straight out to sea."

-o-

August 23
Pentagon

Lillian rushes to Rogers's office at mid-morning, having already worked for four hours to confirm a breakthrough in the case. Rogers was just getting off the phone with Mac after discussing the key implication of Abbott's interrogation—Abbott's word wasn't enough to establish that the final Drone was gone.

"The new Lions are recycling the old Lions," Lillian says.

"You found the connection?"

"They're the same."

"You can tell from the websites?"

"Yes, but even more—they're no more than a website fake, and they're in Russian. There were no old Lions, or new Lions."

"How can you tell?" Rogers asks.

"The guy who created it signed his work. I looked him up. He's a website designer, Russian ex-pat living in Prague. Looks like he does freelance videogame design, which fits. We need to confirm he thought he was designing what he thought was a video game, but I can't imagine him signing his name if he actually knew he was working for terrorists." Lillian has visuals on a tablet that she holds up for Rogers to see. First she displays the Lions of Jihad of Pakistan website—crossed golden scimitars against a green and red background, logo written in Urdu with an English translation beneath. The effect is garish and amateurish, like a 1980s 16-bit video game. She toggles to various screens with messages, praise for Allah, and the like.

"Watch what happens when I change this red background to white," Lillian says. With a few keystrokes, the red foreground drops out and red Cyrillic letters appear. "That's the developer, name, address, and email. It's on every page. My guess is that he didn't trust whoever he did the work for not to try to steal it, so he hid the proof under the background color. This is the same image that appeared in the original Lions website in Iran, and the same messages, but they ran the Farsi through a translation program to change it to Urdu. But in both cases, the underlying signature that didn't show is still in Russian, hidden."

Lillian is smiling broadly and Rogers joins her. "Nobody went back to look at the coding in the old Lions website, since they disappeared so quickly. I suppose it's possible that an Islamist group could have hired Russians to do their website, but the better explanation—the more direct explanation based on what we know—is that this is Zaroff's doing." Rogers doesn't mention Abbott. "And Zaroff has a home in Prague."

Rogers congratulates her on a job well done. He is going through the Herakles financial records to match the payments against the event timeline. His confidence is growing. The evidence in favor of the Drone conspiracy is accumulating.

-o-

August 24
New York State

Sullivan Downey gets back to Mayfair about the $2 million check from RossTech to Cain.

Cain's secretary lost the letter that came along with the check. As the check was written from a Herakles investment fund account, she told Cain the check was from Herakles, and described very distinctly how agitated Cain became at the mention of the name. Cain refused even to look at the check and told her to send it back. She sent it to the Herakles office address, which was printed on the check.

Mayfair keeps a straight face through the phone call, then bursts into laughter as he hangs up. He sees immediately what happened: Cain's secretary misread Ross's check, Cain ordered it returned to Herakles, and then Cain the Lesser forged his dad's endorsement on the check to keep the money for himself.

Mayfair thinks, Nice work, asshole. Good luck in court trying to make that look like an achievement.

-o-

August 24
Washington

For the first time in days, Rogers starts his morning with exercise rather than at his desk. He finds a rowing machine adapted to give his artificial leg proper leverage for smooth exercise. Moving back and forth, listening to the hum of the flywheel coiling and uncoiling, Rogers doesn't try to organize his thoughts, letting the rhythm of the machine and the muscles take over. Rogers likes the rigor of the workout, even if it is only a machine and not actually on the water. Within minutes his pores open.

There are other amputees in the gym, the lucky ones, the ones who came back to the world. Their presence reminds Rogers of Germany, his time in rehab and the other men there who, like him, had been maimed in battle. Some dealt with their changed circumstances with dignity and others lashed out in frustration. Rogers had done both, depending on the day. Others of the newly injured men were still gung-ho and wanted to return to active service. He had not.

As he pulls against the machine, his muscles strain and his mind relaxes. He allows the events of the past several days to fall into place. The FAA is monitoring and auditing autopilots and autopilot maintenance and shutting down little-used frequencies in case they were the ones carrying signals to the Drone. Boeing is rolling out software patches to harden autopilots and communications systems. At Thorpe's request, Mac is preparing a selective report laying out how the Lions are a fiction and how the airline attacks were for-profit sabotage benefiting a Russian citizen who compromised a Middle Eastern official. There are still open points in the investigation—Zaroff is still in the wind, and no one can rule out the chance that the Drone is being mass-produced and still a danger.

Rogers remains uneasy. He'd wanted a challenge beyond academic life and got more than he'd expected. The work will soon be over, he hopes. Thorpe is supportive, but not fully open and could still be holding back information that would undercut or derail the work he and Mac have done, or send it careening in a different direction. Rogers can't define what is missing but has a vague and prickling sense that something is.

As he wipes down the machine at the end of his workout, the thought crystallizes: Abbott said Zaroff was recruited without knowing about the Drone. And before Zaroff was brought in, the CIA already had a high-level Iranian source, so the Agency didn't need either Zaroff or Sanjani for Iran.

Zaroff was recruited for something else entirely—and nobody was looking at what that was.

In the afternoon, Rogers takes part in a video conference vetting Mac's draft report. Thorpe participates, as do FBI agents Brooks and Mayfair, along with FBI counter-intelligence lead Robeson. "We need to be mindful that we have multiple constituencies for any material we produce. As much as we can, we want to avoid having our report put to uses that we don't intend," Thorpe says. "And when it's done, I'll need time to walk it through the CIA."

"It sounds like you're expecting this report to leak," Rogers says.

"I'm planning to have the CIA leak it," Thorpe says. "They should be happy to have their names left out of some of the aspects of the story less flattering to them."

For hours the group picks apart the contents and the wording of Mac's report. Nothing can be allowed suggesting the source of information or the method used to collect it. The process is painstaking.

As the session ends, Mac leaves to finalize the document wording and Rogers asks to call Thorpe back for a private talk. "I'm worried we're solving the wrong problem," Rogers says when they resume by video.

Thorpe looks skeptical. "I'm of the opinion that restoring world aviation is a pretty good use of our time, but go on."

"I went through the Herakles financial records. Abbott says the CIA paid $1 million to recruit Zaroff, but that money didn't go through Herakles, even though all the other payments we've seen did. We're missing something. CIA's recruitment of Zaroff had nothing to do with planes. And if we don't know what it is, there's a chance we don't know how much trouble we have left."

Thorpe's face remains impassive.

"Mac doesn't like Abbott's claim that Zaroff's call to the Israelis was enough to convince Saudi Arabia to shoot down the Mecca plane. He suspects the call to the Saudis had to come from a source they trusted more. Maybe even the U.S. So there's that, too."

"No promises," Thorpe says. "But you raise fair points. Most of our counter-intelligence work on Abbott to date has been dedicated to confirming he wasn't selling secrets to Zaroff. I'm planning a personal briefing for the White House on what we're leaving out of this report, which I'll want you and Mac to conduct along with the CIA. We're coming up to the moment of truth."

-0-

August 25
Washington, D.C.

Talbot Mundy and Maureen Dallas meet again at the hotel near the
DuPont Circle, for breakfast this time, nearly two months since the Burj
attack. The meeting is initiated by Mundy, and Maureen is curious what
he has in mind. As usual, she arrives early.

She keeps one eye on the door, while reading the paper. The Journal
has finally printed her husband's piece on money laundering as a strategic
threat to U.S. interests, but he'd already told Maureen the high points:
Stolen money from around the world finds its way to the West, whose
strong economy and strong private property protections make it a haven.
Russia is not so much a government as it is a crime family that has made
Vladimir Putin richer than Bill Gates and Warren Buffett put together. A
vast river of dirty money flows from oil states, drug cartels, and
kleptocrats, and what that money touches it corrupts.

Still, she finds the print version engrossing and is startled when
Mundy taps her on the shoulder.

"Excellent work by your husband," Mundy says, nodding toward the
paper. "An important story."

"In Washington-speak, 'important story' means you get booked in the
'B' block on cable news a couple of times before everybody forgets about
it," Maureen says.

"Is that cynical, or pragmatic?"

"Bitter. No one in this town acts ahead of a crisis, only after.
Sometimes not even then." Mundy slides into the seat across from her in
the booth and she finishes her coffee. "A lot has changed since our last
chat."

"More than you know," Mundy says.

"Hopefully I will know, once we finish talking today."

"Yes."

"On the record?"

"How about, 'individual with access to high-level intelligence'? I'm giving you the sneak preview of coming events."

"Soon to be unclassified?"

"Soon to be communicated officially to the President. In a summary fashion. A longer classified version will be made available to assure the international community that the perception of threats in the world is exaggerated, and that air travel can safely resume."

"That sounds impressive. Burj? Mecca? Vatican? All three?" Maureen asks.

"They're inter-related. The headline is Russian sabotage, and Russian intrigue."

"Not terrorism?"

"No, and your group that you asked me about before, the Lions of Jihad? They were a fiction, part of the Russian intrigue."

"Really? Because they were just a rumor before, but they publicly used their name to issue the Vatican threat. Or someone did."

"Originally the name was used in connection with an effort to advance an individual within the government of a Middle Eastern country, who had ties to Russian interests. The group is a fiction, but the intelligence community has been treating the threat as real."

"I'll have a lot of questions as we go along, not least of which is why Russia would even want to be involved in this."

"Where do you want to start?" Mundy asks.

"Let's go with what happened, and then go on to why."

"We have evidence that shows there is technology designed to take over an airplane autopilot, installed surreptitiously into the planes' operating equipment."

"So, the planes were hacked."

"The planes could not be hacked, at least, not in the usual sense. Without installation of a device we're calling the 'Drone' for short, an outsider couldn't take control of the plane away from the pilots. It's not like someone with a laptop could take over a jet anytime they liked. But once the Drone was installed, it was possible for someone other than the pilots to control the plane. From the evidence we have, the person responsible wanted to hit the Burj, and may not have been trying to hit the Grand Mosque, although that last point isn't clear."

"When you say evidence, what evidence is it?"

"We have evidence about the creation of a Drone. We have evidence of the installation of the Drone, by individuals in the employ of an individual associated with Russian intelligence. More than that I won't go into, since it involves disclosing intelligence sources and methods," Mundy says.

"Person associated with Russian intelligence. What about Russia itself?"

"We aren't necessarily tying the attacks all the way back directly to the Russian government. We are solid on the specific individual, and solid on this individual's history with Soviet intelligence, dating back to the KGB."

"So maybe not Russia, but a Russian? Is that what you are saying?" Maureen asks.

"I am trying to confine myself to what's in the evidence. We have a Russian who is active in this matter. We know that this individual was associated in the past with Soviet intelligence. So, if you believe that there is such a thing as an ex-KGB agent, then sure, a Russian. My experience is that involvement in the Russian intelligence services tends to be a lifelong commitment, with a very short leash."

"This individual has this thing, and he has it installed in a plane—two planes—and then crashes them in Saudi Arabia and Dubai. How does this tie in with the internal politics of a Middle Eastern country? Does this country have a name?"

"Not in the report. Not hard to guess, though."

"Iran," says Maureen.

Mundy stays impassive. "The official in that particular country essentially was turned into an agent for Russia on certain matters. The Russian in exchange created the appearance of a terrorist attack, to give his agent the opportunity to remove political opponents, in the guise of cracking down on suspected terrorists. In fact, there were no terrorists, just faked communications regarding the Lions of Jihad. The Lions never existed. Just digital fakery created by the Russian."

"Is that evidence, or guesswork? I mean, there must be less extreme ways for career advancement than mass murder, even in the Middle East," Maureen says.

"I can't tell you all the agendas promoted by the attacks. Advancement of the Russian agent was one purpose. Maybe the primary purpose, maybe not. But we can show the Lions were Russian fakes."

"And where did the Drone come from?"

"Provided to the Russian, but by whom is unproven. No physical Drone was ever found, so we have just an evidence trail pointing to it being created."

"By Russia?"

"I can't disclose sources and methods. But as I said, Russian intelligence is a lifetime commitment. Where else would it come from?" Maureen notices Mundy's deflection of her question without commenting on it.

"But Mecca involved the Russians trying to advance their agent inside the mystery country?"

"Correct."

"Then, what about the Burj? Same motivation?"

"More or less. The evidence shows there was also a profit motive— manipulation of the securities markets."

"My husband covered that, back at the time. There were rumors, but that trail went cold, as I understood it."

"Not so much cold as...unadvertised, until we had more evidence in hand," Mundy says. "The money trail in the Burj attack leads to the same individual we connected to the Mecca attack, that is correct."

"Thousands of people died and billions of dollars of property were destroyed. How much do you think he made?"

"We estimate this particular individual gained more than $50 million in stock trading profits in the Burj attack. Maybe more from other activities."

"That...that...just seems like relatively little, to kill so many people and create so much destruction. This is monstrous."

Mundy finishes his coffee. "The act was always monstrous. Does having one man behind it make it more so?"

"It makes it more—personal, I guess. When it's one person. You try to put yourself in their shoes, to understand how they could do it. A country or a bureaucracy is more faceless, you don't have the same reaction."

"Hmm. Where I've been, everything ultimately always comes down to one man, one person," Mundy says. "Somebody who said, 'I want to make this happen.' Or sometimes, one person who is in a position to stop it, and doesn't. And there's always a reason, whether you agree with the reason or not."

"And you know who this is? This one man?"

"There is a main individual, who operates his own organization with some others who helped him, but yes, he is the one who took home the money. And, you know, there were benefits for others, whatever Russia gets out of it in arms sales, or regional influence from the disruption created. That sort of thing."

"So, what happens to him?"

"That may be up to the Russians to decide. Once he's exposed, and his agent is exposed, he may be less effective. The cost-benefit analysis for Russia in having him around might change."

"You knew this all along, when I asked about Lions before, when the Burj happened."

"About the Russian? Oh no, of course not," Mundy says.

"But the Lions, you knew were fake."

"The CIA didn't know. It was buried in another agency."

"I need to confirm this. Which parts of this can I confirm?"

Mundy pulls pages from his leather folder. "You can read the summary report, right here and right now, in front of me. You can't make a copy, or a picture, or take notes. Or quote directly from it."

"There's more to the story than what's in here," says Maureen.

Mundy shrugs. "Isn't there always?"

-o-

August 26
Washington, D.C.

Thorpe wakes quickly and is instantly alert—there are no routine calls at 4 a.m.

"Your Russian is here and wants asylum." The call is from the U.S. Embassy in London. Thorpe is already standing and walking from the unmade bed to the kitchen, where he will make coffee and set up an impromptu command post.

"Get him on a plane. I need him here by this afternoon."

Thorpe makes an initial list at the kitchen table of people to notify and actions to put in motion. He has time while Zaroff is on the plane.

Voluntary walk-in suggests Zaroff wants to cooperate, but it doesn't mean Zaroff will be truthful or complete in what he has to say.

After coffee, Thorpe showers and dresses, then drives the not-completely-deserted freeway in the dark to his office. He can begin making calls by dawn.

Thorpe shares the news first with Nadeau. Thorpe has been pleasantly surprised by the former politician's ability to keep his mouth shut about confidential information, but Thorpe nonetheless sees him as a man whose brief time leading the CIA leaves him under-equipped for handling the emerging disaster within the Agency. Neither man knows yet if Abbott is a one-off bad apple, or if the CIA has other problems. The Agency needs to be compartmented until they do.

FBI counterintelligence will lead the Zaroff interrogation, with input from the team that handled the securities trading. The initial interrogation might be productive, but it might not.

Thorpe waits until mid-morning to notify the White House that

Zaroff is in hand, cautioning that the early rounds of interrogation are unlikely to be fruitful. Events are moving quickly and Thorpe dares not give the politicians details too early—they will either develop unrealistic expectations or lie in public for purposes of their own. Nothing good can come involving the White House blow-by-blow in the questioning. Whatever Zaroff says initially could turn out to be a lie later.

The security team tells Thorpe that Embassy staff members are accompanying Zaroff on the flight, with instructions not to ask questions or make small talk. Zaroff is still wearing the same clothes he'd worn when he walked into the Embassy, without a bag or other personal possessions. Zaroff seems content to remain quiet and even doze for part of the flight. Their guess is that Zaroff knows he has a long day and night ahead of him.

Once Zaroff arrives in the United States, the FBI provides Thorpe with a closed-circuit feed of his intake and processing at the Marine Barracks, where Zaroff will be held and where the questioning will take place. Zaroff's first statement, obviously composed during the long trip, is to tell the agents that he recognized from the news that U.S. authorities connected him to the Burj and Mecca attacks.

He adds that his life as a wealthy businessman is over, "because I don't like the Russian intelligence services retirement plan." Despite himself, Thorpe cracks a half-smile at Zaroff's almost jovial use of the term "retirement plan" in lieu of "assassination."

As the interrogation begins, the FBI doesn't share with Zaroff the full extent of the evidence against him, but they let him know the stock trading is traced to him, and that the Lions of Jihad are a fake. And that Abbott is his contact.

"Yes, poor Abbott," says Zaroff. "Not really cut out for this life. He wanted to be rich, but he didn't know anything about money. And not the right personality to be a proper spy." Zaroff says he resurrected the Lions to throw intelligence agencies off the scent to steady the nerves of his worried co-conspirator.

As the interrogation progresses, Zaroff reveals a great deal and holds back or conceals a great deal as well. Zaroff is cagey about what he knows about the Drones, and when he knew it, and about his role in installing the Drones in the planes. But he is adamant he didn't control either attacking airliner, deflecting questions about who did by simply saying, "Not me."

Zaroff's version of his CIA recruitment is that Abbott approached him, holding himself out as an intermediary for a Western businessman. "I expected that he was a complete liar. I was surprised to find that he was not." Abbott actually delivered on his promise of face-to-face contact with David Cain. Abbott was looking to insert himself into the semi-retired Cain's business, just as Zaroff had done in acquiring companies in Europe. While Zaroff regarded Abbott as hopelessly naïve, he played along to explore the opportunities.

Then Abbott presented Zaroff a chance to collaborate with Sanjani, funded and instigated by CIA. Zaroff demanded $1 million upfront, in part because he needed the money and in part to test the CIA's willingness to pay him. Other than the payment at the start, the only CIA money Zaroff got was what Abbott diverted from money meant for Sanjani.

Teaming with Cain, and promising Sanjani lavish bribes, Zaroff negotiated the multi-billion-dollar Ports project. Zaroff said he and Sanjani had a shared view of human nature: "I trust a man I can buy, because I can predict what he will do. Anyone else is too risky."

Sanjani's bribe from Cain was to be $35 million, but Abbott over-charged Cain and embezzled the balance. Not all of Zaroff's numbers square with what the FBI knows from the Herakles financial records, but the constant petty thievery by Abbott and Jared Cain might account for discrepancies.

"You see, the whole thing is all about doing legitimate business," Zaroff explains. "In my experience, bribery is essential to secure the business. It is a line-item cost. That is my focus. I have been a businessman for a long time now, longer even than I was a spy. But the tradecraft from my former line of work has always been valuable."

The FBI interrogators ask about the CIA money. "When I saw Abbott stealing the CIA money, after that first payment, it was wonderful news. It meant Abbott did not have access to CIA cash and was truly acting on his own on the Ports deal. An honest man pursuing a hidden CIA agenda would not have been comfortable for me."

"How does a businessman like yourself come to tie in with the short sales from an airliner attack on the Burj?" an FBI interrogator asks.

"Ah, that is the great tragedy in this story," Zaroff says. "The man Abbott used to make payments to Sanjani and me was Jared Cain, the son of David. Jared did not manage his money well, and I used a very large portion of my own cash to support what was supposed to be a brief problem. But then I faced my own issues with my bankers, and we needed to raise money quickly. And so..." Zaroff shrugs and holds up his palms.

"Yes?"

"We had billions of dollars on the line with the Ports deal that we had to protect," says Zaroff.

"By crashing an airliner into the Burj?"

"By making a good investment, based on knowing that the airliner would crash, yes, that's correct," says Zaroff.

"How did you obtain this knowledge, about the airliner crashing?"

For a moment in the interview room there is only silence. The FBI has reached the nub of the matter, details about how the attack was conducted. If Zaroff invents a story about the mythical Lions of Jihad telling him about the attack, his claim of wanting to cooperate will be exposed as a sham. For his part, Zaroff wants to downplay his role and avoid confessing to committing mass murder. But everyone at the table knows Zaroff is, at a minimum, an accomplice.

"You understand that my business is construction and shipping, yes?" Zaroff says.

"Does this have to do with a crashing airplane, and how you knew about it?" the FBI man asks.

"Yes, yes. But I need to paint you the picture. I encounter people in my business who are involved in smuggling, or criminal enterprises, and I must work with them from time to time. Some of them are my former colleagues from the intelligence services, even. And so when the question came up of how to install a control into an airliner cockpit—the Drone, as you call it—I knew men who could do it," Zaroff says.

"Go on."

"Well, these men made the installation of the Drone into the planes, and when I knew that the attacks would occur, I used that knowledge to make money in the stock market, so that my capital would not be impaired when it came time to sign the deal with Iran."

"You're skipping over a few details here."

"Such as where the Drone came from?" Zaroff says.

"That's one."

Zaroff sighs. He chose to confess his misdeeds in America, rather than remain in London and face punishment for them from the Russian security services. Still, he hesitates to volunteer the damning details.

"From Abbott. He didn't tell me where he got the devices. He sent three to me. Two you know about, and the third is gone. So you are correct that the threat claimed by the Lions is toothless. But David Cain knew about the Drone. Cain and I talked about it. It was...it was, a condition of Cain's participation in the Ports deal."

"What was a condition?"

"Using the Drone. Cain was becoming more detached from his business. Perhaps early stages of dementia. It is hard to get him to focus on a pure business decision. He was obsessed with vengeance for 9/11, where one of his sons was killed. And so, one day, that is what he said. He told me that unless I arranged to have the Drone placed in a plane to attack Mecca, there would be no Ports deal."

"Cain said that?"

"Yes."

"And what else did he say?"

"That the command to fly the plane into the building—he wanted to be the one to enter it," Zaroff says.

-o-

August 28
Washington, D.C.

The transition from the cells to the courtyard is brief. It is a mistake, the left hand unaware of the right. Neither the single guard escorting Abbott nor the two-man team with Zaroff know the men share a connection. The Marines are escorting Zaroff inside from a brief period outdoors when they pass Abbott being taken for exercise.

Surprise at seeing Abbott alive and in custody does not slow Zaroff. He isn't handcuffed or chained. Zaroff quickly leaps across the corridor, knocking Abbott to the ground, and with a knee on Abbott's back Zaroff twists Abbott's head back and sideways to break his neck. The spinal cord is severed. The guards, taken by surprise, pull Zaroff away, but it is too late.

"You know," says Zaroff, "I wasn't really sure I could still do that. It has been a long time."

Abbott dies in the infirmary.

"Why kill Abbott?" Zaroff's captors ask.

"My life is ruined, from working with him. I've done you a favor. You would have had to put him on trial, and what would that accomplish?"

"He can't corroborate what you've told us."

"No. Or contradict it. I am under no illusions about my value to you. I can tell you what I did with the CIA, and you will want to confirm it with proof, not the unreliable babblings of a novice spy like Abbott. I told you that I think the CIA recruited me for something to do with Russia, not Iran. Unless you catch Abbott's accomplice in the CIA, I am now the only one you can talk to." Zaroff says.

"And I wanted revenge on Abbott, of course. A man can have more than one motive." Zaroff shrugs. "The world is complicated."

-o-

August 28

Hudson River Valley

Rogers is home for a day to see his family. He doesn't find it restful. He isn't back to stay and he is preoccupied, going through the motions of a reunion. Rogers spends the afternoon with Dub and Stevie, then shares a quiet dinner and evening at home with them. He will return to Washington in the morning. The briefing for the President's chief of staff is set for the day after that.

At twilight Mac calls to tell him that Abbott is dead. "For real this time," Mac says.

Rogers takes it in. After a brief silence he says, "We live in a dynamic world."

"You're here tomorrow, right? I'll fill you in on the rest ahead of our meeting. Short version: You and I were right, about the phone call and the payment. Details when you get here."

That night Rogers and Dub finally get time to themselves. "Maureen got the scoop," she says. "Did you give it to her?"

"No. That would be way above my pay grade."

"But it's true?"

"True enough. There's plenty missing."

"There's more? Is it better, or worse?" she asks.

"It's all bad. I'm just hoping everyone at fault for the attacks is brought to justice."

"You know who it is?"

"We know the cast of characters is bigger than just a nameless Russian. I don't want the other guys to get away free. I came in to help sort out information on Mecca and the Burj. I don't get to decide what happens next. I'd probably make different choices from the guys who will. But it's hard to know what the right path is." At the start Rogers told Mac he wouldn't provide cover for a rogue spook, but he doesn't know which part of the operation is rogue. He declines to share that problem with Dub.

"Is it almost over?" Dub asks.

"Maybe. My part will be, soon, I hope."

"You look beat."

"It's hard to sleep down in Washington. There are so many questions I keep turning over. It's hard to stay in the right place mentally."

"Told you so." Rogers gives Dub a glance of mock irritation. "I've been watching," she says. "You're okay. I know what it looks like from the outside when you're really having trouble."

"I was thinking about the Bible," Rogers says. "If God sees the fall of every sparrow, then God spends every day dealing with loss, lets us die and fail and doesn't even try for a perfect outcome. Sooner or later, we all get to experience the same kind of rotten day God gets every day."

"The Gospel of St. Tony."

"There were a lot of lives on the planes, and in the tower, when the plane hit. A lot of pointless loss."

"Well, maybe these other conspirators aren't getting off completely free. Everybody pays for what they do, in some way."

"It figures you would say that," Rogers says.

"What?"

"You're an accountant."

Dub frowns. "I was actually trying to make a philosophical point."

"Works either way."

They hold one another in bed lying above the blankets, neither of them ready for sleep. The weight and warmth of Dub's body, and his familiarity with her touch, comfort Rogers greatly. She knows the Burj secrets wear on him, whatever they are, even though he can't tell her the specifics. "You don't have anything to prove."

"I know. Force of habit. Chip on my shoulder."

"Well, you don't have to feel that way," Dub says.

"I know."

"You say you know, but you don't."

"You could pretend to believe me," Rogers says.

-o-

August 30
Washington, D.C.

Mac and Rogers again meet in a Pentagon SCIF, this time to plan the final presentation on the Mecca and Burj attacks. The summary report set out core facts that were true without being the complete truth. Tomorrow will be the day to paint the rest of the picture.

FBI forensics analyzed all computers and phones from Cain's home. None showed the Drone control software. The FBI tried and failed to use ISP records to trace a history of connections between devices at the house and air traffic control signal sites, and Cain hid or destroyed any computers that made those connections. Proving Cain sent the command to attack Mecca is impossible.

Still, the money trail locks down the Abbott/Zaroff/Sanjani connection—nearly all the trading accounts have been found. And the Saudi Defense Ministry, confronted with what the U.S. knows about the communication ahead of the Mecca attack, has finally confirmed that it took a phone call from Langley, Virginia, prior to scrambling jets.

The money for Zaroff's initial recruitment payment traces to a CIA cyber-intrusion program named PM HOTEL VICTOR. The FBI found no PM country digram, requiring that they search for an operation with that prefix. Initial details on HOTEL VICTOR are scant. For now, what they know is that the PM account is controlled by Talbot Mundy.

-o-

August 31
Washington, D.C.

Sangar Rainsford has skipped all the Burj Action Group meetings, but Thorpe arranged a smaller session for a conference room in the Senate Majority Leader's office. Thorpe wants to ensure the President's Chief of Staff gets a fuller version of the BAG's thinking than what appears in the report leaked to the press. CIA Director Nadeau will attend, along with Deputy Director Mundy. The meeting will not be logged anywhere. For official Washington purposes, the meeting isn't happening.

Rogers arrives early. He sees Robeson, the FBI counter-intelligence lead, in the hallway along with three other men he doesn't recognize.

Robeson pulls Rogers aside. "Col. McCaulley will be providing some updated information. The punchline is that Abbott communicated the impending Mecca attack using the HOTEL VICTOR email. So...ahead of the event."

"Yeah, Mac told me," Rogers says. "These guys?"

"U.S. Marshals." Robeson nods at the three men. "They'll join the meeting later."

"Are you coming in?"

"Yes. You and the Colonel will do the heavy lifting. I'm there for technical support, if details on the counter-intelligence side become pertinent."

Rogers holds a printed copy of the expanded report. He sits in an antique chair in the anteroom, waiting for others to arrive. He riffles the pages, glancing without reading. Nerves. He doesn't need to read it. He knows the contents cold, as well as what has still been left out.

Rogers is prepared, but not over-confident. He'd felt prepared before the BAG meeting ten days ago, too. Planning is indispensable, even though every plan falls apart once the action actually starts. He's never met Rainsford, doesn't know his habits. Rainsford might be on time, or be one of those people who is chronically late.

Mac and Nadeau arrive. Rainsford arrives with Mundy, the CIA's chief liaison to the White House. When Rainsford arrives, Rogers lets out a breath he didn't realize he'd been holding. Okay, he thinks. Showtime.

Rainsford is a clotheshorse. Not showy. Just puts more into his clothing budget, so the cut and fabric and stitching are all top of the line. No wrinkles, no parts that don't lie perfectly flat. Not even obvious at a conscious level, really, but he is ready for a photo op at every second. He'd been House whip before joining the president's staff. He is hard with fellow politicians, smooth with constituents, and switches modes effortlessly. He is a polished politician, his thick graying hair always perfectly groomed, and he is as accomplished as a Broadway actor in delivering a convincing smile or sneer as the situation requires. Right now, he's smiling.

They enter the conference room. Rainsford shakes hands all around.

"Colonel McCaulley. My understanding is that you and Professor Rogers are delivering a supplement to the ODNI's report on the airline attacks at Mecca and the Burj," Rainsford says.

"That's correct sir."

"Mr. Robeson, I understand you have additional background on a counterintelligence effort that grew out of the matters covered in the report."

"That's correct."

"Professor Rogers, I am further informed that even though you are not an intelligence officer, you were active in developing the information that ultimately is included in the report."

"The entire intelligence community was..." Rogers begins.

"And I understand that in light of your investigations, your personal contribution to developing this report, and your personal insight into the situation, the DNI wants you to be involved in presenting me with certain information not included in the report."

"That's correct." Rogers takes the hint to shut up. Rainsford isn't looking for expanded answers.

"Before you get started, I want to go over a few things with you. Would that be all right?" Rainsford asks. Rainsford summarizes the report information accurately. He captures nuances that were glossed over in the Post story. It is clear he has actually read the material and mastered the details.

"The report concludes that the likelihood is very low that non-state actors, like terrorists, developed the technology to sabotage an airliner, or deployed it," Rainsford says.

"That's what the report says, yes, sir. Low, but not eliminated," Mac says.

"Now, ahead of our meeting this morning, I've received additional information that was not covered by the report. I'm going to run it by you. For example, I've been told that the CIA once operated a program to develop a device that could have controlled an airliner, like the one described in the report. There was a CIA operative named Hugh Abbott involved in that development. Is that accurate?" Rainsford asks.

"Yes, sir." Clearly Mundy made a bureaucratic play to be the one to break the bad news to Rainsford.

"I also have information that there is an investigation of a U.S. national who traded on airline stocks ahead of the Burj attack, which led to some of the information developed in the report. That trading also is linked to Abbott. The trading investigation was left out of the report, as well."

"That's correct," says Rogers. Mac keeps his expression blank. They all understand the routine—right now it is Rainsford's show.

"Are you here to tell me that the summary report excludes information about U.S. connections to the attacks?"

"Beyond what you have just mentioned? Yes, sir," Rogers says.

"Really? From the briefing I got, the facts I mentioned should have covered what you knew from your own involvement in the investigation." Rainsford's face has lost its initial smile and seeming friendliness. Rainsford's attempt to make the briefing cover solely what he intended, based on Mundy's coaching, irritates Rogers. He draws on his experience of the control and cold-bloodedness needed before combat. Maybe Rainsford's stunts work better on his fellow politicians, or those seeking his favor.

"Colonel McCaulley and I are prepared to provide you with what we know, sir. We assume you wish to hear it," Rogers says. The last may have sounded unnecessarily provocative. But Rogers needs to say it—he wants to draw Rainsford's commitment to listening.

"That's why I'm here," Rainsford says smoothly.

Mac says, "We're on firm ground stating that the Lions of Jihad threat is a hoax. The Russian saboteur, Ivan Zaroff, is in U.S. custody and has confessed the Lions threat is his work. We also got a communications intercept, days before the threat—Abbott on a burner phone the FBI had previously discovered and tapped. Abbott was worried the CIA was looking at sabotage, not just terrorism, and Zaroff decided to disrupt the inquiry with the Lions threat. Do you want to hear the intercept?"

Rainsford shakes his head. "Not unless it's critical to what you have to say."

Mac says, "We're planning to cover a few gaps in the report. The DNI wants to make sure the White House knows in advance that these gaps will be covered in a separate highly classified version of the report." Mac holds up his copy of the expanded report. "We'll provide you with a copy at the end of the briefing. It covers only what the intelligence community can confirm right now, and it's possible additional information could be developed in the future. Mr. Rainsford, you seem already to be acquainted with the essential facts. One other point that the DNI wants to stress is that the key recommendation in the report stands, on hardening airliner autopilots."

"Yes," says Mundy. "A sound precaution. But because of the way the Drone device was developed, it is less likely that we face an active or ongoing threat from Russia." Mundy faces Rainsford. "Professor Rogers is responsible for a very large break in the investigation, finding an autopilot control device made by an American company, RossTech."

"Actually, the report states that we don't have hard evidence of who created the device that sabotaged the planes used in the attacks. We identified evidence that the sabotage could have been done with the RossTech device, and we believe that it was. But Russia could have developed its own, or taken the original prototype and put it into mass production," says Rogers.

"It's still possible that the actual Drone used is Russian," says Mac. Mac and Rogers have seated themselves on opposite sides of the table, forcing Rainsford to swivel to see the person speaking. "You're correct that Mr. Abbott was a critical person in the airliner attacks. But he is also involved in a number of other activities, and the way those activities interact is important to understanding the full picture. I have to ask you to bear with me, as I peel back the various layers on this onion."

"Please proceed," Rainsford says.

"Abbott was critical to the development of the Drone. He recruited David Cain—yes, it's the David Cain you're thinking of—to finance the Drone development. Once prototype Drones were developed, Abbott routed them from Cain to Ivan Zaroff. Zaroff is former KGB, and we're confident he still has connections to his old crowd, now in Russian intelligence. The summary report didn't mention Zaroff by name," Mac says.

Mac looks at Rainsford as he speaks. He knows Rogers is monitoring Mundy. "The Mecca attack and the Burj attack had Abbott and Zaroff in common, but they were staged for different reasons. The Burj attack was conducted to raise money for Zaroff, who was under pressure from his bankers and from lending money to bail out Abbott's paymaster, who happened to be David Cain's son Jared. The Mecca attack was made at the insistence of David Cain, as a condition of his joining Abbott and Zaroff in a transaction worth billions of dollars."

"Zaroff created the fictional Lions of Jihad, and used Russian criminal elements to install the Drone in the airliners that attacked Mecca and the Burj. Abbott and Zaroff both claim the Mecca attack was actually conducted by Cain, but there's no independent confirmation, and Cain has made no confession. Zaroff orchestrated the Burj attack to make money, and Abbott helped set up trading accounts around that attack, but we may never know who actually operated the Drone controls for it."

"If the Burj was done for money, then why was Mecca attacked?" Rainsford asks.

"That takes us to the next layer of the onion," Mac says. "Abbott and Zaroff had teamed up to compromise the transportation minister in Iran. Once this minister, Sanjani, became an intelligence asset, Abbott and Zaroff conspired to bribe him into delivering a multi-billion dollar project to Zaroff's company."

Mac leans forward. "Zaroff needed Cain's money and partnership to obtain the project. Mecca was attacked because Cain made the attack a condition of his participation in the project, and also because Zaroff dangled the attack as an opportunity for Sanjani to move into the interior ministry."

Rainsford says, "Working with the Russians to compromise an official in a third country is not standard procedure for intelligence operations, I would think."

"You're correct. This brings us to yet another layer of the onion. Abbott was on the CIA's operations desk for Iran. He was given the job of recruiting Sanjani, but the underlying objective was to lure Zaroff into working with the CIA. Zaroff claims he suspected that Abbott's approach was intended to compromise him, as much as to compromise Sanjani. But Zaroff agreed anyway, because he wanted to turn the American money and connections to his own advantage. Which, in striking the deal for the Ports business, he did."

"Why would the CIA want to compromise Zaroff, if he is no longer actively part of Russian intelligence?" Rainsford asks.

"Now we have arrived at the tragedy at the center of this whole sequence of events. It's the reason for this face-to-face briefing." Rainsford folds his hands on the table, waiting for Mac to continue.

"The goal in recruiting Zaroff was not to gain intelligence from him— he'd been out of Russian intelligence circles for too long to have fresh or accurate information. But there was a separate CIA covert operation, having nothing to do with the Middle East, or with terrorism. The name of the operation is HOTEL VICTOR. Zaroff's recruitment, either as an active or passive CIA asset, was in furtherance of CIA efforts to penetrate and overcome Russian cyber-security as part of the HOTEL VICTOR program. They dangled information and money to Zaroff as bait."

Mundy maintains his poised expression, but says quickly, "What's your clearance level? I don't think...."

Nadeau cuts him off. "They're cleared for all discussions in this room," he tells Mundy.

"HOTEL VICTOR is overseen by Mr. Mundy. He is signatory on a project account used to make a $1 million payment to secure Zaroff's participation." Mac pauses.

"I'm listening," Rainsford says.

"My predecessor as CIA director authorized the operation, and delegated full authority to Mundy," Nadeau says. "I was unaware of it until days ago. The FBI and I are still working to get the complete story on the operation."

"You're not saying the attacks were CIA operations, are you?" Rainsford asks.

"They were not. No U.S. official other than Abbott was involved in planning or executing either of the airliner attacks. HOTEL VICTOR was separate from any of Abbott's activities in Iran, either legitimate or illegitimate, and except as an internal Agency email address to contact Mundy, it appears Abbott knew nothing about it," Rogers says.

"But there is a connection between the attacks and HOTEL VICTOR. Abbott wrote to Mundy on the encrypted HOTEL VICTOR email to inform him in advance that the Mecca attack was coming. Abbott claimed at the time that Sanjani had discovered the pending attack—which was a lie—but Abbott also told Mundy it was urgent to warn Saudi air defenses to ensure the attack didn't succeed. Zaroff gave Israeli intelligence the same warning to pass on to the Saudis, but there was no certainty that warning would succeed. We have the phone records from the CIA offices for that day, as well as confirmation from the Saudis. The call to the Saudi ministry of defense to shoot down the plane came from the conference room next to Mundy's office, and was made by Mr. Mundy," Mac says.

Rogers can detect no change in Mundy's demeanor, even at Mac's delivery of this key allegation against him. Mundy has shifted his gaze to the wall, away from the meeting participants. He's disciplined, Rogers thinks, he knows I'm watching him and still looks straight ahead.

"We knew the Saudis wouldn't stay quiet simply to protect a mid-level guy like Abbott," Rogers says. "The call had to have come from somebody senior, who could do them favors in the future."

No one speaks. Rainsford and Mundy turn to face each other, both men expressionless. Finally, Rainsford says, "This is news to me."

Rainsford says, "It sounds like you're suggesting that Mr. Mundy could have just called the airport in Iran to stop the plane from leaving for Mecca. Or that he could have cut Abbott off early and prevented the Burj entirely." Mundy remains quiet.

"Mundy can speak for himself on his reasons. Zaroff told us he was always suspicious about Abbott's recruitment of him—that the CIA had a secret objective that didn't involve Abbott. We think Mundy didn't want to alert Zaroff that Abbott was connected to anyone truly senior in the Agency for fear of compromising HOTEL VICTOR." Mac stares at Mundy as he says this, but Mundy has resumed his stoic wall-gazing. "Mundy knew about the Abbott and Zaroff machinations for the Ports deal. Maybe not about the Drone, but when Mundy found out about the Mecca attack at the last second, he let it proceed."

Rainsford turns to Mundy. "Do you have any response?"

"Nothing at this moment," Mundy says. Mundy finally looks at his accusers. A blank expression, preserving his options. "I'll let the facts do the speaking for me, as they emerge."

"We have a few facts that are talking already, Mr. Mundy," Rogers says. "You let attacks that cost thousands of lives and billions of dollars of property damage go forward, because you were trying to maintain the secrecy of HOTEL VICTOR. Sort of like the way England let air strikes continue in World War II rather than alert the Nazis to the Enigma code being cracked. That suggests that HOTEL VICTOR must be a very important operation. And since Zaroff is involved, Russia must be the focus."

"You should know by now not to speculate, Rogers," says Mundy.

"What I know, sir, is that there is a reason you're not supposed to give an operation a name that might let someone guess its purpose. 'HOTEL VICTOR Papa Mike' works out to the initials HVPM in the military alphabet. And if you think about Russia, and you think about something major, and you think about the initials 'VP,' then Vladimir Putin starts to sound like the target." Mundy does not change expression.

Rogers looks at Mundy. "Maybe the other letters stand for 'hacking' and 'money,' as in, Hacking Vladimir Putin's Money."

"Just quit spec—" Mundy begins.

Nadeau again interrupts. "The records show that HOTEL VICTOR personnel and contractors were mostly coders and individuals with financial institutions and cyber-intrusion expertise."

Rogers looks at Mundy and shrugs. "Lucky guess."

Mac says, "Actually, FBI counter-intelligence checked." Rogers remains silent.

"Zaroff was recruited so the CIA could gain access to bank account and funds flow trends among Russian oligarchs, including—we believe—Putin himself," Mac says. "Communications from HOTEL VICTOR accounts to Zaroff contained a computer virus, which let the CIA penetrate Zaroff's personal and corporate computer systems and from there spread the computer intrusion virus to those Zaroff contacted, including his fellow oligarchs, who in turn would spread the virus further. The goal was to establish first-hand knowledge of the finances of Russia's political and economic elite. You can learn a lot from knowing the leadership group's habits with money, and maybe get leverage on them too."

"Mr. Mundy," Robeson says, "We're not unmindful that protecting another operation may have led you to keep quiet in advance of the Saudi attack. Not necessarily a good choice on your part, but events can have their own momentum. That said, after your team went rogue once, you were reckless not to prevent additional harm. I'm going to be bringing in some U.S. Marshals. The FBI will be asking you questions. You should know, the U.S. Attorney right now is considering charges, including accessory to murder of a U.S. citizen, espionage, and participation in terrorism."

Robeson rises to summon the Marshals, who lead Mundy away. No one speaks until he is gone.

Nadeau tells Rainsford, "I've already confirmed that Mundy has been quietly doing a lot of back-checking, within the CIA, since the Burj attack. It looks like Mundy was worried that Abbott was selling secrets to Zaroff. Always a risk with running a double agent like Abbott. They might do what you want, but they might also do things that you don't want."

Rainsford says to Nadeau, "I see. Beyond his involvement in the attacks, are you finding evidence that Abbott leaked other secrets to Zaroff?"

"It's still being checked," Nadeau says.

"The CIA is going to have to clean up its own mess. You and I are going to need to talk later," Rainsford says to Nadeau.

"I'm prepared to resign, if it comes to that," Nadeau says. "Or I'll stay and clean up the Agency, including developing processes to prevent future directors from being kept in the dark as I've been."

"This meeting isn't the time or place to settle that. I appreciate your discretion in excluding the HOTEL VICTOR information from even the classified version of the report," Rainsford says. "Word of Abbott's involvement in an act of terrorism will harm the national interest, if it ever comes to light."

"I'd say Abbott's involvement harmed the national interest even if it never comes to light," Rogers says. "Thousands of deaths aren't a numbers game."

"That's where my position gives me a perspective that's different from yours," Rainsford says. "I have to take a strategic view about where the United States' interests lie. Russia will deny involvement in the attacks, but Zaroff's fingerprints are all over it, and we can take advantage of that in the future."

Rainsford's face is stern as he speaks to Rogers. "I don't like to sound hard-hearted, but it's not my job to worry about the victims of these attacks. I care about the United States. You teach history, Mr. Rogers. Who makes policy for the victims? Nobody, ever. The nameless dead stay nameless, and they stay dead. Stalin's purges, the Holocaust, the Killing Fields, the Middle East. The dead can't be helped, the living keep living, and the planet keeps turning."

As Rainsford walks to the door, he says, "Gentlemen, I expected your supplemental report was going to be dull. You surprised me. Is there anything else?"

Mac stands, silently, and then says quietly, "Only if there's anything further you'd like to say, Mr. Rainsford."

"The air travel crisis is over," Rainsford says. "That's plenty."

As the meeting participants file out, Mac and Rogers stay behind. They wait for the door to close. Neither smiles. Mac says, "Verdict?"

"We didn't tell him anything that he didn't already know," Rogers says.

"He didn't know that the intelligence community had caught on to Mundy," Mac says, gathering his papers from the conference table. "And I think the marshals escorting Mundy out was Thorpe sending Rainsford a message."

-o-

September 1
Maclean, Virginia

Thorpe receives the phone call roughly ten minutes ahead of time: Rainsford is coming to ODNI headquarters for an unscheduled meeting and Thorpe needs to clear his schedule to meet with him privately. Thorpe finds the demand unusual, but in the circumstances, something he should have foreseen.

"This won't be on your calendar," Rainsford says as he enters Thorpe's office. "Just a short, informal meeting."

"Go on."

"Visitors logs at the CIA will show that I was there around the time of Mundy's call to the Saudis, on the day of the Mecca attack. I'm telling you now so that you and your team don't get surprised when you find out, or start drawing the wrong conclusions. It would be best to limit your final report on Mundy's role in the attacks and HOTEL VICTOR to the President's eyes only. No broader circulation." Rainsford's claims of informality were a sham. He had come to give orders, not talk.

For a second, Thorpe says nothing. "What took you to the CIA that day?"

"Meeting with Mundy on a separate matter."

"HOTEL VICTOR?"

"A separate matter." Rainsford flashes his rehearsed and unfriendly smile.

"All right," says Thorpe, who pauses, then says, "I didn't go to the meeting yesterday."

"I noticed."

"I was saving some ammunition. First, Mundy can't be in a position of authority after what he's done. If he doesn't resign from the CIA, I'll find a way to work past you to explain things to the President in person, not just by memo." Rainsford is silent. "Second, if Mundy isn't gone, my resignation letter is already written, ready for public release, with a copy to the Congressional intelligence committees and an offer to testify in classified session."

Rainsford nods slightly. "I shouldn't imagine it will come to that."

After Rainsford departs, Thorpe writes down detailed notes on their interaction. Thorpe's secretary keeps an electric typewriter at her workstation to prepare documents whose existence won't show in the computer network. After hours, Thorpe types up his notes and puts the pages in a plastic file folder he keeps in a locked drawer in his desk. He wants the contemporaneous record in case he needs it later. He leaves out mentioning that Mac and Rogers had come to him after their meeting with Rainsford, stating they would blow the whistle to Congress unless Mundy was removed.

It isn't their job to take the bullet, Thorpe reasons, it's his.

-o-

September 2-6
Washington, D.C.

Rogers stays in D.C. for several days. World air travel begins returning to normal and Thorpe announces dissolution of the BAG. Dub and Stevie come down for a visit, and the family does the things that tourists do. It is a temporary replacement for the postponed family trip, although Stevie finds Washington a poor substitute for Disneyland.

Stevie is old enough to appreciate Arlington National Cemetery. The family tours the Pentagon, and sees the Lincoln Memorial and the Vietnam and Korean memorials. They see Ford's Theater, and the National Cathedral, and the Smithsonian galleries, and Georgetown and Chinatown, and they tour the Air and Space Museum. They take photos in front of the White House and the Capitol and the Iwo Jima statue, and the Jefferson Memorial and the Washington Memorial and the King Memorial.

Rogers recalls a joke he likes: When Washington D.C. was founded in 1790, the area was merely fetid swampland—and now, after two centuries of effort by politicians and lobbyists, it's so much worse. Still, the architecture and the parks, museums, and monuments all embody something uplifting about the American heart. However the politicians fail, the city still holds much that speaks to what is best about the country.

At the end of the week, Thorpe invites Mac and Rogers to join his staff for karaoke night, which this time is being held in celebration of the end of BAG operations. Mac shows surprising vocal abilities on the Motown oldie *My Girl*. Rogers delivers an earnest off-key rendition of *Bridge Over Troubled Water*. Thorpe steals the show, updating his repertoire with *We Are Never Ever Getting Back Together*.

Thorpe tells Rogers he spoke to Klamber at West Point. "I told him that you were instrumental in resolving a national security problem. He sounded impressed. I told him you're the kind of person who understands things by implication, and that if you were to leave the Academy I could find a spot for you here."

"I appreciate the vote of confidence," Rogers says, "but I'd rather you didn't put ideas in his head. I like the Hudson Valley quite a bit."

"I thought he might value you more if he knew you had options."

-o-

September 15
Phoenix, Arizona

Rogers is never at ease in Arizona, where the dry air, or the scent of desert wind, or a random combination of heat, light, and shadow might suddenly summon an unwanted memory of his time in Iraq. But his father Matt had turned seventy months before, and now the family has gathered for the deferred celebration.

"I hear you were responsible for stopping the guys threatening the Vatican," Matt says.

"Team effort. I did my part." The full story remains classified. The misplaced gratitude makes Rogers uncomfortable.

Rogers' brother James and his wife had travelled from Rome with their children. The birthday is a nice ad hoc reunion, since the siblings haven't all been together for years. Rogers' nephew is now six, and prone to ask questions out of innocence and curiosity, like what had happened to Uncle Tony's leg.

"I was in a war. A piece of a bomb hit my leg. My friend saved my life by shooting the bomber, to keep him from getting close enough to kill everyone. And then when I came home, I felt sad, and your Aunt Dub saved my life all over again."

"Did the bomber die?"

"Yes."

"Did any of your friends die?"

"Yes."

"Is that why you were sad?"

"Some of it. I was very sad for a long, long time."

"Not now?"

"Sometimes. Not as much. Not the same way."

Rogers keeps his answers short for the boy. The longer explanations can wait, the truer ones. The family moves outdoors, and Rogers remains quietly behind.

Cain Senior faces charges for foreign bribery, according to Mac, but not murder. Mundy let people die and is banished from the CIA. "It's like jailing Capone for taxes," Mac told him. "Just take the win."

Rogers resents that protecting the secrecy of HOTEL VICTOR allows Cain and Mundy to escape more serious consequences. The punishments are too small for the crimes.

After weeks of searching for why thousands had died, he's made himself complicit in burying pieces of the truth. Rogers hates discovering that he has the capacity to bend in the face of moral ambiguity. He'd always despised that trait in others.

He broods over what he could have done differently, over what he can still do differently. He tries to imagine how exposing the entire story to Maureen Dallas would create a better outcome. He can't. The prosecutors have already decided to let some conspirators escape trial—that bell isn't going to be unrung. And telling the full truth simply for its own sake: Who would benefit from it, in the end? The world didn't need the truth, it needed the saboteurs stopped and they were stopped. He'd help stop them. Revealed, the rest of the story would turn into nothing but Washington gossip, to no good purpose.

The quest for truth resolved as a bureaucratic "best case" outcome. No victory, simply a balance of competing priorities. All Rogers can do is learn to live with it, live with himself.

Dub enters from the patio, where the group is increasingly noisy and gay. "It's time to come out for cake." Rogers doesn't immediately respond. She's read his downbeat mood. In a matter-of-fact tone she says, "Things didn't go the way you expected."

Rogers shakes his head. "No they did not." Still sitting, he reaches up to put an arm around her waist. He leans his head against her side.

" 'Don't be angry,' the guy said, back in Fallujah." He looks up at Dub. "It felt like, I don't know....Prophecy. Or a curse."

"Maybe it was just advice," Dub says.

"Nobody listens to advice."

For a while, Dub says nothing. Then she takes his hand to guide him to standing, where she holds him with a fierceness as though he'd returned from war. "You're home," Dub says. "I'm good."

They hold hands walking toward the backyard.

"I was thinking. You get the rest of the term off, and I'll be working from home, and Stevie is going to be in school all day during the week." She smiles at him, and Rogers returns it with a smile that includes his eyes.

-o-

Washington D.C.
March 2017
(10 months after Mecca)

Mac is promoted to brigadier general in an afternoon reception in the Pentagon, in the room restricted to ceremonies attended by flag officers with three stars and above. It is a happy event: Friends and family, plus the mandatory official attendees. He has been responding to the name "Mac" for so long that it is odd to hear his full name read in the ceremony: "Johnston McCaulley." He isn't sure his fellow officers even know who that is.

After the Burj investigation, Mac had continued to lead the Defense Intelligence Agency on an acting basis. The announcement of his promotion in rank includes the announcement of orders making him the assigned head of DIA.

Before the ceremony, Mac sees Rogers and Dub in the crowd. Mac makes it a point to pull Rogers aside to update him on new developments. He knows one-on-one time with anyone in this melee will be scarce.

"The senile rich guy in the middle of it got left alone," Rogers says.

"His company's going to fall apart. He's not getting away completely clean." Mac leans in closer and lowers his voice. "Latest rumor is that Mundy's going to get a presidential pardon, very quiet, not even published publicly. No charges, no trial, everything swept under the rug. And he's working as a White House consultant, for a fee twice his salary as an employee."

"HOTEL VICTOR, still?"

Mac grimaces. "No one knows. What I heard is that HOTEL VICTOR tracked Putin's money laundering, but that snapshot is getting old. I don't like it. Supposedly Deadbolt was shut down, too. We didn't learn it continued until after thousands were dead."

Shayera, Mac's ex, is in attendance, bringing Brandon. Brandon is impressed with the ceremony and with his dad. His smile lifts Mac's heart. They sit at a table and talk, but since Mac is the star of the show, he is soon drawn back to the reception to make sure he greets everyone. Brandon and Mac part with Mac falsely promising to see him more.

Angie and Elston are down from Brooklyn. Mac finally gets to talk to her as the reception winds down.

"I met that nice Lillian Charles," Angie says. "She says she liked working with you, but she isn't in the chain of command with you anymore."

"And...?"

"Isn't it nice that they have ambitious intelligent women who work with the military, who know first-hand what the life is like? That could make a pretty good match for an important man like you. Mr. General."

"I knew you were headed there," Mac says. "Tony tried that line on me too, last summer."

Angie stands firm. "Makes him a good friend, then, I say."

-O-

PROLOGUE TO PART IV

ROGERS GETS a letter from Chris Leinheimer's mother.

It has been too long since I have been in touch with you. Chris so looked up to you. He told the story of how you drove into a machine gun to save him. Each time he told the story your heroics got a little bigger. If he had kept telling the story you would have been fighting the entire Iraqi army single-handed.

Chris was impressed not only by your bravery but by your even temper under pressure. He often said he wanted to be like you.

I have heard from Mac—now General McCaulley!—that the respect ran both ways, and that you remember Chris as a brave man committed to his duty. That is what Chris wanted to be. It is what I had always hoped for him. There is not a day that goes by that I do not think of him and miss him.

Mac suggested that I tell you about my recent encounter with a young woman who works as a therapist with wounded veterans. Her name is Fatima Abdullah. She lived in Fallujah during the war, but now she is a U.S. Citizen. I don't know how she found me.

She told me that many years ago, her father was compelled to carry a suicide vest into a group of American soldiers in Fallujah. For many years she believed that no one other than her father had been killed. Then she learned that in fact he had killed an American, my son. She said she only knew of her father as good, and I only knew him as bad. She wants to dedicate her life to continuing what she remembered as good about him. She said to me, "You and I share the experience of loss, and I am sorry. I cried all my tears for myself long ago. The tears I have left I shed for the suffering of others, like you."

I spent a lot of years going through the 12-step programs, to get myself right. For the loss of my son, and other things. I told her that after meeting her, I felt something less than forgiveness, but not an anger, and she said she understood. Maybe that is as much as we can do, until all of us become saints or angels.

Chris Jr. loves football. He doesn't look exactly like his dad, but I see a lot of his dad in him, in certain things he does. As I said, not a day goes by without me thinking of Chris.

Rogers knows who Fatima is. He can find her if he wants to try. He never has. Her experience of her father was that he saved her life at the cost of his own. To Rogers, he is the man who killed Chris Leinheimer and left Rogers without a leg. Rogers has no need to meet Fatima, to reconcile their fundamentally different understandings of Hassan. Rogers made a kind of peace with her father's actions, the way Chris' mother had. He couldn't have recovered if he'd held on to all his anger over the years. He's forgiven himself for work left undone on the attacks. He doesn't want to have to forgive Hassan too.

-O-

PART IV
"HOW MUCH WILL THIS COUNT TOWARD OUR FINAL GRADE?"

Cain Industries is charged with violation of the federal Foreign Corrupt Practices Act. The evidence is substantial and compelling. The prosecution offers a plea deal, and is confident the company will take it, but nothing can be taken for granted. Prosecutors leave some charges out of the indictment to avoid public disclosure of facts with national security aspects. They have enough evidence of bring a case on crooked business practices alone.

The deal requires the company to pay fines of $125 million, with no individual fines or jail time for Cain Senior or Pfennig, who get probation if they admit participating in the crime.

Pfennig knows he is blowing a massive financial hole in the company, but fighting the charges will only delay the inevitable and be far worse. He wants to enter the plea, but there is the question whether Cain will overrule him or dispute the plea after the fact.

This becomes the heart of the negotiation with prosecutors. Given Cain's physical and mental capacity, there is no good reason to charge him, and probation is a formality. Cain won't be in a position to violate the law again. Ultimately, prosecutors don't charge Cain, and while

Cain's bribery is part of the indictment's statement of facts, the prosecution is silent about Cain ordering or executing the Mecca or Burj attacks. As Cain's campaign contributions run dry, none of his former political allies see an upside to defending him, and they drift away.

The authorities find the phony vendor names Pfennig used to hide additional payments he'd made to himself over the years. Because Pfennig has power of attorney, the payments were not technically theft from the company—he always had the power to pay himself whatever he pleased. But the IRS brings tax evasion charges, and the payments violated the company's bank loans, putting the company in technical default. The company undergoes a cascade of financial failures and what survives is a shell of its prior incarnation. Cain lives on the annuity that the company bought for him, insulated from the consequences of it all.

As Cain Industries collapses, Jared Cain tries to intervene in court, claiming Pfennig's mismanagement erodes his expected inheritance. Jared's forgery of Cain's name on the Ross check comes to light. Betsy Ross demands the $2 million back. Jared agrees to give it to her rather than being portrayed in his litigation with Pfennig as the guy who took money away from a widow by forgery. Then in the ensuing litigation Jared learns his father cut him out of inheriting anything.

Jared's cooperation with the FBI on the Burj case allows him to plead guilty to reduced charges, but he still receives a lifetime ban from the securities industry and six months of prison time. When he gets out, his wife Maryam is on the prison steps, waiting for him wearing her hijab.

With the decline of Cain's empire, support for the Americans for Common Sense in the Middle East ends. For a while, Thomas Cutler is forced to make a living from guest fees on cable news, appearing mostly on morning shows as his afternoon drinking begins earlier and earlier in the day. Then, even though Muslims were the targets of the recent attacks and not the perpetrators, right-wing media ignites a new wave of anti-Muslim campaigning, and Cutler is in demand again.

In the West, the woman whose family had died at the Burj, and who had become the face of the tragedy, is forgotten. She rejoins her sisters and family in Kabul, to live as quiet a life as is possible to live in that city.

Lillian Charles returns to duties at the NSA. She and Mac are cordial, even friendly, but their relationship is solely professional.

Nadeau remains as CIA Director, and implements several reforms on the internal reporting of operations. The goal of the new rules is to prevent a repeat of the Abbott situation. He pauses data harvesting under HOTEL VICTOR, but directs the operators to assess whether Zaroff's exposure has led to the compromise of their work.

Prosecutors consider charging Mundy as an accomplice to murder, or an accessory, before offering Mundy's attorneys a bargained plea of negligent homicide. Everyone is hoping Mundy will quietly accept a plea deal so that information on the CIA's role will stay buried. Mundy turns down the plea deal. In the end, no charges are filed.

Russia's public statements at first try to paint Zaroff as a pawn of the CIA. Once Americans release evidence of other Russians sabotaging the airliners and Zaroff's communications with Sanjani, the Russian public stance changes to claiming that Zaroff acted for himself alone, without any Russian help or approval. Zaroff remains in U.S. military custody while his legal status is sorted out. There are rumors Zaroff is at the Supermax prison, but court records are under seal, with even Zaroff's name redacted. Those who know don't talk, and those who talk don't know.

Rogers keeps a low profile, other than being part of two sidebar profile stories that appear on inside pages of the New York Times and the Washington Post. He is described in both as having "made key discoveries" in the investigation of the Mecca and Burj attacks, without any specifics being mentioned. Maureen Dallas tells him to get his story out while everyone is excited, but he passes. "I don't even tell Dub," he says.

While still on leave, Rogers holds an informal symposium on campus in the fall, using the unclassified details of the Burj attack. Klamber hires a full-time replacement for Jerry Howard, so in the spring, Rogers does a case study seminar at West Point based on his fall symposium. Cadets who can't get in are forced to settle for the course on thinking biases conducted by the guest lecturer from Columbia. Rogers receives a flattering letter from the research foundation about how proud they were that their journal can print his paper on terror group leadership succession.

Maureen Dallas prepares a book on the Mecca and Burj attacks that substantially tracks the official version of the story. Ross does not figure into the story, and the origin of the Drone is vague but implied to be Russian. In her book, Zaroff is the prime mover behind the airliner attacks. She comments on the suspicious timing of Mundy's departure from the CIA, but no one tells her the story about that, on or off the record, and she never hears anyone mention Abbott's name.

She has a certainty that the government has held back important parts of the story, particularly given how many of the players in the attacks overlap with the mysterious foreign bribery case against Cain Industries. Stopping the saboteurs was a good outcome, but she doesn't like the lack of transparency, or how some political leaders have gone back to the old playbook from post-9/11 to fan hatred against Muslims.

As she gets closer to finishing the book, Maureen presses Rogers to tell her the part of the story that is missing.

"I can't help you," he says.

"Can't, or won't?"

"You know how it is."

"You need to stay up at West Point, Tony," she says. "When you spend too much time down here you start acting like just another Washington puke."

-o-

West Point
Fall 2017

In the new term Rogers gives the cadets a pop quiz with a single question.

He provides the students with two passages. One is from Maureen Dallas' book, praising the intelligence community's swift action to find and neutralize the saboteurs, while criticizing the re-emergence in the country of anti-Muslim political sentiment. The other passage is an argument from Thomas Cutler's book, calling for an aggressive posture against the Muslim world.

The test question reads, "Please explain which author's argument you find stronger, and why."

A cadet in his late teens—who looks significantly younger—raises his hand after reading the question.

"How much will this count toward our final grade?" the cadet asks.

Rogers thinks: Someday you'll be an officer in a military that has to deal with these questions in the real world, so maybe the answer should be 100%.

What he says is: "I haven't decided yet. Just do your best."

-o-

ACKNOWLEDGMENTS

Many people read many versions of this book as it was being formed. I've benefited greatly from their insights, their objections, and their thoughtful reading. The Off Campus Writers Workshop of Winnetka, Illinois, and the Chicago Writers Association supplied many of those beta readers, as well as extensive programming that has enhanced my experience as a writer. Among those who have seen earlier versions of the book are Diana McInnis, Steve Hagen, Ryne Misso, Alison Hagen, Tom Sundell, Terry Brennan, Linda Buyer, Paco Aramburu, Donna Urbikis, Jerry Olesky, Tonya Coats. Peter Happock, Abby Saul, James Olsen, Nancy Myers, Susan Cherry, Cheryl Reed, Ed Sarna, and Nancy Ullrey.

Particular thanks go to my wife and patient repeat reader, Liane Anderson, and to my brother, USAF Maj. Gen. Brian Dravis, Ret., who not only read the book but provided valuable access to the Pentagon and to the dedicated professionals there.

ABOUT THE AUTHOR

Bruce Dravis is a former journalist and retired corporate and securities attorney whose career advising public and private technology companies included a focus on corporate governance. He has authored and contributed to numerous non-fiction books, articles, and podcasts on law and business. *Confirmation Bias* is his debut novel, blending his insider knowledge of media, finance, and power into a gripping work of fiction.

www.ingramcontent.com/pod-product-compliance
Lightning Source LLC
Chambersburg PA
CBHW020140120726
47903CB00007B/2349